DAYLIGHT DIMS

VOLUME TWO

DAYLIGHT DIMS

VOLUME TWO

EDITED BY J.W. ZULAUF & KRISTOPHER MALLORY

STEALTH
FICTION

Baltimore, Maryland.

For ebook and audiobook downloads, visit DAYLIGHTDIMS.COM

Cover Illustration by Luke Spooner

Graphic Design by Phillip Gessert

For information, email: PUBLISHING@STEALTHFICTION.COM

ISBN: 978-0-9897572-2-5

FOR THE WITCHING HOUR

THANK YOU

*Abbey Northcutt • Amanda Herron • Andrea Box • Anonymous
Anton Scheller • Danielle Horvath • David Cummings
Donovan Corrick • Elle Hama • Em Petrova • Eileen Lynch
Griffin Morgan • Hunter Lowe • Jammin Jenny
Janelle Littlejohn • Jason Norton • Kelly Hoppenworth
Laura Quevedo • Matt Wenzinger • Matthew Strange • Myst
R. Sherborne • Rafael Estrada • Richard Claycomb
Samuel Malachowski • Scott
Shenoa Carroll-Bradd • Stina-Lisa Nelson • Tom Baker*

SPECIAL THANKS TO JUSTIN MARROW

DEAR DAYLIGHT DIMMERS,

As we did last year, we will start with the facts, and if you care to read more, continue on to "A Deeper Understanding: Part II."

In short, thank you for joining us this year. We are glad to have you aboard!

THE FACTS

Who: J.W. Zulauf, Kristopher Mallory, and a talented crew of authors, artists, readers, and proofreaders.

What: *Daylight Dims Volume 2*—a hand-picked collection of horror stories.

When: October 1st.

Where: Hardback and online.

Why: To help create a community for horror authors and readers.

A DEEPER UNDERSTANDING: PART II

The Daylight Dims horror community keeps us going. We're happy to report that the foundation is indeed strong. Nearly every person who had a hand in crafting volume one came back this year. All of our artists and most our authors offer support whenever possible.

Much has changed this year. For starters, we've increased our team. We gained thirteen new authors, three new artists, three new proofreaders, and an even stronger reading staff. A new graphic designer has joined us, as well. Talent all around, and it's unbelievable that everyone is in it to see the success of this anthology.

We wish we could say creating an anthology like this is easy, but it's not. There is nothing easy at all about it. From the first submission we received, we've worked hard to make the right choices.

Did you know that the editors read every submission that comes through? Even the stories that are marked as rejected. This year, we even had cross pollination among our staffing. Carrie, one of our artists, also read. Amber, one of our proofreaders, read every submission and then helped tighten up on the backend.

The point is that real passion went into this book, and it's important that the readers know they come first. We care about you. So welcome back return readers, and hello to all the new ones.

Here's another cliché-ish intro: Darkness thickens as daylight dims ☺

Yours truly,

J.W. Zulauf
Kristopher Mallory

I WILL SHOW YOU FEAR IN A HANDFUL OF DUST.

Artwork: Chrissy Spallone

CONTENTS

Artwork: Alex Hewitt

PERMANENT RESIDENTS

R.K. KOMBRINCK

Amanda caught sight of the Murder Motel as her sister drove onto the bridge that crossed the highway. The old building squatted on a kidney-shaped plot of pavement, surrounded on three sides by trees and dark hills, with nothing and no one else around for miles.

"There it is, Wendy."

Amanda grasped her sister's hand, squeezing tightly. She had done the silo facility in Chillicothe. She'd walked the three-mile track to the derelict rail depot in Hartwell. She'd explored the single-room schoolhouse in Cleves, the old factory in Hyde Park, and the deserted neighborhood off the highway behind Lookout Acres. All had been thoroughly boring and Amanda wanted something more—a place with a rich, dark history. She'd almost given up on finding a new location when she'd overheard two girls in her university's common area talking about the Murder Motel. She'd asked some questions, dug around the web, and discovered that the motel had been hiding right under her nose.

The motel had been something of a nine-day wonder back in the fall of 1983. News outlets across the state had run the story of how a man named Terry Loughton had stumbled into the front office of the Royal Motel just after sunset, waving a pistol. He'd murdered six employees and two guests before turning the gun on himself. The police discovered his wife's body at the couple's home—a hunting knife jammed deep in her belly, her intestines spoiling on the kitchen floor. Their seven-year-old daughter, Jackie, was never seen again.

The motel was shut down quietly and left to rot. No investors came to rehab it. No developer offered to bulldoze it and build something else in its place. It sat...empty and waiting.

Over time, people forgot the name Terry Loughton and his victims. The story was relegated to late night conversations in bars and truck stops, and even *that* eventually dried up. For years the history lay as dormant as the motel itself. Then, decades later, it found a second, vivid life amongst the kind of people who appreciated gruesome tales of blood and tragedy.

"All the kids say that a group of devil worshippers used the place for rituals. That they had orgies, called up demons, and communicated with the ghosts of others who'd died there." Amanda grinned as she spun the yarn. "Another story says a group of paranormal investigators wanted to stay overnight and study the place. They ran out screaming after only three hours, then disbanded the group."

Clark leaned in from the backseat, pushing his face between the two sisters. He squinted at the bright sun from beneath his red knit cap. "That true?"

Amanda shrugged. "Who knows? Probably not. The only thing I know for sure is that nine people died there. The rest are just rumors." She raised her eyebrow theatrically. "But there are a *lot* of rumors. Everybody at Bridlefield has a story about this place, and there's a couple of websites that mention it."

The car bumped along, nearing their new adventure, pines thickening as they left the road. A thick, metal pole poked up from the scrub, topped with a sign proclaiming: '*Royal Motel: Air Conditioned • Free* H B O.' Just beyond the rusted welcome sign lay their destination.

The sagging, two-level affair sprawled in the shadows of the encroaching woods. Its paint had faded and turned yellow. A check-in office sat at one end, and a walkway cut through to the rear. Rooms stretched the length every ten feet. Each closed door accompanied large, naked windows. Further down, two stairways led to the second floor and a glass enclosure where a long-dead ice machine hulked.

As they drove into the parking lot, the car stirred drifts of dead leaves. The empty lot proved that they had the Murder Motel all to themselves.

Clark said in a hushed and respectful tone, "Damn. This is legit."

"Yeah," Wendy agreed, shutting off the ignition. "But I wish it was closer to home. It's gonna be dark soon. We should've left earlier."

Amanda undid her seatbelt. "We can spend the night in my dorm if you want. It'll be quiet. Everybody's gone for the holiday."

Amanda opened her door and stepped onto the pavement. A smile spread across her face as she drank in the atmosphere. The chipped and peeling paint, the empty flowerbed outside the office, the ghosts of parking space lines—she fell in love. She pulled her pack from the front seat and rummaged through it.

Clark got out of the car, stood next to Amanda, and stretched. He looked back in the car at Wendy. "Yeah, that's a good plan. We can all spend the night together. In your dorm room I mean. Makes sense to me."

Amanda glanced at him, amused to see that his face had gone bright red beneath his scruffy beard. "Yeah, we can't use my roommate's bed, so we're all gonna have to squeeze into mine." She pulled her camera from her pack and began snapping pictures.

Wendy stepped out of the car. She wrapped a scarf around her neck and sniffed the air. "Ugh. What's that smell?"

The artificial click of Amanda's digital camera went off and the flash bloomed. "I don't smell anything." The grime on the windows fascinated her. The patterns resembled handprints.

Clark stepped around to Wendy's side and leaned against the car. "No, there's definitely a smell. It's like dead leaves, moldy carpet, and raccoon shit." His voice dropped to an ominous growl. "Or maybe it's the lingering stench of death." He chuckled and lit a cigarette.

"Don't be a dick, Clark. People died here." Wendy shut the driver's side door and sidled over to her sister. "Is this one creepy enough for you?"

Amanda kept taking pictures, her eyes on the view screen, but she spoke as she moved. "Another thing they say is that, sometimes, people driving by at night see lights on in the windows. And sometimes, they see shadows in those lit up rooms."

Wendy hugged herself and shivered. "Maybe people are staying here. Squatters or something."

Amanda looked up from her camera. "Then who's paying the electric bill?" She slipped the camera's strap over her shoulder and hoisted her pack. "You guys ready to explore?" Without waiting for an answer, she strode across the parking lot toward the front office.

She stepped over a parking block and onto the sidewalk. Stubborn weeds clawed their way up the cracks in the cement. She pressed her face to the plate glass that fronted the office and put her hands to either side–the room where Terry Loughton had gunned down four of his eight victims.

Actually, it was ten, counting the wife and little girl, she reminded herself.

She felt a morbid thrill knowing that blood had been spilled only a few feet away. Dust and grit coated the glass, making it impossible to see anything at all. She tried the door and found it locked, just as she'd expected.

No big deal, she thought as she opened her lock picking kit. She heard Wendy and Clark shuffling up behind her. She turned to face them.

"I say we start with the rear of the building, then cut through the tunnel. Maybe try a few rooms. Finish with the office. What do you guys think?"

Wendy chewed at her lower lip. "How many rooms do you want to go through? We can't stay here too long. It's already 3:30."

"Jesus, Wendy," Amanda replied. "We drove all this way, we're gonna check out as many rooms as we can. We've got flashlights."

"Sorry. I was just asking."

Clark tossed his cigarette and put his hand on Wendy's arm. "Don't worry about it. We'll be alright."

She gave him a withering look and shrugged his hand off. "I know."

Amanda stepped into the tunnel-like walkway. An overlapping and confusing roadmap of graffiti spread across the dark walls. She stepped back, observing.

The graffiti turned out to be mostly childish vulgarity: depictions of huge penises, impossibly large breasts, pot leaves, and heavy metal band names. She particularly liked the one that read, *'April Priest + Beer = Blowjobs.'* Some of it, however, was quite strange. She took her camera and began snapping pictures. Each time the flash went off it illuminated a small piece of the chaotic puzzle.

FLASH

Eight small figures holding hands, their eyes round, white holes.

FLASH

A crude drawing of a little girl in a dress and pigtails. Blank white eyes with her mouth drawn in an exaggerated frown.

FLASH

'!!!La niña quiere comer su alma, salir y permanecer fuera hermanos!!!'

FLASH

A bouquet of thorny stems crowning a girl with crescent-shaped eyes.

FLASH

A huge scorpion with human hands gripping the words, 'I'm sorry I came here.'

FLASH

Jacky ate my baby.

FLASH

Jackie RULZ!

FLASH

'Jackie sux dix.' Below this the addendum, 'Jackie EATZ dicks. Get it straight fucker.'

FLASH

A chain of white eyes surrounding the words, 'Everybody up. Amanda's here.'

Amanda nearly dropped her camera. She leaned forward, so close her nose almost touched the wall. The circle of eyes still stared, but the words just looked like a greasy black streak. Her mind had played a little prank on her. She smiled as she turned and examined the writing on the opposite wall. *This is exactly what I wanted,* she thought as she shouldered her camera and headed to the rear of the motel.

Stepping out of the tunnel and into what had once been the motel's recreational area, something caught her attention. To her right, a small structure stuck out perpendicular from the main building with no windows and a gaping doorway. Faded paintings of Pac-Man, Q-Bert, and Space Invaders decorated the front wall. She wondered if any of the old arcade cabinets remained. She doubted it. Surely someone would have spirited them away if the motel owners had been stupid enough to leave them in the first place.

A concrete courtyard spread out from the arcade. A few old, weather-stained chairs scattered the area. To her left, a bit further back, stretched a small swimming pool surrounded by a low fence. A child's deflated, pink inner tube floated listlessly on the surface, proving to be the only spot of color. Everything else sat in a shrouded grey.

Wendy and Clark emerged from the tunnel.

"Smells like dead fish," Wendy said.

Amanda hunkered down and set her pack on the ground. She opened it and began removing items, setting a flashlight on the concrete, then placing a small plastic box next to it. As she unpacked, Clark said, "Oh shit, is that an arcade?"

"All signs point to yes." Amanda flipped the lid of her case, revealing a set of small tools. "Why don't you go check it out? Here, take my light."

"It's alright, I've got one." He padded off to the arcade.

Wendy wore an expression of boredom mixed with unease. Amanda knew the only reason her sister went on the excursions was to show everyone that she was more than just a pretty face. Even though she gamely clambered through garbage-strewn trailers, rodent-infested basements, and crumbling factories, Amanda knew she had no real interest in these places.

"You okay, sis?" Amanda pulled off her gloves and stuffed them into her jacket pockets.

Wendy shrugged. "Yeah. Just tired. And cold. What happened to the sun? Feels like the temperature dropped twenty degrees since we got here."

"Well, the trees keep it pretty shady and it's breezy." Amanda started toward one of the rooms. "Wanna come with me?"

Before Wendy had a chance to answer, Clark came out of the arcade. His eyes sparkled. "You guys gotta see this. There's a bunch more of that crazy shit all over the walls and ceiling. Names, little nursery rhymes. Weird drawings...no games though." His tone lowered for a moment but bounced right back. "The handprints are the creepiest part. Give me the camera."

Amanda placed it in Clark's outstretched hand. "I'll see it in a bit. I want to get into these rooms before it gets too dark"

Wendy turned to Clark. "I'll come with you." Clark smiled widely, and Amanda felt a sting of annoyance. She watched them go into the arcade, and a moment later the flash of the camera began.

Walking past an iron stairway, Amanda stepped beneath an overhang and approached a door: Room 21. Through the window she saw the shape of what looked like a bedframe. She tried the knob. *Locked.* She selected one of the little tools in her case and slipped it into the keyhole, wiggling it back and forth. After some work, a click signaled that the knob had unlocked. Her heart sped up as she pushed the door open and stepped inside.

She switched on her flashlight and guided the beam across the room. Other than the metal bedframe, the room had been stripped of furniture.

Even the carpet was torn up in a few places, showing bald cement. It felt empty and disappointing.

Of course, she thought.

She pulled the door shut, hearing it lock automatically. She walked to the next room and jimmied the lock without even trying it first.

In that room, the bed came complete, mattress and all, with a filthy blanket scrunched up at the foot. A side table with two drawers sat beside the bed, and a long, low dresser sprawled beneath the window.

She moved to the side of the bed and touched the mattress. A cloud of dust puffed up around her hand. The springs screeched as she lowered herself onto it. She settled in and looked around the room.

Amanda had hoped to find some personal items. Artifacts left behind by guests who had stayed, or even junk that transients and squatters left. She wanted anything connecting to a human presence. She trailed the flashlight's beam downward and swept it along the floor. More dust. More cobwebs. Nothing else.

She opened the dresser drawers, finding the first two empty. The third contained a very large, hairy spider and Amanda slammed it shut with a gasp. She uttered a little giggle and drew the last one open cautiously, shining the light in. A pencil rolled across the bottom.

With a disappointed grunt, she opened the top drawer of the side table. Inside sat a thick, cheaply bound book.

Now we're getting somewhere, she thought as she lifted the book out, giving it a good shake to dislodge any creepy-crawly stowaways.

Someone had tried to blot out the title using black ink, but the stamped lettering pushed through, clearly legible: *Holy Bible.*

"Well shit."

Amanda felt a queasy wave of excitement. She tried to flip through it but found all the pages stuck together. Intrigued, she turned the defaced scriptures this way and that. She ran her thumb across the pages and found that it opened from the center. She laid it open on the bed. Notebook paper, with tight little letters, covered the original text. As she held up her light to examine the book, two shadows passed by the dirty window. She heard the door to the next room open and close, followed by muffled voices and thumping.

So much for not wanting to explore the rooms.

Somehow Clark had coaxed Wendy into a room when Amanda could not. His crush was becoming unbearable. It had sneaked in and devoured a part of their friendship. It didn't matter, though, because Wendy would never give him what he wanted.

Another part of Amanda wondered why it never even occurred to him to see if *she* would.

Because Wendy is the pretty one. That's why.

She shook the sour thoughts away, ignored Wendy and Clark, and focused back on the writing. The print seemed to be in a language that Amanda couldn't even guess. She read aloud, pronouncing as best she could:

"Briiecxo gullis bub soom-neilsgh'h alarkcrit upharsin, mene-tekel bubb marked by its lividity shub gomthog Yoth Kamog sybl naahg bub-heilsgh'b aggrieved and unburied lesh coulerig sebs."

The thumping next door suddenly intensified, like someone was hitting the wall.

Ugh, is she actually...? Amanda grimaced, disgusted at the thought. *God, they know I'm in here.*

It was like they were doing it just to mess with her. Normally she would find the idea ridiculous, but there, in the dark room, with dust floating around her like dirty snow, it seemed completely reasonable.

She stood, snapped the Bible closed, and stuffed it into her jacket pocket. She explored the rest of the room, shining her light in every gloomy corner and crevice. The bathroom and closets held nothing but a couple of theft-proof wooden hangers. It seemed that room had given her all it had. The Bible was a nice relic, though, and she couldn't wait to get it home and start researching the writing on the notebook paper. Someone, somewhere, had to have an idea of what it meant. More thumps beat on the wall as she reached for the door to leave. She rolled her eyes.

She opened the door, expecting the onrush of daylight to dazzle her, but the sky had dimmed considerably. In fact, the sun had sunken low behind the hills and the shadows of the pines stretched out long.

Amanda pulled her phone from her pocket. The clock said 4:28. She stared at it for a few seconds and then looked stupidly back at the sky, trying to reconcile the two. It couldn't have been much later than 3:45 when she'd gone into the room, and it felt like she'd only been inside for five minutes. She moved toward the next room, intending to ask Wendy and Clark if they'd noticed her long absence.

Of course they hadn't.

She knocked on the door but received no reply. No sound of any kind. She knocked again and called out, "Guys? Hey, guys. You in there?"

Nothing. No more thumping, no more voices. She decided to walk in and hope they'd finished. The doorknob felt cold against her hand as she closed her fingers around it and turned. She jiggled the knob, but it wouldn't budge. She leaned in closer, placing her ear against the door, straining to catch any sound from within. She swept her hair back and pressed her ear more tightly.

She pounded on the door. The sound of her fist rapping against the mute wood echoed across the pavement, startling some birds from the trees. "Hey! This is bullshit, and it's not funny!" She turned slowly and surveyed the courtyard. She took one last look at the door and considered letting herself in with her pick. After a moment, she decided to instead try the next room down.

Amanda turned on her flashlight and swung the beam around the room. She felt hurried, less genuinely curious and more anxious about being caught there after sundown. She didn't bother with the bathroom. The room lacked a dresser or table to explore, just a bare bedframe. As she turned to the door, something on the dingy grey carpet caught her eye–a small, bright business card. She knelt and picked it up, shining her light on it.

N.O.P.E.

Northern Ohio Paranormal Examiners

"Getting to know the unknown"

Matt Lauritsen M.S.

Bridlefield University

A paranormal group really had come out here? Shit. She shoved the card into her pocket next to the bible. Not bothering to take a last look around, she stepped out of the room, pulling the door closed behind her.

"Guys?" Her voice sounded small. *Where the hell are they?* Amanda went back to the arcade, very aware of how quickly the sky continued to darken. "Wendy? Clark?"

She stepped through the doorway and switched on her flashlight. Dust swam in the air. She looked around the room, and her breath caught in her throat. Graffiti covered the walls and ceiling, just as Clark had said, but he'd gotten it wrong. There were no words, no obscene pictures, but hundreds of eyes. All shapes and sizes, some detailed, some simple, all staring at her.

She backed away from the wall and tripped over something in the middle of the floor. She landed hard, dropping the flashlight. It spun a few times and came to rest with the beam trained on what had tangled up her feet: her camera.

She snatched it by the strap and stood. After thumbing the power button, the little green light came on with a mechanical whine. She didn't understand why Clark had left it lying there. She turned on "View" mode.

She thumbed through the pictures, most were of the eyes, but there were a few of Wendy from behind. *Of course, the perv.* The last picture showed Wendy in the doorway, framed by grey daylight. She wasn't smiling, and a strange smudge hung over her shoulder. Amanda pressed the little plus sign, enlarging the picture, and scrolled to the right. It wasn't a smudge but a shadow. A person stood behind her sister.

Amanda stepped into the shady courtyard and yelled as loudly as she could, "Wendy? Wendy, *please!*"

She desperately hoped they were messing with her. She wouldn't even be mad. She was ready to leave. Her footfalls smacked hard as she hurried across the pavement. She turned and went into the tunnel, calling for her sister. A knot of dark worry bloomed in her chest.

The car still sat in the front parking lot, running with the headlights on and the front doors opened wide. Amanda was about to exit the tunnel when she noticed something. She shined her flashlight across the tunnel walls and gasped.

Mute, indifferent eyes had replaced the writing. A scream crawled up her throat, but she struggled fiercely to keep it inside. She did not want to lose control.

What if they start blinking?

She turned away and rushed to the car.

Amanda stuck her head in the driver's side and glanced in the back. Only Wendy's scarf, lying abandoned on the seat, gave any indication she'd been there.

Amanda's heart pounded as she looked back at the motel. *Where could they be?* She sat behind the wheel and cut the ignition. She pressed the horn, letting it blast for a long time, and slammed her fist in a staccato beat. *Why aren't they coming out, laughing at me for being scared?* It would be hilarious. Mean, maybe, but amusing in a dark way.

The cold crept in. Amanda pulled the doors shut, and watched the windows fog up. She called Wendy's phone but it went straight to voice-mail. She thought about dialing the police, but what would she say? That she was trespassing on a piece of property where a bunch of people had been murdered years ago, just to poke around for laughs, and now her sister and friend had disappeared? That maybe they were playing a cruel joke on her but she was terrified that they weren't? That the eyes were watching her and she thought she was losing her mind? The longer she waited in silence, the idea seemed less and less crazy.

She had just pressed the "9" and the "1" when Clark's voice called from the hotel.

"Amanda! Hey!"

She flung the door open and jumped out. At first she couldn't tell where his voice had come from. She scanned the front of the motel and found him hanging out of the open office.

How the hell did they get in there?

Trying to sound angry, she yelled, "Asshole! What's wrong with you?" But the relief in her voice became impossible to hide. She almost wanted to laugh. "Come on. Tell Wendy the game is over, and let's get out of here."

"Not yet. There's something you've got to see."

Amanda rolled her eyes. She had lost all desire to explore the motel. As far as she was concerned, it was time to look for a new hobby alto-gether. She shook her head and called back, "No, come on. I'm cold. Where's Wendy, anyway?"

"She's in here. She wants you to see this. Hurry up." His form, barely visible in the dark, disappeared into the office, letting the door click shut.

Amanda felt annoyed all over again. Those two were real pieces of work. She strode toward the door. They were probably hiding in there, waiting for her to enter so they could jump out and scare her. She wasn't going to give them the satisfaction. She would steel herself for the shock and offer no reaction. She pulled the door open. Taking in a deep breath, she stepped into the heavy darkness and readied herself for whatever they had in store for her.

The door closed on its own, engulfing her in darkness, but she saw that people filled the room. Arms, legs, and eyes swam in and out of the shadows. With a choked scream, she threw herself against the unyielding door, pounding her fists uselessly. She cried and called for help. No one made a sound behind her. Not until she slid to the floor, tears streaming down her cheeks, sobs turning to exhausted dry heaves. Then a voice spoke, a voice she'd never heard before…the voice of a little girl.

"No time for that now, Amanda. Everybody's here," the voice said, followed by a childish giggle.

Light suddenly filled the room. Ancient, dead bulbs in the ceiling glowed with phantom power, revealing the small crowd before her: five men, three women, their clothes filthy and tattered, stained with age and blood. One of the women had lost the right side of her face, including her eye. Her hair hung over the dark wound like a curtain, bugs squirming inside the wrecked flesh.

A man wearing a plaid sports coat and jeans also wore a ragged hole in his shirt, just above his belt. Something hung from the tear, something that looked like grey-black sausage clotted with dark sludge. He regarded her from behind lightly tinted glasses, unperturbed by her scrutiny.

She looked from face to face. They all watched her wordlessly, their eyes sad. Flies buzzed everywhere. They landed on her cheeks and brow, then flittered away again. And there was a smell…thick, rank, and horribly sweet.

I'm trapped with ghosts.

A gravelly voice came from a corner, "I *wish* I was a ghost." Against the wall, with knees drawn up to his chest, sat a broad-shouldered man covered in dust. A spray of maroon spread across the wall above him, stark in the sallow light. The revolver he'd used lay at his side, garlanded with cobwebs. "Ghosts don't know they're dead."

"Oh stop being so grumpy," the young girl said.

Amanda snapped her head around and found herself face-to-face with a child. A girl of seven or eight with long blond hair pulled back in a ponytail. She wore a Strawberry Shortcake t-shirt with frilly sleeves over a pair of red gym-shorts. The shirt appeared faded but clean, as did the girl's hair and skin. Her eyes shined bright, a complete contrast to the other things that shared the room with her. It was perhaps in deference to this distinction that their dead eyes glowed with adoration as they gazed upon the little girl. She smiled. Her teeth gleamed white and perfect, but her breath—oh, her breath smelled vile.

"Jackie," Amanda said, knowing who the girl was the moment she spoke, but right then, looking at her, breathing in her foul reek, it seemed necessary to say out loud. "You're Jackie Loughton."

The girl's face lit up, delighted. "Yep. And you're Amanda Corcoran. I'm glad you came."

From the corner, Terry Loughton moaned miserably. "I'm so sorry. I thought they brought her here to kill her. I didn't know."

The mirth drained from Jackie's eyes, and she spoke through clenched jaws. "Daddy, I told you to stop. Being. So. *Grumpy!*"

He sobbed, or maybe he chuckled, it was hard to tell, but words kept spilling from his spoiled lips. "They brought her here, but that's what she wanted. It's what she was waiting for. How could I have known? Oh Sharon, I'm sorry. I'm so, so sorry. I didn't know she had that knife. I could've stopped her maybe…." His voice gurgled and rasped.

Jackie flew toward her father, carried on a neck grown suddenly long and thin. Her ponytail flew behind her head like a poisonous comet's tail, and her teeth chomped together as she shouted, "Shut up! Shut up! Shut up! I told you never to talk about Momma. Never, ever, *ever.*"

Terry clearly laughed this time. "Or what? You can't make this any worse. I'll say what I want. You're the one who killed her. You were a terrible daughter." His words dissolved into a series of wheezing coughs that lapsed back into sludgy underwater gurgles.

"I spared her." Jackie's voice sounded like the buzz of summer cicadas. "Because I loved her best. I loved her *only*. I spared her so you would suffer *this*, Daddy." Her head pulled back on the serpentine neck, a triumphant sneer wrinkling her lips. "My flock is coming with me, but you'll stay behind with the new residents."

Terry's face crumpled with fear and terror. "No! I'm sorry, sweetie. I take it back. Please don't leave me here with them. *Please.* Jackie. Please!"

With horrifying speed, Jackie clamped her open mouth over her father's as if sharing a deep, lover's kiss, but when Jackie pulled back,

Terry's tongue dangled between her teeth. She tossed her head back, letting it slide down her gullet like a pelican swallowing a fish, then smiled.

"I told you to stop talking." As if that pronouncement held another significance, the other dead people in the office all raised their hands above their heads in unison and chanted in low, hissing tones: "Medhor chogro lor shub Kamog."

Jackie swung her head back to Amanda, hovering above her like a jack-o'-lantern. Her eyes had become huge, empty sockets that glowed bright white, and her teeth had grown long and sharp, but when she spoke, her voice sounded like a little girl's again. "I'm sorry to leave you with him but he should be quieter now."

"What do you mean? Where's my sister? *Where's Wendy?*"

Jackie's grin spread to an impossible width. Even in that form, childish glee capered on her face. She sang in her high, sweet voice, "*Wendy, Wendy, arms all bendy.*"

Amanda's hand flew from her side and struck the monstrous face hanging in the air before her. It was like striking warm, wet clay. "Where's my sister you fucking *whore?*"

Jackie's crooning ceased. She closed her mouth and regarded Amanda solemnly. Silence crept in. The dead watched impassively. Terry remained still, his head cradled in his arms. Amanda suddenly realized she was dreaming, maybe sick with a terrible fever. As relief began to flood through her, she caught a strong whiff of Jackie's breath and knew that it was no dream.

"My flock...my *friends*," Jackie said. "They picked this place because they were waiting for me to be born. They knew I would be special. In fact, they helped bring me to this world." Her human voice vanished completely. Her words buzzed and rattled. "They spent years reading books, learning languages. They hurt people. They killed people. They watched for the signs, and after I was finally born, they found me. Daddy didn't know what I was, but Momma did. She knew and she didn't care. She loved me anyway. That's why I let her die free."

Terry moaned but Jackie continued to stare deep into Amanda's eyes. "They didn't expect Daddy to show up here with his gun. He thought they killed Momma and kidnapped me. He followed them here. They thought he spoiled their plans, the ritual. But I knew it was going to happen that way. There always has to be a sacrifice. I told them they'd walk out of here in darkness and glory, but I never said they would walk out alive. This place has to be *fed*. It has to be tended to. Always. Someone always has to stay behind. That's just the way it is."

Jackie stretched her tiny hand out, far beneath her floating head, and reached into Amanda's jacket pocket. She grasped the defaced Bible and pulled it free, clutching it against her chest. "People have come and gone before. Some sensed us, and some saw us. We always show little bits and pieces of ourselves…whispers…visions. No one ever stayed very long, though. But you pressed on and found this book, our absolution."

Amanda's thoughts became a muddy swirl of fear and confusion, but the memory of reading the words from the Bible cut through the haze with cold clarity. Fresh tears spilled down her cheeks. She'd never felt so lost before in her life. She whispered, "Wendy."

Jackie nodded, her ponytail bobbing joyfully to and fro. "Yes. Maybe it's time for you to see your sister and friend. Would you like that?"

The words sounded like poison dripping from the demon's mouth, but Amanda nodded. She didn't care what came next. The idea of seeing Wendy had become everything.

Jackie reared up off the floor. Her neck retracted, bringing her head closer to her body, while the rest of her body changed shape. Her arms and legs multiplied: six then eight. It became hard to tell how many limbs had grown. Her back bowed inward and elongated, tearing the Strawberry Shortcake shirt. She appeared fuller, plumper. The Jackie thing, now standing six feet above the filthy floor, skittered with arthropodic grace across the room. Her retinue of dead worshippers stepped to either side, allowing her passage into the room behind what had once been the check-in desk. Amanda waited, trying to ignore the flies landing in her hair, the chill of all those lifeless eyes upon her, and the way Jackie's abdomen undulated underneath her spindly legs as she moved. She tried to focus her thoughts on Wendy.

Two shadows emerged from the room. Shoving past the small, silent congregation they stopped in front of Amanda, swaying gently.

Amanda took one look at her sister…the girl she'd built tents out of blankets with when they were little…the girl who'd been the first person she called after losing her virginity…the girl who she'd confessed her stupid, useless crush on Clark to…and screamed.

Wendy's face had been smashed in. Her jaw hung wrenched horribly to one side. Her lips split wide, exposing shredded gums and a jumble of teeth. Her beautiful dark hair lay matted to her face with dark, tacky blood. Something had reduced her nose to a red, wet channel, but her eyes shined bright. They stared at Amanda with hatred.

Beside her, Clark stood with his head twisted backward, his skull crushed above the right temple. Blood and brains leaked from a gash in his head and down onto the collar of his coat.

Jackie reappeared, standing so large she almost filled the room. She had sprouted long, dragonfly-like wings that shimmered in the sick light. She'd shed her clothes and her body had become further segmented. Eyes like white toadstools opened up all along her sides, lidless and glistening. The worst, though, was that her face still resembled that of the little girl.

Amanda howled at the creature towering over her sister and friend, "You killed them! Oh God, you killed *them!*"

The creature opened its mouth and laughed in its nightmarish drone. "*Me?* Don't be silly. I've never killed anyone. *You* did that."

Amanda's fear and grief hid buried under an avalanche of cold fury. She could stand no more lies. She would beat the monster into the floor with the heavy, blood-soaked flashlight she held in her hand before finding a way to—

When had I picked up the flashlight? I left it in the car with my pack. How had it gotten bloody? Whose hair is matted to the front plate?

She looked around to find the room empty. Jackie and her acolytes had vanished. Terry Loughton was gone. She still gripped the flashlight in her hand. She thumbed the switch, the light filtering through a red haze.

Wendy and Clark lay on the floor in pools of blood. They didn't move. After all of that, it felt strange to see dead people actually dead. She aimed the beam around the room, resting it on Terry Loughton's pistol. She moved to where it lay and sat up against the wall, drawing her legs up to her chest. She set the flashlight down and picked up the gun, wondering if any shots remained. She pulled the hammer back and heard the chamber click into place. Her curiosity grew. She wondered how the barrel would feel in her mouth. After a moment, she put it between her lips and found it to be cold.

She sat that way for a while before realizing someone else was in the room with her. She saw the silhouette of a young girl just inside the door. A voice that reminded her of summertime and mosquito bites whispered to her, "*This place feeds on tragedy.*"

Amanda nodded. She finally understood. The flashlight sputtered out as the batteries died. She didn't know if her eyes were open or closed, but the gun remained in her mouth. With a sigh, she leaned her head back against the wall and pulled the trigger.

❖

"There it is," Jake said as they rode their bikes across the bridge.

The old building squatted on a kidney-shaped plot of pavement, surrounded on three sides by trees and dark hills, with nothing and no one around for miles.

"She killed her sister and boyfriend in room 23 but pulled their bodies into the front office. Their heads were busted open. She beat 'em both to death with a flashlight and there were brains *everywhere*."

Sam paled. "Brains?"

"Yeah. *Everywhere*. And more brains where she killed herself next to them. That's where we should go first. Dibs on any cool stuff we find."

"Alright."

Sam had no qualms giving up dibs on anything they might find in the motel. It had gained a nasty reputation after the murder-suicide, and he couldn't for the life of him remember how he'd let himself get talked into such an excursion. His goal was to get in and out as quickly as possible, but he knew that it would not be easy to dissuade Jake from exploring every room.

Jake stood on his pedals and began his descent to the deserted road below. "Last one there eats dog shit!"

After a moment of hesitation, Sam followed, hoping they'd be done before dark. ◆

R. K. Kombrinck is a writer and artist who lives in Cincinnati, Ohio with his wife and two sons. He is a founding cast-member of the popular horror podcast "Night of the Living Podcast." He enjoys iced-tea (unsweet) and genuinely believes in Sasquatch.

Artwork: Carrie Will

TO FETTER THE FENRIS-WOLF

CHRISTINE MORGAN

Sheep lay slaughtered across the yard: flesh torn, guts strewn, wool blood-matted in the churned mud. By the small sod hut was the shepherd's dog, which had fared no better. Within was the shepherd, who had fared far worse.

The shepherd's eyes bulged and his mouth gaped, horror-struck. His body was split from throat to groin. His ivory rib cage, pulled apart in splintered shards, exposed a dark, glistening hollow. His limbs splayed outward to the hut's four corners. The thick meat of his thighs and upper arms had been mauled.

Men from the village gazed upon the grim scene. They were farmers and fishermen, not warriors. They clutched axes and cudgels, not swords and spears. They wore no coats of mail, no leather. Their faces were ashen and their knees quaked.

What some had suspected, and others had feared, could no longer be denied in the stark, raw face of this savage butchery: A wolf had come to their lands.

Not a normal wolf, though. No shadow-slinker or lone-lamb-stealer had caused this type of damage. This was the work of something else–a great wolf, a god wolf, a chaser of Mani, whose brightness last night had been white and full.

The townsfolk knew it as truth, as well as they knew their own names, as well as they knew the name of the slain shepherd: Utli Olafsson, their neighbor, their kinsman, and their friend. Like Utli the shepherd, Baudr the huntsman has also been their neighbor, their kinsman, and their friend. Baudr had gone missing, vanished along with his dogs from his cottage without a trace. His uncertain fate now seemed undeniable.

❖

All the able-bodied folk of Vidrtoft worked to make their village ready for the coming darkness.

Gottar did what he could to guide them and to assuage their fears. They looked to him as if he were a lord, for he was the wealthiest and most prosperous. He'd made a modest fortune through trading, then married the sole daughter of a man land-rich but poor in silver.

Gottar had no lofty aspirations, comfortable in the small authority of being the one before whom disputes were brought, the one whose counsel was sought, and whose advice was followed. When he spoke, men hushed to listen.

The barrier surrounding the cluster of huts and houses was a mere low fence of sticks to which they added logs and brambles. They secured the cows and oxen in their byres and penned up the goats and pigs.

Men and strong boys, armed with staves or pitchforks, stood watch while others took their turns seizing what scant sleep they could. Torch poles jutted from the earth, waiting to be set ablaze.

Vidrtoft had no longhouse, no great jarl's hall. Gottar thought sometimes of building one, but the lodgings he'd gained from his father-in-law served him well enough, and he preferred to save his money and not spend it on meaningless displays.

The village did have at its center a wide round ring of cut stones topped with logs and a shingled roof. In ordinary times, this was used as a place for gatherings and feasts, as well as working. It served now as a fastness, where the rest of the folk could be brought–the children and eldren, the ill and unfit and infirm. But even they had their tasks. Only the smallest babes and frailest invalids were not expected to lend their hands. The grain must be ground, the fires must be tended, the wool must be spun, and the chores must be done.

Word of Utli the shepherd's fate had spread rapidly, details exaggerated in each telling. Whispered recounting of Baudr's disappearance was no longer attributed to simple accident or mischance. Some mentioned the savaged remains of boar and deer recently found.

The prospect of night loomed a darker and more ominous shadow than ever before.

❖

A month before….

The snares had done well that day, so Baudr the huntsman ate well that night, as did his dogs. The beasts sprawled in a companionable pile by the fire, and Baudr stretched himself out on the raised platform that served him for sitting and sleeping.

He smiled, content in the quiet.

Now and again he did think of marriage–he knew a fine widow, the wide-hipped Andin, who'd let it be known she would not mind another husband–but few women would be willing to leave the village for the solitary life that he enjoyed.

He'd long since had more than his fill of company. In his youth, he'd served a jarl. He'd bent his back to the oar of a dragonship and had been paid in good coinage. The closeness of such quarters had not suited him; the press and stench and ceaseless talk of his fellow sailors weighed on him like a heavy cloak. And he found that he far preferred putting his skill with a bow to good use against game rather than men.

His cottage sat, small but snug, in its hollow between a boulder and tree. When the mood or need took him, and he had ample pelts and smoked meats to trade, he could travel to Vidrtoft. Sometimes folk came from the village to hunt or cut timber, so he was not always without visitors.

For the most part, however, the villagers avoided the forest wilds and feared what superstition had taught them since the cradle–whispers of witches and trolls and other strange monsters.

Baudr could not deny that they were wholly unfounded; he'd had moments of unease himself. Once, some years back, he'd found a man's skull, badly battered, with no explanation of who he might have been or how he came to be there. Another time, more recently, he had glimpsed in a glade what he thought was a woman, tall and proud-breasted, beautiful, naked…but he remembered stories of sorceresses and did not call out or approach her.

Thinking on fables of old, Baudr dozed into a deep sleep, but he woke to his mutts, tails tucked, hackles raised, whining while staring at the door.

Baudr rose from his bed, troubled. These were hunting dogs, fierce and fearless, harriers of boar and bear alike.

Then he heard a loud rustling and thrashing, a crashing through the brush. He judged by the direction that something had fallen into one of his snares, something large.

He secured his bow and knife and walked around the trembling dogs. When he opened the door, they did not rush out barking and baying but scrambled backward with piteous yelps.

A pale full moon shone down through the boughs, guiding him toward the source of the disturbance. A musky, pungent, wild scent hung in the air.

Before him, tangled in the snare, was a great beast, a wolf larger than any he had ever seen. Enormous. Immense. Bunched with powerful muscle beneath a thick coat. Its eyes glowed like embers. In its struggle to escape, it had only become further ensnared.

He could hardly believe his luck. The pelt off this brute would make a cloak fit for a king, and the story alone would ensure that he never lacked ale or mead.

As he stepped forward, nocking an arrow, the wolf's ember eyes found him, burning, searing in their heat and hatred. Baudr faltered at the keen intelligence he saw there.

As he moved closer, the snare broke, leather cords snapping like twine. With a heave, the wolf righted itself and shook off the tattered restraints. It growled, a low and furious noise that Baudr felt vibrating through his breastbone.

He loosed the arrow. It landed in the wolf's side, buried fletching-deep between ribs. But he might as well have just pricked the beast with a thorn; it lunged at him before he could make another move.

A sharp, slashing agony opened his belly. His entrails tumbled out in a slippery, stinking tangle, slapping wet and heavy against his thighs. He fell hard to the ground, clutching at his insides to try and hold himself together. From some vast distance, his dogs wailed.

As his life flooded out of him to darken the forest floor, the wolf's muzzle lowered. The burning-ember eyes seemed to drink in his pain. Then its jaws closed on Baudr's throat, and he saw nothing more.

❖

"Old Father?" asked Ferilke, looking up from her spindle.

Vjan, warming his bones by a hearth where bread baked on flat rocks in the coals, met her eyes. "Hmm?"

Even at such a tender age, how like her mother she was becoming–the same chestnut hair and clear gaze. She would be as beautiful, but if she proved even half as spirited, she would have a tough time finding herself a husband able to withstand such willfulness.

"Will you tell us a tale, Old Father?" Ferilke asked.

Vjan learned forward. "A tale?" He stroked his white beard.

"Please?"

The others in the room took up the clamor, voices rising in excitement. "Please, Old Father, please!"

"A tale, a tale," Vjan said, still musing. He asked the air before him, "Are these good and diligent little workers deserving of a tale?"

"Yes!" came a begging chorus.

He glanced beyond the circle of their eager faces, seeking objections from his fellow eldern but finding none. "What manner of tale would you have?"

"Freya and her Cats!" Kjarte cried, her golden, tousled curls bouncing.

"That's a girl's story," said Tygg, his plump face twisting into a sneer. "I want battles and blood!"

"Sigurd and the Dragon!" another voice called out.

"Longships and Plunder!"

Once the commotion died down, Ferilke whispered, "What of wolves?"

At her words, the clamor arose anew, led by Hrugar, Gottar's son. He often took to his half-sister's suggestions as if they were his own.

Vjan hesitated and frowned. He glanced around. Bjolf snored, drooling onto his scrawny chest. Uma, swaddled in blankets, coughed weakly. Deaf Lindis hummed to herself while she carded fleece. Neunn was oblivious to all else as she cradled her precious new grandson. Thura, kneading dough, nodded at him. So did Suthor, his gnarled fingers coaxing the shape of a horse's flowing mane from ivory.

"Wolves, yes, wolves!"

"Old Father, please?"

"Tell us of wolves!"

"Yes, a scare-story!"

"With blood!"

"And killing! Lots of killing!"

Vjan lifted his hands to calm them. "As you will, as you will," he said, relenting with a laugh. "Sit now and hush. Hear me well as I tell The Saga of the Fenris Wolf."

❖

Once it was that Loki, the wicked god-tricker
Made a visit to Jotunheim, land of the giants
There, with Angrboda, she who brings sorrow
He sired three children foretold of great mischief

These were their names, that monstrous brood:
Jormungandr, the Serpent of Midgard, world-circling
Hel, flesh-hued of one half and ash-black of the other
And Fenrir, the Fenris Wolf, ever-hungry for fame

By prophecy, the three offspring boded ill for the gods
From the nature of their mother and their father worse still
So the Aesir resolved to do what they could
To fend off this end fate and delay the destruction

The Serpent, they cast into the depths where Njord rules
And wave-maidens polish the bones of the drowned
Hel was made queen of the cold grey corpse-halls
Hunger upon her table and sickness for her bed

Fenrir, they took to Asgard, high home by the Ash-Tree
To be raised under watch of the All-Father's eye
Fed and cared for by Tyr, who alone of the gods
Could stand safe his ground in the very wolf's lair

Odin saw with concern how each day Fenrir grew
The muscle, the sinew, the breadth of his chest
Becoming a larger and more fearsome brute
Destined to cause all the Aesir much harm

It was then decided that the wolf must be bound
Tethered and fettered to tame his fierce temper
Something to which they knew that he would not consent
So they sought instead to ensnare him with wile and guile

First they brought Leyding, of leather, greatly strong
"Try yourself against this," said the gods,
"For one such as you, famed as you would be,
A simple strap such as this should pose little challenge."

And Fenrir, judging it not beyond his strength
Gave the gods leave to bind fast his four legs
At his very first kick did Leyding break and snap free
Loosening him easily from the fetter's grasp

Next they brought Dromi, the iron-forged chain
Twice as strong as Leyding had been at the least
"True fame," the gods told the wolf, "cannot be had without risk.
"If these bonds will not hold you, then nothing will."

Well, Fenrir saw that this chain was strong, of stout make
But he knew as well that his own strength had grown
So he again let them bind him, four legs fettered
And the wolf set himself once more to the test

He pushed and he pulled and Dromi still held
He clawed and he kicked until foam flecked his lips
He heaved and he strained with all of his might
Then the iron links shattered, the pieces flew high

Now, bolder in boasting than ever before
He went with the Aesir across the dark lake
To Lyngvi, the island, the place thick with heather
For a feast-day as the fresh wind blew

There, he was shown Gleipnir, the silken band
Slender and fine, finer than Freya's fair hair
The gods passed it about amongst themselves
Marveling that they could not rend such thin cloth

"Oh, but the Fenris-Wolf could," some of them said,
"For did he not snap Leyding, the stout strap of leather?
And did he not shatter Dromi, the iron-forged chain?
This wisp, this mere ribbon, this would be nothing!"

The other gods, laughing, said, "If even we, even Thor,
Odin's son, thunder-maker, cannot break this thin band,
Then surely it is beyond the wolf Fenrir's famed strength
And we need have no fear of him for evermore."

"I will consent that my legs be bound again," Fenrir said,
"If one of you, high Aesir, great gods and wise,
Will set his hand whole within my mouth
And let it rest there as a pledge of good faith."

For although the Fenris-Wolf's pride felt the sting
He suspected deception, some clever craft
Demanding this proof against any misfortune
Which, of course, none of the gods were eager to do

At last there stepped forth the brave god of glory
Settler of duels, justice's champion, bold Tyr
Who placed his hand between the wolf's jaws
To hold it there as Fenrir's legs with Gleipnir were tied

This then was when the trickery came revealed
The fine band had been in Svartalfheim dwarf-made
Fashioned by them from six impossible things
So Gleipnir would be just as impossible to break

Of the beard of a woman and the breath of a fish
Of a bear's sinew and a bird's spittle and a mountain's roots
And the sound of the footfall of a cat was it forged
Which is why these things are found nowhere else in the world

The stronger the wolf fought, the stronger the band grew
Until Fenrir lay helpless, well and fully bound
The gods, relieved at this, made joy and celebration
All save Tyr, whose hand had been in one bite taken off

They brought next a stone slab pierced with holes
And strung a cord through it, anchoring it with a deep peg
Gjoll, was the slab named, and the anchor-peg Thviti
To the cord, called Gelgja, Gleipnir was tied

Fenrir, fettered such that he could not fight free
Howled wild howls and bit wide in his wrath
Teeth gnashing until his mouth was sword-struck
Slicing his gums so that the wolf's blood ran red

Then it was that a fury filled Fenris-Wolf's heart
He summoned his son, known as Hati, moon-chaser
The hater, the enemy, black wolf of the night
Brother to Skoll, who gives chase to the sun

In Hati and in Hati's sons he stirred madness
A ravenous craving to devour and destroy
A blood-lust, an unspeakable hunger for flesh
Sated only by making them eaters of men --

❖

"Vjan!" Gottar's voice crashed through the hall like a hammer blow on an anvil.

They all were startled, young and old alike. The baby let out a sound somewhere between a wail and screech, then began to cry. Even the crone, Lindis, deaf as a stump, dropped her hand-carders so that the fluffs of fleece fell smutty in the soot and dust.

Gottar strode past them without acknowledging their distress. "What, by Thor's thunder, are you doing, telling them tales such as this?"

Children scattered, all except for Gottar's own.

Hrugar looked as if he would have liked to join the scatter, but Ferilke stayed where she was, beside the old man, and this seemed to have shamed Hrugar into staying as well.

Ferilke. Gottar could hardly look upon her without seeing the face of her mother, Ulrika.

"There's no harm in tales—" began the old man.

Gottar clenched his jaw. "Men are dead, livestock slaughtered! Wolves roam the woods! And you sit here spinning tales of Fenrir?"

"It'll be a caution to them to not stray far from home."

"It'll be night of no sleep, if they're up all the night with the terrors!"

"I'm not afraid," said Ferilke.

Hrugar's eyes were wide, but he bobbed his head. "Nor am I, Father! They're just stories."

"Well, of such stories, we've had enough!" Snorting, Gottar turned away.

The storyteller had gone from placatory to indignant. "These tales serve a good purpose!"

Gottar spun to face him. "To cause panic with foolish superstitions? To distract men from their honest and profitable labors?"

"Not all in this world can be reckoned by money!"

"All that matters can be," Gottar told him. "You'll see for yourself; tomorrow in the clean light of day, when this rogue wolf lies dead like any other, they'll laugh at themselves for their meaningless fears."

❖

Outside the fence of logs and brambles, a lone goat bleated plaintively in the dusk. The moon rose fat and full, shedding a silvery shimmer through the night mist.

The men and boys waited. Hands gripped tight to the hafts of pitchforks and rakes, palms sweating, knuckles aching from tension. Their expressions in the torchlight were drawn and grim-set.

They had dug pits in the fields, covering them with stretched hides pegged down and disguised by a thin layer of dirt. Beneath these were stakes, roughhewn ends jutting upward.

A goat, tied by a rope, continued bleating.

Women served meals that went largely uneaten. Children fretted, too overwrought for sleep. A hushed expectation hung in the air.

Clouds crept across the sky, veiling the moon's white face, obscuring its pale shine. The goat's bleats became screams. A huge shape moved swiftly in the shadows. There was a sudden violent commotion, the goat brutally silenced, a thudding crunch followed by a pained, piercing howl.

Men rushed from the village, armed with their tools and torches, to the place where one of the pit traps had collapsed.

They brought ropes and chain, intending to haul up their prize from the hole after they stabbed and hacked every last trace of life from it. But when they peered into the pit, they saw only the goat's bloodied carcass impaled across the many stakes.

A hot, snorting chuff of breath made them turn.

The wolf sprang among them, teeth flashing. It tore flesh from bone and ripped away one man's scalp, leaving a ragged hairy flap. His skull gleamed all along the side of his peeled head. Some men stumbled into their own traps, sharp wood punching into their throats and guts.

Pitchforks jabbed, scythes and cudgels swung, and two men tried to sling chain over the beast. But a twist of the wolf's body yanked the end from one of the men's grasp. The other held on, shouting for help. A weak link gave with a crack; iron flung against the man's chin with such force that his lower jaw shattered into a dripping red ruin.

With a leap and a bound, the wolf fled from the field, leaving corpses and carnage in its wake.

❖

So many had died. Youths and men alike, gutted, dismembered, lifeless in pools of blood. Others lived, though for how long remained uncertain. Few had escaped only with scratches, and fewer still had survived unscathed.

Gottar himself was among the latter. The wolf had merely knocked him aside in passing.

A mother, whose barely-bearded twin boys had fallen beneath savage bites, wailed over their corpses. As for the rest, their lamentation had to be set aside for later. Too much else remained that needed to be done.

The wounded were brought to the center of Vidrtoft. The dead were lowered into the very pits intended for the wolf.

Vjan, bent over his gnarled walking stick, moved to and fro among the gathered, offering words of comfort.

With some, he joked and was jovial, telling them they would have proud battle scars to boast of. With others, he made promises to see that debts would be settled and messages delivered. He spoke quietly of the gods or warmly of times past.

It was only much later that Hruga, Gottar's woman, burst through the door to ask if anyone had seen her son, Hrugar.

A quick search was made, the children questioned, but it soon became clear that both Hrugar and Ferilke were gone.

❖

"You see?" Ferilke asked. "I told you. I was right. You shouldn't have doubted."

"I didn't," objected Hrugar. "I came along, didn't I?"

They had slipped from the village during the bustling activity, Ferilke confident that no one would notice their absence until mealtime at least. It was an easy matter for her to guide Hrugar through gaps in the fence, cross the fields, and enter the forest.

In the dense trees, Ferilke unloaded the dried meats stolen from the town's stores and waited. Finally, the wolf had come. Sun-dapple and leaf-shadow played over its pelt, dark grey streaked with silver and ivory and black.

Ferilke withdrew a long, thin ribbon of silk.

The wolf's amber eyes regarded the ribbon warily.

"Just like in Old Father's story," she said. "No iron chain or leather strap…this will be as nothing to one of your great strength. You could break it with ease."

The wolf's eyes narrowed. Its lips skinned back, baring sharp, blood-stained teeth.

"Open your mouth, then," Ferilke coaxed the wolf. "Let Hrugar put his hand between your jaws."

Hrugar jumped back. "What? Why?"

"To prove our trust and good will, as Tyr did," she said.

"What if I won't?"

"Then you'll be a coward, not brave like Tyr."

"You wouldn't tell!"

Ferilke pointed at his chest. "I would and I will."

Hrugar looked from the waiting maw to his hand, curling his fingers again. "It'll bite me."

"Only if it can't break the band."

"But, in the story–"

"That was Gleipnir, made by dwarves," she said, impatience becoming exasperation. "This is a plain silk ribbon my mother wore in her hair."

Still, the wolf waited, slaughter on its hot, damp breath, amber gaze fixed upon the boy.

Hrugar slowly extended his arm. His hand shook, fingers trembling as he unclenched to slide them between the sharp, pointed rows. He glanced once more at Ferilke, pleading.

"You see?" she said to the wolf. "We trust that you mean us no harm, so you must trust that we mean none to you in return."

She crouched and brought the silk band close to the wolf's foreleg. The fur was warm and soft to the touch. She slipped the ribbon once around and tied a loose knot just above the broad paw.

"Ferilke…" whined Hrugar.

"Hush." She began to stretch the ribbon toward the other foreleg.

The wolf's jaws snapped shut with a vicious crunch. Skin ripped and blood sprayed. Hrugar shrieked.

Ferilke recoiled from the wet, red spatter across her face. She landed hard on her back, struck breathless as much by the impact as she was by what she saw happening before her.

Hrugar attempted to pull his arm free, but the wolf held fast, clamping down all the harder so that there was a terrible grinding and cracking of brittle bones.

"No!" Ferilke cried, but the wolf paid no heed.

More blood gushed as the boy struggled in the relentless toothy grip. Urine soaked the front of his breeches. His free hand slapped madly at the wolf's furry head. He fell, feet tangled, to thrash and kick upon the ground.

"I didn't bind you! I didn't finish! And it's only silk. It would have broken!"

To this, as well, the wolf paid no heed. It stood over Hrugar, powerful shoulders bunched. It gave a mighty wrench of its neck. With the gruesome tearing of meat and gristle, the boy's hand came loose from his arm, trailing veins and tendons, vanishing in a single gulp down the wolf's gullet.

❖

Gottar, angrier than he'd been in years and more afraid than he was willing to admit, stalked grumbling through the trees.

This was all the girl's doing, of that he was sure. She'd goaded the boy into it, willful creature that she was.

It was unfair and unwarranted, he knew, to hate the daughter as much as he'd hated the mother. Ferilke had been little more than a toddler at the time, blameless. But now the wretched girl might cost him his son. For that, he could hate her as freely as he'd grown to hate Ulrika.

Ulrika had been opposed to the marriage, in love with some wood-cutter whose father was poorer than her own. What began as unhappiness soon became bitterness. Not even the birth of their child had softened her resentment.

When Gottar had forsaken their cold and unwelcoming bed for Hruga's, Ulrika had taken this to mean she could return to her own lover's arms without consequence.

That was an insult Gottar's pride would not bear.

At the boy's first shriek, Gottar's anger and weariness were forgotten. He plunged ahead, hearing more screams, Ferilke's cries, and a terrible guttural growl.

Hrugar lay on his back, blood spouting crimson from his stumped wrist. The wolf's forelegs straddled the boy's body, muzzle burrowing beneath his chin.

A raging madness fell over Gottar, such as he'd not known since that day he'd followed his faithless wife to meet with her lover in a similar wood-grove. He'd meant only to give them both a sound beating. He had not intended to drive the man's head again and again against a boulder, but he did not stop until blood smeared across the stone. What else could he have done but finish the act, conceal the crime, and let folks think instead that Ulrika and her lover had run off?

Gottar flung himself on the wolf, fists flailing. The boy's screams ended in a bubbling gurgle. Gottar tore clumps of hair from the wolf's pelt and pummeled its body. The wolf uttered a roar. It spun, hurling him aside.

When he raised his head, it was to see Ferilke huddled nearby, arms wrapped around her knees. Her face was tear-streaked, eyes brimming with piteous fear. He lunged at her, swinging his arms. Twice more did his fists strike his daughter's face before the wolf's jaws hamstrung him.

Gottar rolled sideways. His vision filled with the gaping black maw of the wolf's mouth.

❖

Ferilke moaned, waking with the slow, sludgy struggle of one fighting her way through a mire. Her surroundings were dark and unfamiliar. Warm, though, and the earthen smell was strange but not unpleasant.

She blinked until she could see clearly. She heard water trickling, chuckling over pebbles. She heard the wind sighing around the pine boughs.

Her head hurt with a low, dull throb. She sat up carefully, then felt at her face, finding it swollen and bruised, and remembered the blows from her father's fists, the stickiness of blood still drying on her skin.

A shadow briefly blocked the cave's opening. A shape entered, ducking under roots. Not a wolf but a woman…naked except for a length of silken ribbon hanging from one wrist.

They looked at each other. The woman's amber gaze was intent. Her head tipped to the side so that her hair swept in a long fall over her shoulder–hair the same chestnut color as Ferilke's.

"Mother?" she asked in a whisper.

"Yes." she nodded. "Yes, Ferilke."

Ulrika knelt beside the bed of soft moss where Ferilke sat. She untied the ribbon and held it out. Ferilke took it, running it through her hands.

"Mother," she said, this time more sure. They embraced. "I thought you were gone. That you'd abandoned us."

"So your father would have had it. He beat me and left me for dead. The sons of Hati found me. They saved me, took me with them, made me their wolf-wife." Ulrika laved blood from the girl's brow with rough strokes of her tongue.

"Wolf-wife?"

"We traveled far through the forests. We roamed high in the mountains where the snow never melts. We raced in meadows, the grass standing tall as our shoulders. I was one with the pack. I hunted. I howled."

"And now?"

"And now," she said, smiling at her daughter, her teeth strong, pointed. "Now, at last, I have come home." ◆

Christine Morgan works the overnight shift in a psychiatric facility, which plays havoc with her sleep schedule but allows her a lot of writing time. A lifelong reader, she also reviews, beta-reads, occasionally edits and dabbles in self-publishing. Her other interests include gaming, history, superheroes, crafts, cheesy disaster movies and training to be a crazy cat lady. She can be found online at www.christine-morgan.org.

Artwork: InkyMcStapleface

THE MUMMIFIED MONK

REBECCA FUNG

Luong knew that it was time to die. Perhaps if he were not a monk, it would be something he approached with apprehension or fear. Perhaps he would not approach it at all. Men of the ordinary world did not embrace death–they ran away from it. The tiniest whiff of it, and they would use chemicals and treatments to put it off, shove it into the future, so they would no longer have to think about dying.

There were people, far closer to death than Luong, who clung to every last second with all their determination…but not Luong. He neither ran toward, nor fled from death. He accepted it as the natural ending to his life cycle and said, "I am ready. I do not fear. This is as it should be."

Luong was not ill. He just knew he was fading. He could feel his body slipping away, and he knew he should allow it to do so. It was the True Way.

Mastery over the mind was one thing, but even more difficult was mastery over the body, for that involved more than just meditation and prayer.

Luong lit incense, took a carved spoon, and sprinkled oil and water over the altar, as was the tradition of his Order. He moved very slowly. Soon he would not be able to sprinkle at all, and he would know it was time to go to the vault. But for the moment he would continue his tasks, although each movement was made with incredible pain.

After completing the simple task, Luong looked down at his hands. His skin was a yellow-brown. The skin was what bound a person to their body, and as such, it was affected first. It was not easy to give up. He had pictured himself shedding like a snake, wiggling out of his skin easily and dropping it to the ground on his way to meet the Winged Ones in the sky.

The reality was far from this airborne fancy. To give up the skin, one must allow it to slowly dry, and instead of shedding, the skin would bind one down. Though Luong had grown lighter, his skin felt heavier as it hardened.

Luong prayed to the gods and the Winged Ones. He would never lose faith, no matter what pain he had to endure.

Some believe that a monk is beyond pain, that the gods protect him, or that meditation allows one to not feel. This couldn't be further from the truth. There are not many monks who could do what Luong set out to do.

Luong was acutely aware of every change to his body. As a monk, he was a man of fine sensitivities and had an alert mind. He had trained to be able to focus on each part of his body separately *and* as a whole. Each tiny pinprick or tingle, he told himself, is proof of the Higher Being's presence. When he meditated, he would often focus on a small part of his body, allowing himself to feel tiny sensations, until those feelings took him over.

But now that he had undergone the ritual, he was only eating certain nuts and seeds, drinking a special tea, and avoiding too much light. Very soon he would lock himself in the vault and undergo the final stage.

He knew the process: Sit in the lotus position with his only access to the rest of the world being an air tube and a bell to ring. Stay there until his body solidified. Once done, the other monks would entomb him.

Luong shuddered.

Only cowardice would cause a monk to shudder at the thought of displaying the greatest devotion, he knew, so he began to pray.

He could feel the effects of the tea on his flesh, the pain in his arms, his legs, and his neck, as his skin shrivelled around him like bandages being wound tight.

Though he could not rid himself of the pain, he could still control his mind. It's this discipline that shows the man over the beast, the monk over the man. Luong refused to allow himself to stop his rituals simply because of the pain. He would not give up his faith, even as he felt his stomach being slashed apart from the tea.

I am leaving this shell of a body, but my spirit will fly, and despite all the pain, all the temptation to break my rituals, I must not, for only the most pure, most disciplined, most noble of spirits will fly so high.

He retched constantly. Mucus poured from the sides of his eyes. His lips crackled in dryness such that blood ran from them. Still, Luong smiled.

Luong went into the vault, closed the door, and rang the bell.

He knew the other monks would look into the vault with awe and trepidation. His carcass would be preserved for a long time, and many monks would pray by it, hoping that some of Luong's extraordinary character would be passed onto them, helping them find their True Way.

Eventually, the bell stopped ringing.

❖

"What a perfectly wonderful story!" Brother Tristan cast a broad smile. Luong's story always got a great response, no matter what class he recited it to. It was one of his favourites to tell. A part of him felt stronger after repeating the tale, and another part of him despaired that he could never be as great a monk as Luong.

Where are all the great monks now?

Brother Tristan saw himself as a very ordinary monk, but he liked to tell stories about the great ones. There were inspirational monks, daring monks, heroic monks, and Brother Tristan admired them all. He contemplated all of them while remaining in the safety of his classroom.

"The story shows the greatness that some monks could achieve," said Brother Tristan. "It is a life we give ourselves to–discipline and devotion–really, boys!"

The giggling and nudging in the back of the group subsided when the students seemed to realise Brother Tristan's eyes rested on them.

"Discipline," said Brother Tristan. "Some have mastered how to overcome the most primal desires and urgent calls of the body in their show of discipline to the Higher Being. And you boys cannot even pull yourselves together for an hour of a lesson!" He sighed. "Now, have we any comments on today's story?"

"Brother Tristan," said one student. "Is the mummified monk *real*?"

Brother Tristan was known for his indulgence in storytelling, not lying exactly, rather lessons through fables and metaphors. None of the students seemed to like Brother Tristan's explanations about metaphors. They wanted real pots of gold, real flying horses, real lions that died, and most of all real mummified monks.

"Of course the mummified monk is real," said Brother Tristan. "Sokushinbutsu was a practice taken up in some areas of Japan and Tibet. It was uncommon, but of course that is what made it so admirable. Not everyone could do that. We admire men who can do great things, don't we? That is why we tell stories about them."

A murmur rippled through the group.

"Have you ever *seen* a mummified monk?"

Brother Tristan shook his head. "No, I have not. But I would like to. It is a great part of our history. There are still monks enshrined in some of the monasteries. Perhaps one day we will visit one." Brother Tristan smiled. "There are many good stories about the powers of the mummified monk. His body brings good luck to the monastery in which he resides. Those who worship him have their minds cleared and see the True Way with absolute clarity. Just seeing him makes many a better monk! While he was in the vault, waiting for the final stage before his soul departed for the Winged Ones, it is said he saw much and learned much, and his soul reached a stage that many of ours never will. Unfortunately, he could never pass it on to us in life. Instead, he passes on some good through death, through his earthbound body."

"It sounds sick," said one student. "Drinking poison tea and throwing up till you die!"

"It is beautiful," said another student, Olaf, quietly. "You didn't get the point of the story at all."

"Beautiful! What are you, a girl?" jeered the others. But Olaf ignored their taunts.

At the end of class, Olaf waited behind. "Brother Tristan, do you believe in the powers of the mummified monk?"

"I believe, Olaf," answered Brother Tristan.

"I'd like to see a mummified monk one day," said Olaf.

"I hope that you will. I hope that his great powers will touch you. Now get ready for your next class."

❖

Olaf was the most promising of Brother Tristan's students. There were a great number who did not make it past the first year. Then there were those who simply went through the motions of being a monk because their family had pushed them into it.

Olaf was different. He was one of the top students, sincere about his lessons. While it wasn't right to play favourites, Brother Tristan could not help but devote more time to this group of boys. *It is as the Higher Being would want it*, Brother Tristan thought. *We must nurture those closest to the True Way.*

Was it right to refer to the group as a clique? They were, in Brother Tristan's mind, a group separate from the others; they were the better students. But they did not band together. They seemed hardly aware they were special. They were intelligent boys; monks of such calibre were generally not stupid, but they didn't use their intelligence to observe each other.

Perhaps that is what makes me so ordinary, Brother Tristan thought. *I spend too much time weighing other monks, and I am not focused on higher thoughts like these boys are.*

He had resigned himself long ago that being a mentor was his talent, even if it did not mean being a great monk. Being so close with his students allowed him to see when things were unwell, and it was obvious to him that Olaf looked ill. He had a suspicion as to why and confronted him.

"Olaf," said Brother Tristan.

"Yes, Brother?"

"I wish to speak to you. I can see that you have not been eating well. You look pale."

"It is nothing, Brother."

"I think it is something. It has to do with the pilgrimage you took to Japan, doesn't it? You haven't looked well since you came back."

Olaf's eyes filled with tears. "It's not right to cry, Brother. But... but...."

"Say it, Olaf, and then we can be done with the tears forever. If you do not say it, the tears will be locked inside you, ready to burst forth at any moment like a thunderstorm."

"I looked for the mummified monk," said Olaf. "I did my research. You know I always wanted to see him. So I found the temple and I journeyed to it."

"Aah," said Brother Tristan. "So you journeyed to the mummified monk and he disappointed you? This happens, Olaf. Perhaps I built it up too much for you. I am sorry. I am an enthusiastic storyteller, but it is not always the best thing."

"Oh no!" said Olaf. "The mummified monk was everything you said he would be. He changed my life, Brother Tristan. He was amazing. I fell to my knees and I prayed. A feeling of cleansing came over me, Brother Tristan, a feeling...so imposing and unworldly. In front of him, I felt I was right in touch with the Higher Being! I felt the Winged Ones brush against my cheeks. Do you know his corpse does not decompose, even now, so long as they keep him in the dimly lit temple? And I felt he has not been destroyed because he has gone beyond what normal men can. I wish you had been there, Brother Tristan."

"I wish I had been there too," he said softly. Olaf's eyes had changed. He had not taken the last steps to being accepted into the monkhood yet, but to Brother Tristan he was further on the way to enlightenment than any other student. When he spoke of the mummified monk, there had been a shift in his expression. He had unlocked a secret world and returned so much richer. Brother Tristan felt a pang of envy.

My job is to create great students and great monks, he reminded himself. *If a monk has found his way, I have done well. Let that be my reward.*

Olaf nodded and turned to go.

"But, Olaf," called Brother Tristan, and the boy turned back. "Why do you look pale and miserable? Surely such a trip should leave you rich and fulfilled?"

"I wanted you to be there," said Olaf simply. "I felt it was not right that I saw the mummified monk but you did not. Did you know that hardly anyone visits that temple? The great glory of the Higher Being, and hardly anyone is taking it in."

"That is very thoughtful of you," said Brother Tristan. "But it is not up to you to feel bad in such situations."

"I did something you mightn't approve of," blurted out Olaf. "I tried to steal the monk. I wanted you to see it so badly, I thought he could do so much good here, and more people would see him! I thought, if I could just push it into a suitcase nobody would know."

"Olaf," said Brother Tristan. "Where is it? Where's the mummified monk?"

"I couldn't do it," admitted Olaf. "I tried. I went to the temple and I broke open the tomb where the monk is kept but he was…. His eyes, they were red and shiny. He was…watching me. I almost lost my nerve right then, Brother Tristan. I tried to grab him and it felt wrong. The monk was somehow very cold. I expected him to feel like stone, but he felt like ice. And I thought, perhaps it's a warning. He scared me. I'm a coward. So I dropped him and I left."

Brother Tristan hid his disappointment. So he would not see the monk after all. He could not blame the boy, but he forced himself to comfort Olaf. "You did the right thing. The Higher Being gave you a sign, and you knew not to take the monk."

Olaf nodded. "Thank you, Brother Tristan. You are a good friend and a good monk." But Olaf's head drooped, and he did not look content.

And now, neither was Brother Tristan. He lay awake at nights, thinking of Olaf, the mummified monk, and the attempted heist. It was a great story that could be added to Brother Tristan's collection. He could see the glowing red eyes as Olaf described them, piercing the heart of the valiant in the darkness.

But the more he thought about it, the more Brother Tristan thought about how they almost had the monk and all his powers in their own monastery.

❖

Perhaps, if he were a better monk, he would have been able to push the loss to the side and continue his work with the same vigour as found in past years. But Brother Tristan brooded. He saw the mummified monk in his dreams. It was strange he had told that story for years and it had never affected him so much. Now that Olaf had made his pilgrimage and added his piece, the monk haunted Brother Tristan.

It was illogical to resent Olaf, but he couldn't help it. Olaf had seen the monk himself, and Brother Tristan had not. Olaf had been so close! He might have brought him the mummified monk, but he had failed!

He had once enjoyed talking to Olaf, but eventually those conversations stopped. Olaf became Brother Olaf, and Brother Tristan merely went through the motions of joining in at the ceremony. He did not offer to play a special role as mentors often did. He began to focus on the younger, newer generation of students and ignored Brother Olaf as much as possible.

Easy enough for Olaf, he thought. *He has seen the mummified monk! But what of those of us who have not?*

He had let his student mentoring slip, but he did not realise how much until one of the elder monks spoke to him.

"Brother Tristan, you have long been admired for your ability to handle the students and your mentoring abilities," the elder monk stated. "But your work has come into question of late."

"My work?"

"You do not seem to be paying attention to the classes or preparing very well," said the elder monk. "What's more, several of the more promising students left the monastery some time ago, before they had a chance to ascend to monkhood, and a few more shortly after."

Brother Tristan was jolted into reality. The elder monk passed him a list of students and junior monks who had left; yes, these were some of the boys that he had thought most highly of. Brother Olaf's name was not on the list. But he saw Francis and Jaspar and a few others, and he wondered why he did not know that they had left.

"When did they leave?" Brother Tristan asked.

"We're not sure, exactly," said the elder. "They did not give notice. Apparently they simply packed their bags and left. We have approximate dates for each. Some left over a year ago, one more than two years ago. It's adding up, Brother Tristan. You need to pay more attention, especially to our remaining top students."

Brother Tristan looked over the list again. "I will, I will."

"Otherwise, I am sorry to say, we will be finding a replacement as a student mentor."

He had always been the one to look after the boys and tell them stories and see them through to monkhood. Losing that would be losing his life.

The problem was that although he viewed the most promising students as a small group, he was not sure they thought of themselves that way.

Brother Olaf was one of the few from the top group of students who remained. Brother Tristan would ask him what he knew.

❖

Standing there with more on his mind than the mummified monk, Brother Tristan felt a surge of emotion. It was like old times when he used to talk to Brother Olaf, and the mummified monk had not been between them.

Brother Olaf and I used to be able to talk openly. We understood each other.

"They left for a higher reason," said Brother Olaf.

"So you know where they went? Why they went? Why didn't anyone tell me?"

"It was a private decision," said Brother Olaf. "But they will do greater good."

"What could be greater than being a monk? They were so promising. I always thought they–and you too, Olaf–were my best students."

"No, Brother Tristan. I am not a great student, nor a great monk. I wanted to be…I tried. I even went on my pilgrimage, but I failed you and I failed this monastery."

Brother Tristan wanted to say something comforting then, but he could not think of anything.

Brother Olaf shook his head. "I can't let it go."

"Don't blame yourself," said Brother Tristan. Only a part of him meant it, but that was a start. Stronger and more sincere, he added, "You can still find your True Way."

"That is all I want," said Brother Olaf. "I go to sleep at night, and wish I was back in Japan. The mummified monk would surely give me the direction I am seeking."

"We need to be able to get on without him," said Brother Tristan. "I was obsessed with him too. But now, I know I need to find out about what happened to my students, so I can fix this. I used to be valued here as a mentor. I cannot let that go. It is not a grand aspiration, but it is for me."

Brother Olaf smiled. "You are a great monk, Brother Tristan."

"Thank you."

"Do you want to know where the other students went?" asked Brother Olaf.

"Yes, indeed. That's why I came to ask you."

"Follow me and I will explain."

❖

Brother Tristan followed Olaf to the basement levels. A hard and foul stench hit him. He wanted to turn and run.

"It is for the Higher Being," said Brother Olaf's voice behind him. "Don't let the stench put you off the work."

Brother Tristan forced himself to look around the dim room. As his eyes adjusted, he was able to make out the shape of a man sitting in the lotus position, and his skin was a delicate flakiness over a hard frame–the mummified monk.

Brother Tristan had told the story long enough and often enough to know. He had always believed that if he saw a true mummified monk, he would fall to his knees in praise of the Higher Being, the heavens would open, and the Winged Ones would dance in front of his eyes.

But now that he had the real thing in front of him, he felt a mixture of awe and wonder, paralysis and revulsion. His knees started to bend. The sight both intimidated him and made him want to vomit.

"Marvellous, isn't he?" asked Brother Olaf. "I believe you, of all people, Brother Tristan, will understand and appreciate. This is why I brought you here."

"But how did you get him here? You said you left him. You said you could not do it. How did he get here?"

"That is Francis."

Brother Tristan took in the words slowly. "Francis…?" He looked up at the preserved corpse, and now he saw something different. Not the frame of an esteemed monk from history, but the body of his student looking down at him. His eyes did not shine with the purity of the Winged Ones, but swam with accusations.

This is the most revolting thing a man could put himself through, Brother Tristan thought.

"The process of mummification takes many years," said Brother Olaf. "I researched it thoroughly during my pilgrimage in Japan. It still does, to do it properly. To reach the enlightenment, the body must take on several years of natural change. I have worked on certain methods to speed up the entire mummification procedure. I believe I've made real progress. For instance, I have found chemicals that can be rubbed into the skin to preserve it more quickly, and I refined the herbed tea they drink."

Brother Tristan's jaw hung open, but he could not speak. He stepped toward Francis and saw three additional bodies in cages, two sitting upright in lotus position. Each was reed-thin and glistening with oil. None of them seemed to notice Brother Tristan. The body lying down was the skinniest with yellow-brown tinged skin. His hands and legs were locked in metal cuffs and chains.

"In the name of the Higher Being, what are you doing to these men?" gasped Brother Tristan. "They need to be released and treated immediately!"

"Don't be ridiculous," said Brother Olaf. "You know what is happening as well as I do. You know the process. You have told me so many times, over and over in class. Though I have refined it, I cannot do what these men are doing. But I can offer some small service to the Higher Being. I have resigned myself to it, Brother Tristan. I may not be a great monk, but I can give great monks to the Higher Being. I have found my True Way."

"It's not right," said Brother Tristan. "These men locked up like this. You're forcing them, killing them, murdering them…."

"It's mummification," said Brother Olaf. "These men all want to serve the Higher Being. They love the mummified monk story. They are good monks. I can tell they are suitable. Brother Tristan, when I explained it to them, they all wanted to serve. It's just that, well, sometimes the body is not as strong as the mind. That is why the cages, the cuffs. Sometimes we struggle, but we know it is wrong. I facilitate. I help turn these men into great monks."

"It is barbaric!" Welts grew on their skin, and their bleeding, open sores gleamed with oil. Their undernourished bodies hung from crooked backs.

"It is beautiful," said Brother Olaf. "Brother Tristan, I am not sure you understand the point of your own story. The mummified monks will bring glory to our monastery."

Brother Tristan shook his head. "Why did you do this? Why?"

"Everyone remembers the mummified monk," said Brother Olaf. "From when you first told me that story, Brother Tristan, I knew I would bring a monk to the monastery somehow. I would find that True Way, as you always described it. Truly, Brother Tristan, you have been a good mentor. Look around you and see what you have created! Look around!"

Brother Tristan lost his stomach and fell to the ground, crying.

"Don't worry," said Brother Olaf. "Everyone does the same the first time they come down. Jaspar and Leslie did. But it becomes easier. After a while, you don't feel your body at all. It takes some time, but you'll barely notice."

Brother Tristan looked at the cages containing his students, rotting away, and continued crying for his weakness. He did not feel Brother Olaf put his arm around him soothingly, nor the cuffs as they clicked around his legs and wrists. ◆

Rebecca Fung is a legal editor based in Sydney, Australia. She loves to edit in the light…but writing brings out her dark side. She has previously had her dark fiction published in Midnight Echo, Voluted Tales *and* Eclecticism *magazines and is a regular contributor to the* Demonic Visions *anthology series. Her work has also been published in a number of other anthologies and her ebook* Dead Lucky *will be published by Perpetual Motion Machine Publishing in their* One Night Stands *series in October 2014.*

Artwork: Alex Hewitt

BONY RIVER

STANLEY B. WEBB

"When you were little," Mr. Thompson said, "you would run away from me every time we came here."

"You could never catch me," said Martha.

"I caught you every time."

"I'll bet you can't catch me now." She grinned like an imp and ran.

Mr. Thompson chased her through the park. He normally felt light on his feet, but today his body felt heavier. He forced himself to run faster but still fell farther behind the giggling Martha. Black spots appeared in his vision. His heart pounded against his ribs. Mr. Thompson stopped and leaned against a tree, laboring to breathe.

Martha ran back. "Daddy, are you all right?"

"Yeah…just winded," he lied, feeling as if he were drowning inside himself.

Martha retrieved her phone. "I'm calling an ambulance."

"Put that away." Once his heart calmed, he pushed off the tree.

Martha clutched his arm. "Daddy, you look terrible."

"Thanks."

She tightened her grip. "I made you chase me. You're too old for that game."

"I'm not too old!" Mr. Thompson faced her. "I'm only 62!"

"I want you to see my doctor," Martha said.

"I don't need a doctor."

Her eyes opened wide, full of tears. "I lost Mom two years ago. I can't lose you, too. Promise me, please, that you'll see Dr. Sing."

After a moment, he said, "Okay, I promise."

Mr. Thompson walked carefully to his pickup. He got into his truck and waited behind the wheel, wanting to be sure that he wouldn't faint while driving. When he felt confident, he started the engine, waved to Martha, and drove away.

❖

While driving down a winding, two-lane road, a 1972 Charger tailgated Mr. Thompson–the same model he had owned when he was a bachelor. Thick smoke blew from the car's undercarriage, rust blended with its dark green paint, and its vinyl roof flapped around in shreds. Cracks obscured the windshield, causing the silhouette behind the wheel to be nearly impossible to see.

He hadn't seen the car approach. Twice he tried waving for the Charger to pass, but it only inched closer.

Mr. Thompson turned onto his street. The Charger followed. One eye still on the rear-view, he quickly pulled inside his garage and closed the door. He got out of the truck and stared through the small window in the door and watched the Charger pass by slowly.

When he pulled away from the window, he glanced up at a fifteen-foot aluminum canoe stretched across the rafters above. Pack baskets, two ice chests, sleeping bags, and paddles rested on a platform beside the canoe. The camping gear made him remember better days. He reminisced, putting the Charger out of his mind, and walked inside the house.

❖

"More tests will be necessary," said Dr. Sing. "But, on the basis of today's examination, and considering your occupational history, I'm certain that you're suffering from asbestosis."

"But I worked in an auto factory."

"Asbestos is common in the auto industry. Did you work with brake pads?"

Mr. Thompson swallowed. "Yeah, but I had a physical every year. I always got a clean bill of health."

"Who was your doctor?"

"The factory's medical office."

Dr. Sing nodded. "Your employer may have had a reason for not discovering work-related health issues."

Mr. Thompson swore. "I just retired."

The doctor paused a moment, then cautiously said, "I'm afraid that it's too late to help your lungs. Scarring has already occurred."

Mr. Thompson's hands trembled. He balled them into tight fists.

Dr. Sing continued, "Your condition *is* life-threatening. Your alveoli are damaged and incapable of passing sufficient oxygen into your blood supply. That explains your sudden fatigue. Those spells can happen any time and can be much more severe if you exert yourself. In an extreme exertion, you could experience complete heart failure. You need to adopt a restful lifestyle."

"My wife and I planned to have adventures after I retired. She passed away…and I was going to take a whitewater canoe trip down the Black River."

Dr. Sing shook his head. "Absolutely out of the question."

❖

Mr. Thompson met his daughter at the food court in the shopping mall.

"What did Dr. Sing say?" Martha hugged him.

"I have a problem in my lungs. Asbestosis," he said, poking around his salad with a plastic fork.

"Is it bad?"

Mr. Thompson shrugged. "He recommended that I take life easy. Watch television. Say, would you help me pick one out?"

After they finished eating, Martha led him to an electronics store. Styles had changed drastically since he and his bride had furnished their home. She pointed out a huge, flat object. "This is a plasma screen, high-definition home theater. It comes with surround sound, and it hooks right to your computer."

"I don't have a computer, and I don't want one."

"Yes, you do, Daddy. All the best shows are online."

He scowled at the appliances. "I feel like I've landed on another planet."

"You need to catch up with the times." She patted his arm. "I'll hook you up."

❖

The next morning, a gaudy van arrived from the mall. Two cheerfully efficient young men installed a television system. His living room resembled the bridge of a science-fiction starship.

After the installers left, Mr. Thompson faced the dark screen. Its presence felt intimidating like it threatened to bring unfamiliar worlds into his home. He sat on his sofa to study the instruction manual. Shortly after, he clicked through channels and found an older movie that he remembered watching with his wife. His eyes filled with tears. He could not enjoy it in her absence, so he changed the channel again and again. He had no tolerance for newer movies, entertainment shows, or documentary programs. They were all the same.

According to the doctor, there seemed to be no option but to sit and wait for death, which only caused him to feel panicked. With a sense of desperation, Mr. Thompson turned off the television then read the instructions for accessing the Internet. Placing his cursor in the search engine, he typed: 'Black River canoeing.' The screen blinked and a column of options appeared.

An advertisement from a whitewater guide caught his eye. An image of a helmeted kayaker cutting through foamy water accompanied the ad. On the left side of the screen stretched another list of options. He selected the first link and watched a video recorded from a kayaker's helmet. The view hurtled through a canyon of white water, dodging grey boulders and dead logs.

Mr. Thompson whispered, "I want to do this."

He clicked a link to a map of the Black River. The access point was over a hundred miles away. He zoomed in and the map enlarged to show the run. The first ten miles meandered through woodlands with numerous campsites marked along the way.

I'll take it slow. I'll spend a day on that stretch and camp for the night above the whitewater.

There was a take-out point after the last campsite. A half mile downstream, the whitewater run began. Mr. Thompson enlarged that section. The Black River ran downhill through a series of pools and rapids. After the final take-out, a shuttle service ran back to the access point.

The map gave no indications on the nature of the rapids, but each had a name: The Staircase, which flowed into a long pool; The Gauntlet, which included wild turns; The Cauldron, which opened directly into the fourth rapid: The Abyss.

He considered the ominous names. Though he didn't want to die, he couldn't tolerate the lifestyle that Dr. Sing had prescribed.

He nodded. "I'm going and no one can stop me."

❖

Mr. Thompson picked up the phone and stared at it a moment before dialing. *Just like her mother,* he thought, knowing that Martha would try and talk him out of it. He dialed the number anyway.

"How are you feeling, Daddy?" she asked.

"I'm fine."

"No more attacks?"

"Nope." He paused, listening to the static on the line. "By the way, I'm going to be gone for a couple of days. I'm taking a canoe trip on the Black River. I'll be leaving early on Saturday and be home by Sunday afternoon."

"Has Dr. Sing given his approval?"

"I don't need his approval," Mr. Thompson snapped.

"Daddy, that river is too rough, and you're not young anymore."

"I'm not old, dammit!" His fist tightened around the receiver.

"Please listen to reason. Your body isn't as young as you feel in your heart. You abused yourself for thirty years in that damn factory. You could die on this trip."

"I'm going to take it easy."

"Daddy, I need to talk with you face-to-face," she said, her voice shaky. "I'll come over first thing in the morning and fix breakfast."

"You won't talk me out of this," he told her, loosening his grip on the phone.

"I love you, Daddy. I'll see you in the morning."

"I love you, too."

He hung up, knowing Martha would put a stop to his adventure. His only chance would be to sneak away.

❖

After loading his camping gear into the back of his pickup, Mr. Thompson drove to the supermarket and parked under a flickering light on a pole. He bought all the essentials–steaks, eggs, bacon, cheese, a stick of pepperoni, a case of beer, and four bags of ice–and loaded his coolers.

A loud engine roared through the air. It idled at the far end of the lot, where all of the lights seemed to be broken. The low-slung shape of a car crouched in the darkness.

Mr. Thompson finished loading his food and drove away. The loud car followed with its lights off. Passing under a streetlight, he saw that it was the same decrepit Charger that had followed him home, and his heart accelerated. The streetlight filtered through the Charger's damaged windshield, allowing a glimpse of a bald, abnormally pale head.

Turn by turn, Mr. Thompson's stalker followed. *What would a bald albino want with me?*

A few years ago, he would have stopped and confronted the stalker. Now he lacked the self-confidence and considered driving to a police station, but he was determined to lose the pursuer.

He pushed on the accelerator. The Charger fell behind. He changed directions several more times, then his tires squealed as he cut the turn into his garage. The door descended, leaving him to wait in darkness.

He heard the Charger pull to a stop and fall silent.

Mr. Thompson gasped, his heart thundered. Dark spots grew in his vision, adding to the shadows in the garage. He waited, but nothing happened. The attack eased. He got out of his truck, found a big pry bar, and peered out through the small window.

No cars were on the street. Mr. Thompson raised the garage door, stepped outside, and walked to the curb. He glanced at the pry bar in his hand and returned to the garage feeling foolish. Perhaps the Charger didn't exist; perhaps he was sicker than he was willing to believe... Perhaps Martha was right.

After going back inside, he locked all the doors and windows. He sat at the computer and opened the Black River advertisement. For hours, he watched different whitewater videos.

❖

He awoke at 1:59 a.m. still sitting at the computer desk. After dressing, he checked that the stove burners were off and turned the water heater down to pilot. He checked all of the locks again, then went into the garage and strapped the canoe onto the pickup's bed rack.

The door opener seemed to make a special racket in the early morning. The street was dark, without even the glow of a television screen behind a neighbor's window. Martha would be angry, he knew, but one day she might understand.

Mr. Thompson smiled as he drove away from his house.

Once back on the two-lane road, he frequently checked his rearview mirror, worried that the Charger would reappear.

Ninety miles from home, he pulled into a truck stop and ordered steak and eggs. As he ate, a young couple entered and sat in the booth across from him. They requested omelets and home fries from the tired-looking waitress.

"You kids heading out to the Black River?" the waitress asked them, piquing Mr. Thompson's interest.

"Yes," the young man said. "We've been looking forward to the trip for some time."

Not as long as I have, Mr. Thompson thought.

The waitress frowned. "Good luck. I've heard that the Black River is bony this year," she said and walked back to the kitchen.

"Really?" The young woman raised her eyebrows. "Jack, you didn't tell me that."

"Bony is more fun, Pam," replied Jack.

"But a pushy river lifts us over more of the rocks and snags."

Mr. Thompson turned toward them. "Pardon me, but I'm going down the Black River, too. I confess I'm new to the term. What is a bony river?"

Pam smiled and said, "Bony means low water, where more rocks and logs are exposed. Those are the river's bones."

Jack added, "Pushy means higher cubic feet per second. You know, if you're not that experienced, consider the upper part of the run…calmer water. There's a take-out point above the first rapids."

Mr. Thompson stood and dropped a twenty on the table. "Thanks, but I won't be taking out. I've been waiting a long time to do stuff like this." He nodded. "Nice meeting you two. Maybe I'll see you out there."

❖

Mr. Thompson drove the last ten miles, reaching the unpaved access road just before dawn. As he made the turn into the dark spruce forest, a motor roared behind him. The Charger was back, a pale green fiberglass canoe on its roof, just like the one his father had once owned.

He pressed on the accelerator and the truck bounced on the rocky road. The Charger pursued, black smoke pouring in its wake as it dwindled into the shadows.

A fallen spruce lay halfway across the road ahead of him. Mr. Thompson swerved to the opposite shoulder. The tree scraped the door.

At the bottom of the next hill, a swamp overflowed the road. He splashed across, drove up another hill, then accelerated down the far slope where the road was a washboard of rocks. The truck shuddered violently.

The road leveled off and he drove out of the forest into the parking meadow above the river. The sun had risen while he was under the trees. He crossed the meadow, turned, backed down the access ramp, and stopped on a bank of ruddy sand. A cluster of boulders stood along the river's edge. The water looked like black glass. Hair-thin lines writhed slowly down its surface. The trees on the far bank were aglow.

The roar of the Charger grew louder as the phantom pursued. He quickly unstrapped the canoe, which seemed heavier than it had the night before. It slipped out of his hands and banged to the sand. He dragged it to the river and pushed it halfway into the water.

Mr. Thompson heard the Charger nearing. Wheezing, he went back and forth, loading the canoe.

The Charger's exhaust burbled in the swamp.

Mr. Thompson loaded the two paddles, the saw, the skillet, and matches. He leaned one paddle against his canoe and slid the spare under the starboard gunnel. He returned to his truck, drove it into the meadow, parked, and locked the doors.

The Charger rattled as it came down the last rocky hill.

Gasping, he ran to the ramp, took ahold of the stern, and pushed. The canoe did not move.

The Charger roared loud and clear.

Mr. Thompson pushed with all of his might. His vision speckled and his heart sped up. The canoe slid deeper and floated. He used his paddle to push out into the river.

The Charger crossed the parking meadow.

Black spots began to steal his vision, while dizziness forced his eyes closed. He laid his paddle across the gunnels and rested. The current carried him around the first bend.

The Charger bellowed like a dinosaur. The noise echoed from the trees on the opposite bank. Tires crunched down the ramp.

Mr. Thompson's heart throbbed. He fought panic while the canoe drifted. The current pushed him toward the outside of the next curve. A tree lay in the water, its roots exposed on the bank, its top slanted downstream. The dead branches sieved flotsam from the river and the canoe drifted to a stop among the debris.

His pulse calmed with the slow and steady bobbing, his breath evened out, and his vision cleared. He looked back at the empty river. If somebody was after him, they had time enough to catch up.

I'm hallucinating. The Charger can't be real.

He back-paddled to get clear of the dead tree, then resumed the trip downstream. The current flowed smoothly, keeping the river glassy. Occasionally a tree, stripped of bark and branches, lurked below the surface. Sometimes the river struck a deep object, and the current rose and pillowed on the surface.

His terror from the access point seemed like a fading nightmare. It hadn't been a dream, though. Even if the Charger was a hallucination, it was real to him, and he was sure their business was not finished.

Daylight seemed to dim.

After an hour, he came to a campsite marked with a numbered yellow tag. He climbed ashore and tied his canoe to a stump. With a can of beer in one hand and a piece of pepperoni in the other, he sat down.

A plastic thump from upstream warned him that another canoe was approaching. He stood. He crackled the beer can in his hand. Then he heard a woman's voice and relaxed. Pam and Jack appeared around the curve. They veered toward the campsite, racing and ramming each other. They beached their kayaks, and climbed ashore.

"You made good time," said Pam, smiling.

Mr. Thompson laughed. "I'm faster than I look. Want a beer?"

Jack shook his head. "Alcohol impairs your performance."

Mr. Thompson glanced upstream. "Have you seen anyone else on the river?"

Pam shook her head. "Nope, it's just us."

Nobody had followed him. Mr. Thompson had been frightening himself with phantoms. He stood up. "I think I'll head on downstream."

"We'll see you later," Pam said.

"If you can catch me."

Jack grinned. "We'll catch you."

Mr. Thompson stepped aboard his canoe. He felt like proving to the young couple that he was just as strong as they were. He could probably gain a mile on them before they got back on the river, perhaps even reach the whitewater run before they caught up.

He was wrong. It hadn't even been fifteen minutes before he heard their voices behind him. He looked back as they came around a bend.

They were racing each other, swerving back and forth across the river. They came up behind him and passed him on either side.

"Tag!" Pam shouted. "You're it."

Pam and Jack swept around the next bend. A few minutes later, the sound of their laughter faded.

Mr. Thompson's good mood evaporated. He was no challenge to the youngsters.

A sharp thump came from upstream. A skeleton sat in the stern of an old canoe, paddling with a T-handled spade. It hunched its shoulders and dug into the river. The skull fixed its vacant stare on him.

Mr. Thompson missed his stroke and slapped the water with his paddle. His next was better. He accelerated around the next curve and scraped the brush on the outside bank, looking over his shoulder.

The apparition was gone from his view.

"Not real. Not real. Not real."

He paddled harder. His breath became short as he entered a long, grassy straight. Dead logs stuck at angles from each bank. He paused to catch his breath and looked back.

The skeleton rounded the last curve, chasing after him.

Panic grew into terror. His only thought was to escape the boat of bones. His senses returned when he heard Pam and Jack's laughter.

If he could catch up with them, the bones would dematerialize again, and he would be safe. He tried to call out but lacked the breath. His terror had granted him a burst of energy, but that was now failing. Black specks whirled across his vision. His strokes faltered.

The laughter faded away.

The black specs in his vision turned into shimmering blobs. He misguided his canoe and rammed into some brush, coming to a stop amid spider-webbed foliage.

The skeleton's spade thumped behind him.

He paddled desperately, flinging water into the brush. His canoe slowly backed out. Twigs scratched along the aluminum. He yawed his bow to point downstream.

The skeleton glided alongside him and reached out its spade, hooking the tread behind Mr. Thompson's gunnel.

Mr. Thompson screamed. He thrust his paddle beneath the spade shaft and struck upward, knocking it free. The blow also broke a splinter from the side of his paddle blade. He stroked the broken piece into the river.

The skeleton stood, smoke rising from its cranial seams. It took its spade in both hands and chopped at him. Mr. Thompson ducked. The spade whistled overhead and banged off the stern. He pulled ahead and rounded the next curve.

His only hope was to catch up with Pam and Jack. The blobs chased each other around his eyes. His mind fogged and his heart slammed. The skeleton still tailed him.

He forced himself to paddle until the skeleton began to fall behind. He eased his pace as his pursuer dropped out of sight.

Mr. Thompson prayed that the young couple had stopped for a break, but he feared that they would go all the way to the whitewater, leaving him at the bones' mercy.

Heart laboring, he sought inside himself for greater strength. He rounded a curve and saw a line on the water ahead–a beaver's dam just below the surface. He aimed for the lowest point. His bow drove across the dam. The keel struck, and he came to a halt. He rocked his weight fore and aft. The canoe slid a few more inches. He pushed his paddle into the water but couldn't touch the bottom for leverage.

He lay his paddle down, crawled forward over his gear, and stepped out onto the dam. Cold water filled his shoes. He braced his feet among the gnawed branches and dragged the laden canoe across the dam. It nearly slipped from his hands.

The skeleton came around the last curve, its bow hissing through the water. Mr. Thompson whimpered. He dropped into his stern seat, took up his paddle, and pushed off from the dam behind him.

The skull fixed its empty stare on him. It drove its canoe onto the dam, where it rode aground.

From behind Mr. Thompson came the sound of old fiberglass dragging over wood. Then came a splash as the canoe re-entered the river.

Pam's laughter echoed from ahead. The blobs in Mr. Thompson's eyes became roiling, lightning-shot clouds. He was about to pass out or die.

The skeleton rounded the curve, a dozen yards away. He couldn't fight anymore. As his canoe drifted into the next curve, he leaned on his paddle and closed his eyes.

Jack yelled, "Hey, look!"

"Oh my God!" Pam cried.

He heard splashing from up ahead. His canoe swerved. He opened his eyes. Pam and Jack were in the water, towing him toward shore. They grounded his canoe then lifted him out, helping him climb to their camp.

"Hold him while I get a sleeping bag," Pam said.

Mr. Thompson said, "Use mine."

She laid his sleeping bag out and helped him to recline, using his rolled tent as a pillow.

"Did you call an ambulance?" Pam asked.

"An ambulance couldn't get up here," Jack replied.

"We should still call! Maybe a helicopter or something?"

Mr. Thompson's vision had cleared. He sat up. "I'm all right. I just got a little short of breath." He looked upstream. The bones were still there, he knew, hiding in limbo behind the last curve.

"Is someone after you?" Pam asked.

His face narrowed and he let out a breath before answering. "Death."

❖

After speaking to Martha, Pam handed the phone to Mr. Thompson.

"Daddy, are you okay?" Martha sobbed. "Why did you scare me like this?"

Mr. Thompson wiped his forehead. "I'm all right, Martha."

"Pam said you were dying!"

"I just lost my wind for a few minutes."

"I'm coming to get you."

He wanted to argue, but Martha and her doctor were right. He had literally given his life to his job. Thirty years in the factory had left him incapable of enjoying his retirement. He had nothing to look forward to.

"I'm miles down the river; there's no road."

She groaned. "You make everything so hard! Put Pam back on and we'll figure something out."

He lay down again and listened to Pam's side of the conversation.

After a few minutes, Pam said, "We can't do it tonight. It would be too dark when we got to the take-out point. We'll break camp at dawn."

❖

Mr. Thompson awoke in his tent. The quality of the light told him that it was just before dawn. He needed only to lie where he was, and Pam and Jack would see that he reached the take-out point safely. Martha would be there to escort him home. He could sell his house and move in with her. She would hire home health aides to watch him, and he would never be alone again.

He would live as if he were an invalid.

In the end, Death would still catch him.

Mr. Thompson climbed from his tent, quietly loaded his canoe, and slipped downstream.

Mist hung above the calm water as he paddled from the campsite. From behind him came a deliberate thump. The skeleton appeared, hunched over its stroke, its skull raised with black sockets intent on him. Mr. Thompson looked forward and ignored it.

On his left, a muddy break in the riverbank's shrubbery caught his attention. It was the last take-out point before the rapids and he passed it.

The current increased. The shrubs dipped and rose in the waves until they surrendered to grey rock walls. Several giant boulders began to break surface, breaching like monsters around him. The river roared downstream.

Mr. Thompson went over a submerged rock. A series of shelves followed, set at odd angles. He entered the first of the four rapids: The Staircase. Below each shelf was an eddy current where the dropping river rolled backward. He had to make an extra effort to drive his canoe out of the suck holes.

Breathing came hard, but he felt alive. His canoe dropped over the shelves, and he fought his way out. He hoped that The Staircase would prove to be too rough for the skeleton's old fiberglass canoe.

After he splashed down the final step of The Staircase, he applied extra power to his strokes. The current held his canoe to the base. Water sprayed over his stern.

Mr. Thompson looked upriver. The skeleton shot down The Staircase, nearly flying across the eddy currents. It aimed its canoe to drop on Mr. Thompson.

Black spots swam around his eyes once more. He leaned back and put his paddle blade vertically into the falling water with the edge against a rock and pushed. He entered the long, foamy pool that flowed from The Staircase to The Gauntlet.

The skeleton dropped from the last shelf. The suck hole gave it a moment of trouble, then it continued after him as if it were a torpedo, catching up to him at the entrance to The Gauntlet. Their canoes banged together. A bony arm swung a spade at Mr. Thompson. He raised his paddle to block, and the blow knocked it into the water. The skull's immobile face seemed to display triumph.

Mr. Thompson retrieved his spare paddle and guided the canoe into the rapids. The Gauntlet was narrow and fast. The river blasted from bank to bank, diverted only by giant boulders. Trees lay pinned against the boulders and reached across the current like brittle claws.

The current pushed Mr. Thompson toward one of the giant boulders. The canoe swept broadside against the rocks. He tried to bear off, but the current pinned him. He pushed forward, forcing his canoe across the face of the boulder and ducking under a tree branch. He reached open water, then switched hands constantly as the current tried to batter his canoe against the staggered boulders. With each stroke, the black spots increased. He made it through The Gauntlet and entered the quiet pool below.

Mr. Thompson glanced back and saw the skeleton steering flawlessly.

He returned his attention to the river as he entered The Cauldron's whirlpool. The Cauldron was the plunge pool of an extinct waterfall. The exiting channel was to Mr. Thompson's left. He followed the current around The Cauldron's sheer walls. His eyes dimmed and his heart raced.

The skeleton entered The Cauldron. Rather than follow the current, it came straight across the whirlpool, rammed him amidships, and drove him hard into the cliff. His vision exploded with dark fireworks. He pushed the fiberglass canoe off just as he reached The Abyss, where the Black River rose in a hump over a submerged boulder.

The skeleton came alongside him, met his eyes, and raised its spade with both hands. Its hard expression seemed desperate as it struck.

Mr. Thompson leaned back. The spade glanced across his canoe, banging a dent in the opposite gunnel. He returned a strike against the skeleton's spade, jolting it free from his bony grasp. Mr. Thompson struck at the skeleton again.

The skeleton feverishly paddled with its bony hands as its canoe turned broadside to the current.

Mr. Thompson went over a hump. The descent beyond seemed nearly vertical. He gave a shout of victory as he went over the crest, then tried to steer around the obstacles as the river carried him. His canoe bumped over submerged logs and scraped alongside boulders. The foamy pool at the bottom of the run rushed toward him. His vision cleared.

He turned his canoe around to look back up at The Abyss. The skeleton's canoe slipped over the fall, crashed into the white wash, and broke in half. Bones scattered everywhere as it fell out. The wreckage washed into the pool. All of the bones sank, except for the skull, which floated near him just below the surface. Its eye sockets glared.

"You'll have to try harder than that," Mr. Thompson said.

Smoke bubbled out of the cranial seams. The skull disappeared into the Black River.

Mr. Thompson paddled to the take-out point and pulled his canoe ashore. He walked across the parking lot to the picnic area, carrying a cold beer and a sandwich.

Martha's car raced into the lot and braked. She clambered out without turning off the engine.

"Daddy!"

"Good morning, Martha."

She rushed to him in tears. "I thought you'd be dead!"

"I only went camping," Mr. Thompson said, pulling her close.

A loud yell came from up the river. Jack flew down The Abyss, paddle held high. Pam followed. They slid into the plunge pool and paddled to the take-out point. Pam ran to Mr. Thompson. "Why did you leave?"

Martha turned on her. "Why did you let him?"

Jack walked up beside Mr. Thompson. "Some ride, huh?"

Mr. Thompson popped the tab of his beer and took a long drink. "Ride of my life," he said, glancing back at the water. "So far." ◆

Stanley B. Webb is a resident of upstate New York. Although he has been writing since childhood, he began his fiction career later in life, after taking early retirement from his factory job. He lives on a small homestead near the shore of Lake Ontario, with his wife and son.

Artwork: Luke Spooner

TRAVEL ADVISORY

MATT WEDGE

Griffin huddled under the awning of a porn shop while cold rain poured from the sky, briefly concerned that the people driving by would think he had just left the store. It was ridiculous to worry, given his bigger problem.

The awning was only half successful in keeping his body dry. The howling wind sprayed rain against his right side. He shifted the satchel slung over his left shoulder as he stared down the street. His bus idled in traffic only a hundred feet away.

He could walk the short distance to the bus. It would get him out of the rain, and he could tell by the way the windows fogged up that the heaters were blasting at full strength. *If I were normal,* Griffin bitterly thought, *that is exactly what I would do.* Not being normal, he refused. He knew that the entire trip to O'Hare would smell like a slaughter-house in the middle of July.

Griffin held his hands close to his face, inspecting them for any out-of-place details. The wind, rain, and chilly temperatures had caused red splotches to cover his otherwise healthy pink skin. Satisfied, he shoved his hands back in his jacket pockets.

A Hummer creeped by slowly, maneuvering around a pothole. He shifted his attention to the decaying corpse behind the wheel, skin and hair burned from its body. The corpse sneezed, blowing blood against the windshield. Despite the grotesqueness, Griffin smirked. It served the bastard right for having one of those monstrosities in the city. Traffic was bad enough without some asshole driving a tank on rubber wheels.

He looked toward the downtown Chicago skyline, barely visible through the rain, fog, and general gloom of the day. He wished that it were beautiful and sunny, so he could have a better last look.

The grating sound of metal scraping metal filled the air as the bus stopped in front of the porn shop. The doors opened with a hiss, re-vealing a burned, bloodied corpse in the driver's seat. A large chunk was missing from its head, where it looked like a bullet had entered. Griffin could not decide what disgusted him more–the stench of decay that flowed from the bus, or the sight of the cockroach burrowing into the hole in the driver's head.

The corpse stared at Griffin for what seemed an eternity before finally yelling, "I ain't got all day! You gettin' on?"

Griffin covered his mouth and nose with his jacket and climbed aboard.

❖

Breathing shallow, Griffin managed to control his disgust. The bus was populated by a full complement of the deceased. Most of them were similar to the driver of the SUV, with charred flesh revealing the musculature and fatty tissue beneath. They were obviously going to be close enough to the initial blast to be cooked alive. Griffin thought of them as the lucky ones. The others, those who would die of radiation poisoning, were less nauseating but more pathetic. They were so skinny that they reminded Griffin of the photos he saw on a high school field trip to the Holocaust Museum. Large clumps of their hair had fallen out and their teeth were missing. Their clothes were stained from the bile they had vomited before their days mercifully ended–or would end, rather.

While the ride had been fairly smooth, Griffin received several odd stares as he held his jacket over his face and occasionally retched. An ironic fact that he bitterly acknowledged also held some humor. Over the last week, Griffin had learned to deal with the absurdity of the situation. In a strange way, he was glad the bus ride was so unpleasant. It only strengthened his resolve to board a plane and fly far from the Northern Hemisphere.

The bus pulled to a stop at the Logan Square 'L' Station. Griffin let everyone else get off first. He didn't want to run the risk of bumping into anyone and having clumps of their decaying tissue stick to his clothes. He had already been through that less-than-pleasant experience on an elevator earlier in the week, ruining one of his favorite shirts.

"You gettin' off?" The bus driver's voice hissed through his permanently bared teeth. The effect gave it a lisp causing the words to whistle. Griffin guessed that a scavenger would gnaw off the driver's lips after its death.

❖

The ride on the L was easier to endure. He chose a less crowded car at the rear of the train. From his seat, he gawked in fascination at a figure that was nothing more than a dark shadow against a window. This certainly was someone who'd be up close for the actual detonation, nothing more than a dusty gathering of carbon molecules burned into a wall. Nuclear graffiti.

A woman yelled, "What's your problem, asshole?" Griffin couldn't find the source, no matter which way he turned. "Don't give me that blind bullshit. You were staring at my tits."

The voice had come from the shadow. Griffin wasn't necessarily surprised to find the shadow speaking; he had encountered several situations that were less than normal in the past week. He was surprised that he still had the ability to be surprised. He looked away from the shadow, focusing all his attention out the window.

"Yeah," she said. "You better look away. You wanna stare at some tits so badly, why dontcha grow a pair of your own?"

Despite the situation, Griffin found himself smiling at the absurdity. The shadowy girl had a sexy voice. He knew that his grin would only infuriate her more, so he kept his eyes glued to the window. He used the soft reflection the window provided to inspect his face. He was still fine.

❖

Griffin decided on Buenos Aires. He would have to catch a connecting flight in Miami, and hoped against hope that the college kids on spring break wouldn't be on his flight. But O'Hare was a nightmare, and hope had taken a permanent vacation.

Energetic corpses in several different levels of decomposition surrounded him. They chattered excitedly with each other about their vacations of booze in the sun, partying, and the promise of drunken sex. Sprinkled amongst the crowd were a few normal-looking people. Just like Griffin, they were going to survive the blast.

The charred woman behind the check-in desk said, "I need to see a government-issued I.D."

Griffin didn't care for her tone in the least. It fell somewhere between snotty and condescending. He handed her his passport and waited as she looked from his picture to his ashen face.

"Are you ill, sir?"

It was obvious she didn't care, but he guessed it was policy.

"I'm fine. I had an allergy attack on the L, but I took some Benadryl."

The charred woman clicked her tongue, spraying a small dusting of ash from her mouth.

"How many bags are you checking today?"

"None, I just have a carry-on."

He couldn't quite tell for sure through the burned facial tissue, but it looked like she raised an eyebrow.

"You're flying all the way to Buenos Aires and you don't need to check any bags?"

Griffin tightened with panic. He should have thought of the suspicion this would raise. He did his best not to let his face fall into that guilty expression he had whenever he was caught in a lie, but the corners of his mouth turned down while his right eyebrow rose involuntarily. He hurriedly put together the best lie he could think of.

"I'm visiting my friend, Pablo…and, uh, he's gonna take me camping. So, he told me not to bring a lot of clothes or anything, because he said the weather's really unpredictable. We're just gonna stop at an outfitter to get what gear and clothing we need for the…uh, camping."

She said nothing as she typed on her keyboard, then reached under her computer terminal and handed him a boarding pass.

"Gate C-10. Have a nice flight."

He'd never felt as much love for a soon-to-be dead woman as he felt for her at that exact moment. Though her tone had been disingenuous, those words were the sweetest Griffin had ever heard. Now all he had to do was get through security without looking like a threat and he would be home free. For the first time in two weeks, Griffin started to feel a sense of optimism swelling in the back of his mind.

While he stood in line to get through security, he inspected his hands again. They were still fine, but he spotted an annoying hangnail on his left pinky. Staring at the red irritation seemed to make it even more uncomfortable. He bit at it helplessly, knowing he looked ridiculous, but he didn't care. Besides, the line was moving so slowly, it wasn't like he had anything else to do.

"Dude, they're just flip-flops," a stoned-sounding frat boy groaned from the front of the line. Griffin craned his neck to watch the commotion.

A student wearing a bright orange shirt and khaki shorts tried to walk through the metal detector without removing his flip-flops. A female security official wearing an unflattering polyester pantsuit grabbed him by the arm. Her expression was all Griffin needed to know that she didn't appreciate being called "dude." The student took one look at her face and put his flip-flops through the X-ray machine.

Griffin dropped his knapsack and tennis shoes onto the conveyor belt and watched as they disappeared into the X-ray machine. He waited impatiently, tapping his fingers against his thigh while a badly burned man kept setting off the metal detector. As if it were some sort of comedy routine, the old man passed through just to return and find another metallic object in one of his pockets.

"Try takin' off your belt," the security official said, pointing a bony finger at the man's waist.

"Oh, yeah. I'll bet that's it," came his chipper response. As soon as he took his belt off, the old man ran his thumbs along his waist. The polyester had melted against his skin. Griffin gagged as the old man's thumbs made a circuit around his waistband. The skin tore free and clung to his pants like melted cheese pulled from a pizza.

Some of the more obnoxious college kids in the line let out a sarcastic cheer as the old man finally made it through the metal detector. Apparently not catching the insincerity of the gesture, the old man turned and waved.

The line moved quickly once the old man was through, and when Griffin finally strolled through the checkpoint, he silently said a thankful prayer. He grabbed his shoes and knapsack from the conveyor belt.

"Ten-four," a deep, male voice said from behind him.

Two huge men in matching dark suits approached Griffin while he slipped a shoe on, balancing on one foot. Both were of the charbroiled variety and carried themselves as though they were ready to spring into action. The one on the left, the larger one, held a walkie-talkie. With a few long strides, they took up positions on either side of Griffin.

"Excuse me, sir," said the large one through a crooked mouth. The right side of his jaw had been fused shut. "Could you please step this way?"

Griffin immediately checked his hands. They still looked fine, and he breathed a sigh of relief. This was going to be nothing more than a minor nuisance and then he'd be on his way.

Griffin asked as innocently as he could, "Is there a problem?"

"There's no problem, sir. We just want to ask you some questions."

Griffin glanced at the second man, wondering why he remained silent. The man had no mouth from which to talk, his face a solid mass of blackened tissue. Any distinguishing features had been twisted and melted into chaos.

"I'm sorry, I don't mean to be rude," Griffin poured honey across his voice as he talked, "but who are you?"

An I.D. badge appeared in the man's skeletal hand as though it had been spring-loaded up his sleeve. "Agent Nicholls, Department of Homeland Security."

A word sprang from Griffin's brain and passed his lips before he had a chance to stifle it: "Shit."

He made no fuss as the men ushered him toward an unmarked door next to the metal detectors. He wanted to be cooperative and to show that he posed no threat.

The room was no bigger than a walk-in closet. A small folding table sat in the center with three chairs. Two chairs on one side, the third on the other. Fluorescent bulbs cast a sickly, yellowish pall over everything.

The pallor gave Griffin a bit of a fright as he glanced at his hands again. His skin appeared jaundiced. Radiation poisoning loomed in his mind before he realized it was simply the lighting.

"Why do you keep doing that?" Agent Nicholls asked as he sat in one of the two chairs.

Griffin stared between the two men. "What do you mean? Doing what?"

"You keep looking at your hands. Is there something wrong with them?"

"No. It's just a habit."

"Are you high?"

"What? No!" Despite the situation, Griffin laughed. He had gone totally sober after the visions began.

Agent Nicholls nodded at the silent agent who left the room. "So, if I were to take a blood or urine sample, you'd pass with flying colors?"

Griffin tried to cover his rising panic with annoyance and sarcasm, saying, "Yes, I would pass because I'm not doing drugs."

Nicholls' face dropped. "You listen here, young man! This is serious business, so you better start taking it seriously."

"Are you kidding me?" Griffin asked. "That's a nice speech, and I'm sure it scares the hell out of your kids, but I don't even know what's going on here. You drag me into a room and start asking me if I'm on drugs with no reason at all. I'm taking this seriously, because if I screw around in here any longer, I'm gonna miss my flight!"

He leaned against the wall by the door and wondered if he had lost his mind.

Nicholls smiled. "And why is it so important that you catch your flight?"

"Um, because I paid a lot of money for the ticket?" Griffin asked before backtracking on his sarcasm. "Look, I'm sorry. I don't mean to be a jerk. I have a lot of plans already set up in Buenos Aires and if I miss my flight, that's going to throw a monkey wrench into a lot of other people's plans."

Nicholls leaned back in his chair and crossed his arms. He seemed to enjoy watching Griffin grovel. "Buenos Aires, huh? You ever been to Chile before?"

"No, it'll be my first time."

"That'll be a hell of a trick if you can pull that off. Buenos Aires is in Argentina, not Chile."

Griffin stared at his hands as he racked his mind for something to say. "So I suck at geography. Is that a crime now?"

"No, but lying to a federal agent is."

"I haven't lied about anything! Tell me one thing that I've lied about!"

"I don't know yet, but I know a liar when I see one. I also know a dangerous man when I see one. So, you can understand why I can't let you get on that plane."

"No! No, I can't!" Other than acting a little stranger than your common schizophrenic homeless person, he had done nothing to make himself appear as a threat.

The door opened and the silent agent returned, a charred woman following. Griffin recognized her from the check-in counter and groaned. He checked his hands. Still in the clear.

The woman gave off no hint of an unusual situation. She had probably done this dozens of times.

Agent Nicholls smiled at the woman. "Why don't you tell me what Mr. Stewart said that caused you to suspect he might be some kind of threat?"

"When I asked how many bags he was checking, he said, 'None, I just have a carry-on.' When I asked him about going all the way to Buenos Aires without any luggage, he said, 'I'm visiting my friend, Pablo…and, uh, he's gonna take me camping. So, he told me not to bring a lot of clothes or anything because he said the weather's really unpredictable. We're just gonna stop at an outfitter to get what gear and clothing we need for the…uh, camping.'"

Griffin stared at her, awestruck. Despite the bored monotone of her voice, she had repeated his every word. She had even paused in all the right spots and dropped in the appropriate "uhs."

"Do you have a fucking stenographer in your head?" Griffin asked.

She looked at Agent Nicholls and asked, "Is that all you need?"

"Yes, that will be fine. Thank you."

The woman left, followed by the silent agent who closed the door behind them. Griffin turned to Nicholls. The smirk on the corpse's face only made Griffin more irritable, and he instantly regretted letting the man see him look so flustered.

Nicholls kicked the other chair from under the table. It was obviously a practiced move because the chair slid to a rest giving Griffin the exact amount of room he needed. "Take a seat, Mr. Stewart."

Griffin reluctantly sat down.

"So now you know why we're here," Nicholls said with a triumphant lilt.

"No, I don't. So I sounded like an idiot when I was talking to the check-in lady. Big deal. I didn't expect to get a game of Twenty Questions thrown at me. I mean, if I were a terrorist–"

"Who said anything about terrorists?"

"I'm assuming that's why I'm sitting here while my plane is probably boarding."

"I never said anything about terrorists. In fact, the only person who's mentioned anything about terrorism is you."

"I'm not a threat! Can't you see that? Look at me! I'm 160 pounds soaking wet! I have nothing on me that could hurt anyone! I just want to get on the plane and get the hell out of here!"

Nicholls leaned forward. "Why's it so important for you to fly out of here? Why are you acting like you have something to hide?"

"I'm not hiding anything, okay? It's just important that I get on that plane. That's the only way I can explain it that sounds sane. I'm telling you, I'm not a threat."

"Oh, I don't think you're a threat. I think you know about something that's gonna happen. And if I let you get on the plane, I'll never find out what it is."

Griffin stared at the agent's blackened face and knew that he couldn't reason his way out of this. The man had an idea in his head, the wrong idea, and it was going to cost Griffin his life. He stared at his hands.

"What's with the hands? Tell me that."

"Nothing," Griffin replied, still staring at them as if spellbound. "There's nothing wrong with them. I'm still okay."

"What's that supposed to mean? 'You're still ok'–oh, Christ! You're carrying something, aren't you?" Nicholls stood up and slowly backed toward the far corner of the room. He stared at Griffin, eyes bulging from their fried sockets. "Am I already infected?"

"I check my hands to make sure that I'm gonna be okay! That I survive it! So far, I do, and I wanna keep it that way!"

Nicholls' body slumped forward, as though a huge weight straddled his shoulders. Griffin could see in the man's distant stare that the agent had mentally checked out.

Griffin checked his watch and figured he had ten minutes to get to his terminal and catch his plane. He could make it if he ran and nobody else got in his way.

Despite his frantic state of mind, it occurred to Griffin that even if he could board the plane, they would never let it take off. An air marshal would drag him off like a criminal, no matter how much he claimed to be the victim, but his gut told him to just walk out the door and make a run for his plane.

Griffin grabbed his knapsack, slung it over his shoulder, and ran from the room.

The airport buzzed along. The silent agent was nowhere to be seen. Nobody paid Griffin any attention as he slipped into the crowd.

Griffin passed under a sign that read: 'Gates C-1 – C-14' and he followed the arrow. He quickened his pace to a trot and checked his watch before he slammed straight into what felt like a cinderblock wall. Griffin fell and gawked stupidly up at the silent agent. Chunks of chocolate and peanuts were smashed against the area where a mouth should have been. The agent's big, meaty hand squeezed the life out of a Baby Ruth candy bar.

The silent agent, apparently shocked, made no move to restrain him.

Griffin kicked against the man's knees, managing to topple the giant. He scrambled to his feet and ran to the nearest door. The agent emitted a deep, moaning noise. Griffin turned and saw him pointing and running in his direction. He pushed through a door and turned the deadbolt.

The smell of urine and disinfectant filled the air. A bathroom. No windows, no back doors, no escape.

A toilet flushed, and a man that looked straight out of a disco circa 1977 exited the stall. He was a survivor. A cheap, black toupee perched atop his head, though it didn't match the grey hair poking out the sides and back of his scalp. His white suit jacket clashed with brown corduroys and black shoes. Three gold chains lay against his over-tanned chest.

Disco Man washed his hands, smiling wide and inspecting his nicotine-stained teeth in the mirror. A sudden pounding against the door made him turn. His face lighted in a recognition that caught Griffin off guard.

"You're a survivor!" Disco Man said in a sincerely delighted tone. "Wow, man! Look at you. No burns, no radiation poisoning, no missing limbs. Let me tell you something, you are one lucky bastard. Most of these other people out there…food for the roaches."

Griffin's mouth hung open. He tried to think of something to say, but nothing seemed adequate.

"I'm going to Rio to ride this thing out," Disco Man continued. "Then maybe catch a ship to South Africa. I've got a buddy in Johannesburg that has the hook-up with all the lovely local ladies. Where're you headed?"

"Buenos Aires," Griffin muttered.

"Great city, man. That's a great idea on your end. Listen, I hate to be rude but I gotta catch a flight. Um, that pounding on the door, is that because of you?"

Griffin nodded.

"See, that might make it a little difficult for me to just waltz on out of here." Disco Man's smile fell and his voice faded as he stared at Griffin's chest. "You, uh, got something on your shirt."

Still in a daze, Griffin walked to the mirror.

Disco Man shook his head. "Sorry, man. That's pretty rough."

Griffin slowly nodded. He wished his mind would cooperate, so he could respond to Disco Man's understatement. Not surprisingly, he was unable to spare any part of his brain for language. It was too busy processing the three bloody bullet holes that had appeared in his shirt.

He wanted to scream, to cry, to rail against the world about how unfair it was. But instead he just stared at his bloody reflection. His face had become waxy. His yellow, shiny arms reflected the light in the room like a highly polished car. He would be dead and buried before the blast, his body embalmed and preserved better than all the walking corpses he had encountered.

"Look at it this way, my man. It's a better way to go than the alternative."

Griffin hated the Disco Man for even thinking that, let alone saying it out loud.

The sound of the deadbolt turning caused Disco Man to jump backward and cower in a stall. Griffin faced the door, determined to make a run straight at whoever was the first through.

The door inched open, frustrating Griffin. He wanted to get it over with. Suddenly, the door flew the rest of the way open, banging against the wall. The silent agent rushed through the entry and grabbed Griffin before he could react. He slammed Griffin to the floor, pressing his face into the dirty tile under the urinals. It disgusted Griffin to think he was going to die with piss on his face. The cuffs clipped around his wrists in short order, far tighter than they needed to be. The agent pulled Griffin to his feet and marched him out of the bathroom, past a crowd of gawking corpses.

Griffin squinted against the lighting that seemed too bright. He turned his face away from the large windows that looked upon the tarmac and saw Nicholls. His crusty face was the picture of madness. He screamed something that Griffin could not entirely catch. As he charged closer, Griffin was able to understand a single word: "Carrier!"

The silent agent marched Griffin directly at the screaming Nicholls who kept repeating the word over and over, "Carrier! Carrier! Carrier!"

Nicholls reached inside his jacket and withdrew his pistol. The silent agent moaned something at Nicholls that Griffin could not understand. He tugged back on Griffin's arm, pulling him away from Nicholls. Griffin dug the heels of his shoes into the tile and fell backward. He sat upright and turned his body toward Nicholls, purposely giving him as wide of a target as possible.

The first bullet ripped into his left lung, just below his heart. The second slammed into his stomach, passing through his right kidney and exiting his lower back. The third went straight through his diaphragm and lodged in his spine, instantly paralyzing him from the waist down.

Griffin's body collapsed, his head resting in a sticky pool of blood that rapidly expanded. He heard screams and crying as corpses stepped back from the puddle. He barely felt the silent agent's hands applying pressure to his wounds. His surroundings grew blurry. The last thing he saw before the light dimmed completely was the triumphant eyes of Nicholls staring down at him.

Griffin left a smile frozen on his face. ◆

Matt Wedge is a writer, film critic, and beleaguered Cubs fan. He lives in Chicago with the harshest critic of his writing: a Russian Blue house cat named Storm.

Artwork: Luke Spooner

LIGHTHEADED

BRENT R. OLIVER

Jack felt horrible. He was certain that the goddamn zombie apocalypse virus was wreaking havoc on his immune system. He'd be patient zero, and soon he'd die and resurrect with the mindless urge to eat human flesh.

He barely managed to drag his sorry ass to the doctor.

Turned out he had the flu.

"Are you sure?" he asked. "I feel like I'm gonna die."

The doctor nodded. "Most people with the flu feel like that. You'll be fine."

"What medicine do I need? Antibiotics or whatever?"

"You have the flu, Jack. It's a virus. Antibiotics only work against bacterial infections. They won't help you. What you need is lots of water, lots of rest, maybe some chicken soup."

"That's it?"

"That's it. People endure the flu. There's no cure or quick fix. You just get over it."

Jack frowned. "That kind of sucks, doc."

"Go home, Jack. You'll be fine."

❖

A week later, Jack felt better. His appetite came back, he could breathe through his nose again, and his muscles no longer ached like they were rotting on his bones. A cough persisted though. It seemed that every breath exploded right back out of him. It was embarrassing to break out into heavy, wet coughs whenever someone told a joke. Not to mention running off to the bathroom to spit out whatever his lungs had sent up.

Jack went back to the doctor. Tossing out another thirty-dollar copay pissed him off, but he'd had enough.

The doc pressed his stethoscope to Jack's chest and back and listened to him breathe. He stuck his tiny flashlight into Jack's ears and up his nose.

"It's a respiratory infection," he said. "The flu weakened your immune system and another bug snuck in."

"Fantastic. So I'm still sick?"

"Well, yes, but not nearly as sick as before. You'll feel a little run-down and it'll take a couple more weeks to get rid of the cough, but you're out of the woods. I'll give you an antibiotic that'll help chase this thing off."

❖

The antibiotic did not intimidate the cough in the slightest. Even after two weeks, Jack still wheezed like a diseased hooker. He refused to shell out *another* copay to have the doctor tell him he was okeydokey.

So he coughed. He coughed at night when he tried to sleep. He coughed at work in between talking to customers. He coughed while watching TV and during dinner. He coughed so much, and so hard, that he would become lightheaded.

The black spots scattering across his vision had been scary the first time. He'd been sitting on the toilet when it happened, sure he was about to Elvis out with his dirty ass in the air. It happened again the next day, too. The coughing had started mildly, with a couple of gentle puffs. A moment later he fell on his hands and knees, hacking breathlessly at the carpet. His head felt as if it were filled with helium, so light that it would float up to the ceiling if not for being attached to his neck.

Sometimes he went an entire twenty-four hours without suffering a single fit; sometimes it happened four times in an afternoon. Nothing seemed to set it off and nothing made it any better.

He became accustomed to the lightheadedness and black-speckled vision. It was an inconvenience that had to be borne, an almost daily distress. He never actually fainted, so he just learned to accept the swim-my-head feeling.

Still, there were a few uncomfortable situations, mainly at work. More than once someone came upon him hunched over the break room table, wheezing and swaying drunkenly. Sometimes coworkers would find him pressed against the bathroom wall, unable to draw a normal breath and seemingly on the verge of collapse. On these occasions, they were sympathetic and full of suggestions: Had he been to the doctor? Well, maybe he should try goldenseal or raw garlic. A shot of bourbon before bed would clear up any lingering flu-related symptoms. Or maybe try Jägermeister, or ginger tea with honey.

❖

Jack left the bank and walked into Freak City, still coughing. He took a seat at the bar, where his best friend Eric poured him a drink. "Any chance that you accidentally aspirated semen while sucking cock behind the bowling alley?"

"Funny."

Eric earned more money slinging Kamikazes and PBR than Jack made working at the bank. It irked the shit out of him, considering he'd gone to all the trouble of finishing college while Eric had dropped out their second year.

Jack nursed a bourbon. It didn't help the cough, but it made his throat feel better.

"Seriously," Eric said, his face somber. "Jizz can clog up the lungs and cause all kinds of problems. Maybe you're sucking dick *wrong*, you know? You're supposed to swallow, not breathe it."

Shawn, the other bartender, set down a case of beers. "That's true, Jack."

"Thank you both, but has it occurred to you that I might have caught AIDS from the two of you handling strange dick in the bathroom, then pouring drinks?"

Eric waved his hand. "What? I always wash my hands. Don't you, Shawn?"

"I dunno. I get busy. I wash 'em…maybe fifty percent of the time."

The wisecracking went on until the bar closed. Jack stumbled home, several slugs of bourbon sitting comfortably in his stomach, enough to put him into a pleasant, dreamless sleep.

His ringing phone interrupted the short slumber. "Hello?"

"Jack? It's Shawn."

"Hey, what time is it?"

"I dunno. Listen, Eric was in an accident on the way home. You'd better come to the hospital."

❖

Jack hated the hospital because everyone there seemed to be dying. People wandered listlessly in the hallways, trailing various tubes and wires. Their expressions said that they'd given up, that recovery was impossible and they were waiting for the end.

Jack walked into Room 308. Shawn sat slumped in a chair, passed out, and something that was supposed to be Eric lay in the bed, head and face swathed in white bandages dotted with pink stains. Plastic tubes stuck up his nose and dangled from his arm. Metal trees loomed around the bed holding clear bags that dripped fluids while odd machines beeped quietly.

Jack stood in the middle of the room, frozen. *That can't be Eric lying there like a mannequin.*

The twisted sculpture of bed, tubes, machines, and mannequin warped as he tried to focus. "What the hell happened? Was he drunk?"

Shawn opened bleary red eyes. He looked like Jack felt. It seemed to take a huge effort for him to speak. "No. We had two beers while cleaning up. Same as always." Shawn's eyes moved to the mannequin. "I was driving right behind him when it happened. He just crashed."

Jack sat in the other chair. "What did the doctor say?"

"That he doesn't know shit about shit." Shawn ran a hand through his hair. "Well, that may not be exactly what he said, but it's what he meant. Once I took out all the self-important medical jargon, all I got was head trauma, coma, and no idea when he'll wake up." He shifted and moved his gaze to the window. "Or if."

❖

Jack sent Shawn home to get some sleep. Ten minutes later, the doctor came in to check Eric's vitals. The information he provided was polite but useless. Yes, Eric could recover fully. No, he didn't know what the odds were. Yes, there could be loss of brain function. No, he couldn't speculate on the chances. Yes, he could wake up at any moment. No, he didn't know how likely that was.

Jack's illusions about the thing in bed melted away. He knew it was Eric now. Jack hadn't cried but he'd spent an hour with his chair pulled close, holding Eric's cool and waxy hand.

❖

The TV on the wall had shown a brain-shriveling marathon of drivel. Jack sat semi-conscious in his chair, leavings of his hospital foraging sprinkled across his lap: an empty bag of Doritos; the crunchy cellophane wrapper from cheese and crackers; a Coke can wedged loosely between his thighs.

The coughing fit slammed into him like a meteor. His lungs convulsed, shoving out air in staccato blasts that bounced him around in the chair. The trash in his lap went flying, some landing on Eric's bed like tornado debris. Jack doubled over, arms wrapped around his midsection while the coughs tore out of him. The black specks blasted across his vision and his head became airy.

Strong fingers grabbed his shoulder and pulled his body upright. He looked up through watering eyes and saw a woman with a hard expression on her face. "No you don't, pal," she said. "Just calm down. Get your breath back."

Sitting up straight eased some of the pressure on his lungs. He dragged in half a breath and coughed it back out. The woman's hand gripped his arm, holding him steady. The next breath came easier. It left his lungs in a wheeze instead of a hack. The sparkles and specks in his vision faded and the lightheadedness retreated.

Jack tilted his head against the wall. The ceiling lights swam in his tears. He took a big, shuddering breath and let it out slowly. Glancing sideways, he saw the woman wore blue scrubs and a plastic badge that read: 'Susan Hicks, RN.'

"Thanks," he croaked.

She smiled. "No problem." She let go and patted his shoulder. "That sounds bad. You should see a doctor."

❖

After Shawn came to relieve him, Jack went home. Though exhausted, sleep wouldn't come. His thoughts lingered on Eric, bandaged and silent under hospital covers. Even with Shawn right beside him, Jack knew Eric was alone, trapped in the dark.

When Jack woke up, his eyes were dry and scratchy, his body sore and sluggish. He drank a pot of coffee and went back to the hospital.

Everything was the same. Eric still looked like a reclining statue.

"Any news?" Jack asked.

Shawn yawned. "Nope. Get any sleep?"

"A bit."

Shawn stood and moved to the door. "See you tonight?"

"Yeah."

Jack settled in. He'd brought his Kindle, hoping he could concentrate on reading, but he just stared at the screen unable to focus on the words. Eventually, he put it down and decided to get a drink.

He looked at Eric. "You want anything? No? Fine."

When he returned, he burst into long coughs, staggering from the force of the spasms. The Coke fell from his hands and soda foamed across the floor. Black spots jumped into his vision, and when he shut his eyes, huge spinning pinwheels and starbursts colored the darkness. His knees splashed down into the puddle of spilled Coke. He jerked back and forth between his chair and Eric's bed, fighting to stay conscious as the coughs racked his body.

The lightheadedness deepened. Through his tearing eyes, the room wavered like a mirage, squirming black around the edges.

In the glimmering haze of his diminishing vision, something on the wall above the bed caught his attention. At first it looked like a mural, but that didn't make any sense. There hadn't been a mural there before. The image jittered in and out of focus like a film from a rickety old projector. Everything appeared fuzzy except the dark grey at the bottom and a lighter, dirtier grey at the top. The faint line of distinction between the two looked like a horizon. Hundreds of silhouettes, like leafless trees, jutted up from the lower portion, jet black against the lighter sky-grey.

Jack recoiled, still coughing, and bumped the chair behind him. He shook his dizzy head, blinking furiously, but nothing changed. The image remained.

He put his head down on the bed and coughed weakly against the blanket. The horrible clutch in his lungs loosened and the lightheadedness faded slightly. He wedged in a few deep breaths and the feeling receded further.

He raised his head and squinted at the wall again–smooth and white, just like it had been before the fit. Below it, clean sheets encased Eric.

Jack felt like an idiot. There wasn't anything weird on the wall. He looked at the mess on the floor then back up at Eric. "I hope none of this is disturbing you."

❖

Over the next week, he and Shawn relaxed their vigil. The hospital had informed them that they'd let the rules slide the first couple nights but now regular visiting hours would have to apply. The staff promised to call right away if Eric woke up.

During their next visit, another attack blindsided Jack, hitting with nuclear force. He doubled over in his chair, hacking desperately. The colors and patterns lit up behind his eyelids and the lightheadedness clawed into him. He struggled to sit up and breathe while Shawn slapped pointlessly at his back.

Jack tried to speak but the words were locked up with his breath. His lungs were about to overload and shut down, drowning him on dry land. The coughs kept rattling out, chewing at his throat. Through the blur of tears and the haze of lightheadedness, he saw the vision above Eric's bed again: a surreal watercolor, dark grey earth, grey sky, and those leafless black trees.

Jack managed a dry croak.

"Jesus!" Shawn said. "Are you having a seizure?"

Jack cranked one arm up and jabbed his index finger at the scene above the bed. The picture above Eric's bed faded into a hallucinatory blur and then vanished.

"Well, fuck me," Shawn said. "What was that all about?"

❖

At home that evening, Jack googled: *'Can people who almost faint hallucinate?'* The answer came back: *'Hell, yes.'*

The fact that his hallucinations centered on Eric actually alleviated some concern. His best friend was trapped in a coma and his chances of recovery were a coin flip. Who wouldn't be messed up?

❖

That night at Freak City, Jack limped through a few glasses of bourbon. The bar was hopping but the party atmosphere didn't suit his mood.

Shawn dumped more alcohol in his glass.

"Well, hell," Jack said.

"What? You trying to stay sober? Weird method, drinking bourbon."

"Ah, not sober. But not drunk, either. Just trying to maintain."

"I hear you," Shawn said. "I'm not feeling so festive myself. This Eric shit is on my mind all the time."

Jack nodded. "You want to meet up at the hospital tomorrow?"

"Sure," Shawn said.

"Sounds good." Jack stuck a twenty under his still-full glass and headed for the door. "See you then," he called over his shoulder.

❖

Room 308 had all normal white walls, and Eric had fewer bandages. His body continued to chug along, healing itself while his mind remained submerged wherever it was.

Jack sat down in his chair, already uncomfortable. His throat had started to tickle as soon as he entered the room. That had to be a mental thing, but it made him nervous. He gave an experimental cough and cleared his throat vigorously. It sounded like he was choking on an outboard motor but the tickle stayed. He tried to ignore it and watch TV.

"Not a lot else to do," he told Eric. "You suck at conversation. Usually it's because your mouth is full of penis, though. I'll cut you some slack this time."

He flipped through the channels and settled on women's beach volleyball. "This'll be good for you. Athletic chicks in their underwear. Just what you need."

Jack heard rubber soles squeak into the room. A nurse bustled around the bed, poking buttons, twisting dials, writing on the chart. "Sorry to disturb you two," she said.

Jack rubbed his eyes. "No problem. I'm sure he doesn't mind."

"How are you doing?" she asked.

"Exhausted," Jack said. "But still not as sleepy as this guy." He nodded at Eric.

The nurse laughed. "It's pretty great that you come to see him so often. I really think it helps coma patients to be close to loved ones and hear their voices."

"I don't know if it helps. He looks pretty bored."

"Well, keep at it. Don't give up."

"Sure thing."

The nurse left, and Jack stood up and stretched. He checked his watch. Shawn should arrive shortly. As he smothered a yawn with his hand, the coughing exploded out of him.

Jack collapsed on the foot of Eric's bed. He couldn't fight it this time. The brutal, overwhelming lightheadedness swept him away.

He looked up to the wall to find that the vision had returned. It was vivid, sharp, and whole in a way it hadn't been before. Jack continued to cough as he stared at it. It formed a perfect rectangle on the wall and Jack realized it wasn't a hallucination. It was a door.

❖

Jack woke up to a howling screech. He was lying face down on a gritty, hard-packed surface. It tasted sour in his open mouth.

He groaned and rocked up onto all fours. The harsh soil scratched at his palms. It was a deep, nasty shade of dead-rat grey.

The screech came again, sounding like a monkey fucking a bald eagle. Jack heaved himself upright and tottered on his feet. He rubbed grit out of his eyes and looked around.

A solid, pewter-colored sky stretched overhead, emitting a muted, reluctant glow. The skeletal outlines of hundreds of trees etched against it, stretching out in every direction, fading into the murk. Squinting, Jack realized they were too symmetrical for trees. And they were all the same, like markers or monuments.

Jack shook his head but the hallucination didn't fade. He heard that awful monkey-eagle shriek again and spun around.

He stared at a crucified naked body hanging from one of the things he'd thought was a tree. The structure, comprised of two rough, unfinished logs, had been lashed together in the shape of an X. The bottom arms were buried in the ground, and those on top jutted toward the leaden sky.

A man's head hung down, his face barely visible. His body looked as if it had been frozen in the middle of a jumping jack, arms and legs bound tightly to the wood appendages. His skin was red and inflamed where the ropes held wrists and ankles, while his hands and feet were bone-white and bloodless. The weight of his body pulled him forward so that his arms stretched cruelly at the shoulder joints. The man turned his head.

"Eric!"

Jack ran forward, but skidded to a halt when a black-skinned monster the size of a toddler peeked from behind Eric's head. The thing hung from the fork of the X-shaped cross, talons on its left hand buried in the wood. Its right hand held the back of Eric's neck. When it opened its mouth to make that horrifying shriek again, Jack saw rows of pointed teeth. It peered over Eric's shoulder, eyes large, bulbous, and pus-yellow with no pupils at all. Its chest was a lighter color than the rest of its black body, nearly the same shade of grey as the soil at Jack's feet.

Jack started forward again, reaching a hand up in Eric's direction even though he was ten feet away.

The black creature hissed. It curled its talons into Eric's neck and pushed his head to the side.

Jack took another step closer and the thing darted its head forward, snapping its teeth.

"Okay, okay." Jack stopped and held up both hands. "What the fuck are you?"

It threw back its head and yowled, not the same screech as before, but a gravelly, urgent sound. Answering cries came from all around. Howls and shrieks and snarls rose into the bleak sky, and Jack's heart began slamming into his ribs.

He shuffled a couple of steps closer while the thing's eyes weren't on him. Dead grey dust puffed at his feet. Six feet from the bottom of the cross, the monster whipped its head back, and Jack stopped, hands still in front of him. The bulging yellow eyes studied him carefully. A smile curved its thin lips.

A thick red tongue flopped out of its smile. It hung down impossibly long, then licked slowly up the side of Eric's face. The meaning was perfectly clear: *He's mine.*

The trail of saliva coursing down Eric's face smoked lightly. Eric's eyes opened and Jack's stomach clenched. He took another step toward the cross and the monster hissed again. This time when it lunged its head forward it nipped the side of Eric's neck.

Eric didn't flinch at the bite but his gaze rolled to Jack who thought he saw a flicker of recognition, a tiny spark in Eric's vacant eyes. Eric's head snapped backward, catching the thing right in its grinning mouth. It gave a rusty squawk and toppled over. The claws on its left hand ripped loose from the wood and the creature dropped out of sight. When it hit the ground, it shrieked.

A rising tide of snarling and hissing filled the air. The other creatures were leaping off their crosses, abandoning their victims, and heading for him.

Jack's spine turned to ice. He looked up at Eric, desperate, but with no plan, no idea, no goddamn *clue* what he could do.

Jack was pretty sure Eric was unconscious; that head butt hadn't done him any good. The thing trembled in the dirt behind the cross. It tried to get to its feet but collapsed and uttered an angry bleat like a demonic goat.

The pounding, howling mob of approaching creatures grew louder. They poured over the tenebrous, cross-studded landscape like a swarm of ants, waves of yowling black monsters converging from all 360 degrees.

Jack had nothing to battle an army of ferocious creatures armed with talons and teeth. He didn't even have a pocketknife to cut Eric down.

Eric blinked. Maybe he wasn't exactly unconscious but he didn't look like he had any helpful ideas, either. Jack ducked under the inverted V of the cross and stepped through to where the monster had almost re-gained its balance. He took a short stride, then a long one, and punted the thing's face as hard as he could, enjoying the brisk, satisfying crunch.

The creature's eyes burst, splattering Jack's foot with green and black fluid. Its head flopped on its neck and it soared several feet through the air before collapsing in a jumbled, motionless heap.

Turning around, he looked at the two logs making up the X-shape. He decided to climb it, unsure what he would accomplish outside of putting him a few feet above the wave of death sweeping in.

He leaped forward and clambered his way up the knobby wood like a squirrel. When he got to the fork where the creature had been, he held onto the right arm of the cross and looped his left around Eric's neck from behind, digging his fingers into his friend's skin.

"Eric, are you awake? I don't know what to do. I don't even know where we are." He craned his head around and saw the horde of pitch-black monsters pouring into the clearing, surrounding them in a sea of pus-yellow eyes and snapping white teeth.

Jack tightened his left biceps around Eric's neck. "I think we're fucked, buddy."

The monsters smashed into the base of the cross like a tsunami, screeching as they dug in their claws and began to climb.

Jack lowered his face to Eric's ear. "I'm sorry," he whispered.

As the victorious shrieks of the monsters rose from the ground, he heard something else. It was faint, almost buried under the gibbering demon chorus. It sounded like his name.

"Jack!" The voice was weak and distant. "Jack!" Louder this time, and he had no doubt it came straight out of the gunmetal sky.

"Oh, fuck," Jack muttered. "It's Jesus."

The creatures were fighting their way up both legs of the cross in a furious boil of thrashing black bodies. They bit and clawed at one another, their own mad frenzy slowing them down. One of the monsters clamped down on another's back with its teeth and viciously jerked its head sideways, throwing the other beast back into the churning mob.

Jack knew it was over. Inter-demon strife or no, they would buzz saw their way up the last few feet of timber in a hurry.

"Jack!" the voice bellowed again from the heavens.

Jack threw back his head and shouted, "Hurry up, Jesus!" His shoulders began shaking, almost knocking him from his perch. He tightened his grip but his body jerked harder, wrenching him back and forth. Jack clung to Eric for support. His whole body moved in harsh twitches, threatening to dump him off the cross and onto the monster-covered ground.

"Jack! Wake up!" The voice sounded closer now.

"Shawn?" he whispered.

"Come on! Wake up!"

Jack realized his unconscious body must still be in Eric's hospital room, and Shawn was attempting to rouse him. The shaking stopped. Jack slumped forward and banged his face against the back of Eric's head. "Sorry, pal. Blame Shawn."

The closest creatures reached up, their long talons struggling to rip at Jack and Eric. They shrieked with terrible, delighted rage, and their disgusting eyes stared with feverish intensity.

Shawn's voice came from the sky again, desperate now. "Come on, man. Please wake up."

Jack stared up at the dull grey sky. He could see the outline of Shawn's face, as if he were standing on the other side of a filthy window. Shawn became clearer, and Jack knew what was coming. He shuffled up a bit higher on the cross and draped himself over Eric, wrapping his arms around him as far as he could. He squeezed with every last bit of his strength.

When his shoulders began shaking again, he gripped Eric tighter and felt himself becoming lightheaded. Fog seeped into his vision, narrowing it to a tunnel.

"Okay," he said. "Okay, pal, I'm getting you out of here."

He looked up and now he could see other shapes behind Shawn: the IV stand beside the bed; machinery bolted to the wall; the chair where he'd spent so many hours.

Jack started to slip. His fingers lost their hold on Eric's skin as he was pulled backward and up. Below him, the demons screamed in frustration. The cross vibrated intensely as their furious little bodies propelled upward even faster.

Jack rose from the cross, his feet floating off the rugged wood. He snatched at Eric, scrabbling for something to hold onto, something to keep him connected. Eric's naked torso gave no purchase. Jack's hands slipped over him like he was made of porcelain. The things would begin tearing Eric apart unless Jack could keep his grip. His fingers skated over Eric's collarbones. The tips of his fingers dug under the bones and his thumbs drove down, grasping Eric's clavicles like handles.

His left hand popped free as his body rose higher toward the heavens, toward Shawn, toward his world and freedom. His right hand, his single point of contact, clenched so tightly he felt his thumb meet his opposing fingers underneath Eric's collarbone, pushing through muscle and gristle.

He felt another tug as his body ascended higher. His grip trembled. The dark world full of crosses and demons snapped to black like a TV that had been turned off, and Jack felt an overpowering moment of disorientation, like he was teetering on the brink of the abyss.

Then he was back in the hospital room, lying across Eric's bed. He took a deep breath, smelling the freshly laundered sheets. He raised his head and looked around.

"Jesus Christ!" Shawn yelled from behind him.

Jack tried to turn but, instead, he slipped from the bed and landed on the floor.

Shawn grabbed Jack under the armpits and hauled him to his feet. When he let go, Jack wobbled. His legs felt unresponsive. He swayed back and forth like a sailor making the transition from sea to solid ground.

Shawn began to ask questions, each one starting with "What the," or, "How the," or, "Where the," but Jack ignored him.

Jack lurched toward Eric's bed but his knees unhinged and he fell forward in a graceless plummet toward the just-departed floor. He threw out his arms and his elbows caught the edge of the mattress. His knees scraped the linoleum, and the momentum caused his chest to whack the bed's frame with a comical *thwang*.

Jack ended up half-kneeling at the head of the bed like a penitent monk, his face inches from Eric's, his hands raised in front of him as if in prayer.

Eric's eyes opened. His mouth moved once, silently, then again. He looked Jack in the eyes and whispered, "Hello, homo." ◆

Brent R. Oliver read Salem's Lot *when he was twelve and blames Stephen King for pretty much everything that happened after that. He has been the victim of irony, repossessed morals, and harsh language. The nine-to-five grind has rejected him and the bank has foreclosed on the tiny little haunted house that is his brain. This bio was penned from his favorite neighborhood bar because his power was shut off and it's cheaper to buy beer than electricity.*

Mr. Oliver writes creative nonfiction as well as tales rooted in glorious darkness. His essays and articles have been featured across a broad spectrum of online and print media including FIGHT! *Magazine, Business Lexington, and Tricycle. In July of 2014, his first short story "One Shot," was published by horror-writers.net. He lives in Lexington,* KY *with his amazing wife Stacey and a mostly underwhelming cat.*

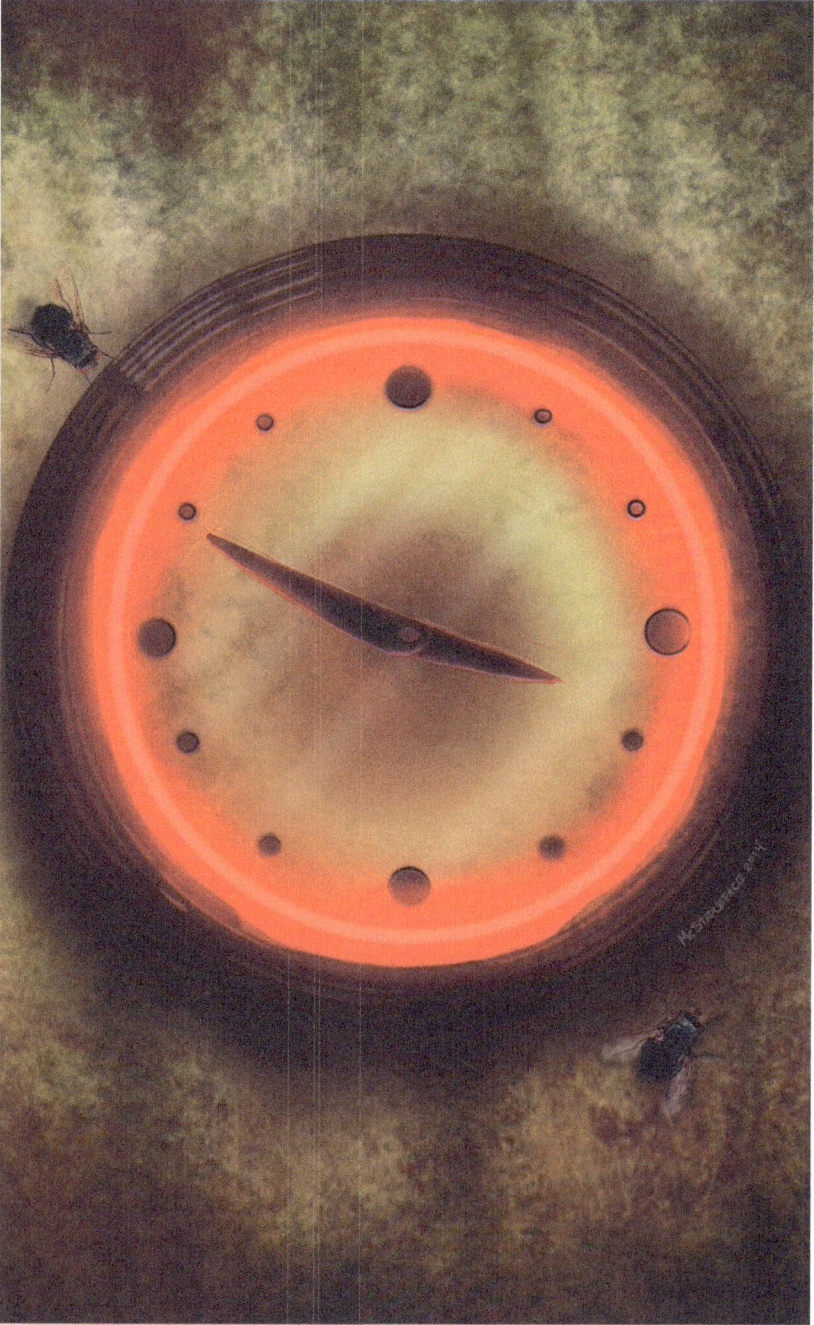

Artwork: Inky McStapleface

THE DEVIL ORDERED AN OMELET

DALE ELSTER

Between the fat guy who'd shit his pants and the waitress bent over the counter, I knew I'd found the place. The waitress and the fatty seemed normal compared to everyone else. I saw a cook's face just beyond the steaming plates waiting to be picked up, a crooked finger jammed into his broad nose.

The food in the window was probably for the guy to my left. He was devouring the contents off the three plates in front of him, while the twenty or so he'd already finished were piled high, ready to be cleared.

As I passed by the fat guy with the shitty pants, I noticed him puking into a bucket and scooping it back out with a giant spoon he most likely pilfered from Chef Boogers. I could even hear his slurping over the moans coming from an orgy a few feet away.

If the sight of this crowd didn't turn one's stomach, the smell sure as hell would have.

I walked to an empty booth in the corner of the diner and sat with my back to the wall. I had a good view of the restaurant, not that I was interested in any of the activity. I was looking for someone. I didn't have a name or a face to pick out of the crowd, but I knew that I would recognize him as soon as I saw him.

In life, I would never have agreed to a meeting where I wasn't in control. In order to do my job effectively, control was essential. Control–and who had it–had been a matter of life and death.

In life, I was the guy someone met. I was the guy who took care of things. I was the guy someone came to when they wanted a certain *problem* to go away.

In life, people called me Angel but not because I was a nice guy. People called me Angel the way someone would call a fat guy Tiny.

To my victims, I was the Angel of Death, only I didn't wear a black robe or carry a scythe; I wore a black leather trench coat and carried a selection of knives.

In truth, I was no Angel of Death…I just arranged the meetings.

I looked at a stain on the floor, wondering if it were blood, semen, or just water, and when I looked up, the man I was waiting for sat across from me as if he'd been there the whole time, but I knew he'd just arrived. His skin was the color of drying blood, nearly black with an oily shine. Elongated horns curved back from his temples. His teeth were like tiny yellow knives.

"I trust introductions are unnecessary," he said. His voice seemed too soft for his hard features. It was like he'd swallowed some pathetic little weakling who spoke from somewhere inside of him.

I stared into his eyes. "You talk like a faggot."

"You speak from experience, no doubt. Considering all your time in prison, naturally."

I relaxed against the red, sparkling vinyl, a tiny grin stretching the line of my mouth.

"Got something for me?" I asked.

"Now what makes you think I'm here to offer you something?"

"Because I don't look like all the other assholes in this place."

Wasn't *that* the truth? My size alone set me apart from the crowd. It had been that way my whole life. Add in the dreadlocks, and there would be no need for a police sketch. A box of crayons and any five-year-old would do.

Smiling, I added, "I figure you for the guy that can make me suffer. Since you haven't pulled the trigger on that particular option, you must have something else in mind for me."

The Devil blinked but not in a human way. Two sets of milky lenses flashed across his yellow eyes. "Very astute, Mr. Stark," he said, spreading out his wings. They looked like a bat's, only red and flecked with black pigmentation. "You don't mind if I forego the use of your nickname, do you? Angel doesn't sit very well with me."

I said nothing.

"I'm not here to offer you anything," he continued. "I'm only here to point out that you have a choice to make."

I listened, but acted like I was blowing him off. "Can you still get a decent cup of joe on this side?"

"Something wrong with the cup in front of you?"

I looked down to find a steaming mug. Lifting it to my nose, it smelled not just normal, but great, black and brewed strong.

"You don't seem to mind that you're here," The Devil noted.

"Why would I? After all the shit I've done, I didn't exactly expect to sail up to the heavens on silken wings." I wanted to provoke him, but he wasn't taking the bait. "So if your plan is to torture me, you best get to it. Just let me finish my coffee."

The Devil grinned. His hands alternated between hooves and human-like fingers with long, black claws. He held them in a steeple before his face. "Remarkable. You just might be the man for the job, after all."

He was finally getting to the point.

"These fools," the Devil said, gesturing to the diner patrons, "they were harvested from the living world, unredeemable, and are now left here to wallow in their sins."

I glanced at the crowd. They seemed content to me.

Look more closely, his voice echoed in my head.

I buried the surprised look, or at least thought I did. I hid it behind a hard stare, the kind of look that used to send even the bad asses running for the exits. Not this guy. I knew he saw the tiny shock in my eyes and could tell he enjoyed it, so I let him have his fun. But I made up my mind...that was the last time he would get to me.

"What's the job?" I asked, taking another sip.

"Doing what you do best, of course."

I liked him but decided to screw with him some more. I wanted to see if he'd show me a weak spot. Weaknesses were like gold in my line of work.

I shrugged. "That's it?"

"Essentially, yes."

"You want me to kill people for you?"

This time I couldn't keep my emotions in check. The place fell church-quiet, except for my laughter. The Devil didn't seem bothered. He remained fixed on me.

"It's not as easy as it sounds," he said.

"What do I get when I pass this test of yours?"

"*If.* If you pass my test." He allowed a moment of silence before continuing. "It's simple. Pass the test and I'll make you a demon. You can continue your life in comfort, walk the Earth as you please, and claim souls in my name. You will possess powers greater than you can imagine."

He talked with his hands, like a lot of Italians I knew. Watching him was like watching an actor in a play. Theatrical. He leaned forward, long enough for me to sample that fresh-as-a-dumpster breath of his, before gesturing to the crowd.

"But if you fail, you'll end up just like all of *them*."

He kept talking, some shit about walking the Earth, blah blah blah. Doing his bidding, blah blah blah. All I could hear in my mind was game show music. Instead of seeing him as the Devil, I imagined him as a game show host, dressed in a red suit, standing behind a little podium, giving away cheesy prizes to a panel of smiling idiots for playing his little game.

That's all it was. Just a game, and one I wasn't willing to play…at least not by his rules.

"Fuck off," I said and finished my coffee.

He laughed. "This is, to use a phrase I know you are familiar with, 'an offer you can't refuse.'"

I got up and walked away from the booth. I expected something to happen. Maybe a mob of those demons the Devil had talked about would show up and rip me apart, or maybe he'd stab me in the back with that tail of his.

That's when I noticed—really noticed—the people in the diner. I heard the Devil's voice in my head again: *Look more closely.*

The waitress and her several sex partners all screamed in agony instead of ecstasy. The guy with the plates stacked up forced each bite into his mouth. When I walked past, he puked across the counter. The fat guy who'd shit himself walked over, as if some invisible man held a gun to his head. When he arrived to the booth, he used his thick arm to swipe the guy's puke into his bucket.

Dead, the Devil's voice repeated in my mind.

I walked back to the booth, where the Devil was waiting patiently.

"Many don't remember how they got here," he explained. "Make the choice and perhaps you'll discover just who killed the legendary Angel Stark. Get revenge."

Revenge. I thought of my brother, Michael. He wasn't like me. He always needed my help with money and protection. With me gone, he wouldn't last long.

"I'll do it," I said. "Send me back, but I want you to do something for me first."

"I'm listening."

"My brother. He's only involved in the business because he's related to me. He's a good kid otherwise. I can save him while he's alive, but if he's dead…."

"You want his soul saved?" The Devil chuckled. "Then you need to talk to Jesus."

"I'm talkin' to *you*. My brother ever comes knocking on your door, you send him back the other way. Give me that and I'm all yours."

The Devil looked away a moment, appearing disappointed. "This weakness you have concerning your brother is troublesome," he said, shaking his head. "You might not be the man for the job, after all."

"Ask my victims if they thought I was weak."

The Devil's eyebrows lifted.

"As long as I know my brother's safe, I'll make all your demons look like grade school bullies. Trust me on that one."

The Devil said nothing. He sat there looking unimpressed.

I leaned forward and tightened my jaw. "Anything happens to my little brother, I'll make you pay for it. I'll find a way."

The Devil smiled, showing every one of his shark's teeth. He gave a single nod, the pointed tip of his chin dipping way down.

I realized he wasn't nodding to me, rather to a plate in front of me. A simple omelet, garnished with a sprig of parsley and an orange slice.

"You can't make an omelet without breaking eggs, as the saying goes," he told me. He stood and stretched out his huge wings and looked dead into my eyes. *Now, let's see if you're the one who breaks the eggs or one of the eggs that gets broken.*

❖

I found myself walking the streets of the city. A power burned within me, different from anything I had ever experienced. In life, I did my job the way it needed to be done. If it called for me to get physical, I would break a neck, stop a heart, or crush a windpipe with a single punch.

In the early days, I often lost my temper. The results were the same, only messier. But I learned from them. I learned not let things get personal. It was just business. Things were different now. With my brother's soul on the line, it could never be anything other than personal.

The first victim was a woman waiting for a train.

I was on my way to see my brother, to talk to him about everything that had happened, to warn him what was at stake.

In life, my client would supply me with a name and photo of the target, along with a short list of information including work schedule, vehicle I.D., and address. Shit like that. I never kept any of the information, never even allowed it to exchange hands from the client to me. I memorized the details and went to work.

It was like that now, only without the client meeting. As I walked along, I found myself drawn to a face in the crowd. I didn't like it. I knew I wasn't in control, that the Devil pulled the strings now.

I needed to reach my brother. Until that time came, I would play the Devil's game. So I stood behind the woman in front of a subway. The fact that she was pregnant and had a second kid strapped to her chest didn't bother me at all.

A little push and off they went, just before the train rushed past. All the police would see on the security tape would be a young mother falling into the path of a passing train. They would witness the crowd suddenly pulling together, trying to help.

Without audio, what the cops wouldn't experience was the collective scream of the crowd, temporarily washed out by the high-pitched metallic wail of the train as the panic-stricken driver applied the brakes.

I moved on, hoping to somehow appear right before my brother's eyes.

It didn't work that way, apparently.

I found myself sitting in the back of a dive bar. The air was thick with smoke, the familiar smell of cheap perfume, and stale beer. I sat alone at a table with a fresh glass of beer. I sipped the drink, taking as much pleasure in the taste as I did the coffee the Devil had provided in the diner. Maybe the beer was a reward for a job well done. I didn't care what purpose it served.

I stared at a man at the end of the bar, cell phone pressed to his ear. He had just lost his job and was lying to his wife about how everything would be okay, working to keep his voice level.

I reached out an impossibly long arm and planted a finger in his back, penetrating all the way into his lung. He never felt a thing, never knew what I left growing in him. By the time his doctor would find it, it would be too late.

As I left, I whispered, "See you later, Mr. C."

The cops, the people at the train station, Mr. C's family–all of them would search for answers. We all try to make sense of the horrors in our lives. Most would console themselves with the notion that this was all God's will or some other nonsense.

I wondered what these people had done to piss God off. Mentally, I shrugged them off and moved on. Everybody gets what's coming to them.

Near the park, I stopped the heart of a runner by squeezing my fist tight as he bounced on by. He dropped like a stone. I could've taken my time with him, using any of my knives to gut him and let him bleed out in the bushes.

I met four different people at once not far from my old neighborhood. Two in cars, the other two on foot–one guy crossing the street, the other walking on the sidewalk. I snapped my fingers, changing streetlights at my will. I heard the crunch of metal. The guy crossing the street got swallowed up in the middle of the two cars coming from opposite directions as they collided. One of the cars in the pileup bounced over the curb and took out the guy on the sidewalk. Of course, the drivers were both dead, too.

The power went to my head like fine bourbon. It was all so much fun.

The next victim to pop onto my radar was at a bar in my old neighborhood, right in my old stomping grounds. *I might get a chance to see my brother after all.*

I didn't look like the old me. I was still big, still intimidating, and still carried the 'don't fuck with me' vibe, only without the dreads, the leather trench coat, or any of the ink.

Once again, I sat at a table in the back corner of the bar, facing the crowd.

I sipped my beer and stared at the guy I was going to take out. I thought about giving him a quick death, maybe a stroke.

A whispering came from the booth next to mine. I recognized the voice right away.

When we were kids, the church ran an outreach program, taking kids like me and attempting to turn us around…setting us on the right path. The service offered free Sunday school, sports programs, and summer camps–that sort of shit. Father Callahan had been the priest then. Two more priests had been appointed since, the latest being Father George. He whispered Psalm 23:4: *"…though I walk through the valley of the shadow of death, I will fear no evil…."*

I stood and faced him. The candlelight from his table drew fear on his face in bold lines, making his skin look as if it had tightened to fit the skull beneath.

"Relax, padre. I'm not here for you."

"You belong to the Devil now, but I am not afraid of you anymore."

Anymore? I knitted my brows in thought.

"You know who I am?" I whispered.

"Yes," he answered, his voice quaking. "I see through your mask. The Devil is a deceiver, but I see you. I see you, Robert Stark."

I passed through the solid wood of the table and part of the booth. Judging by the tiny puddle around the priest's shoes, he was impressed by my little trick. I grabbed him by the shirt. His stiff white collar buckled under my grip.

"Like I said, I'm not here for you, Holy Man. But you're gonna do something for me. You're gonna help my brother."

"Your brother? I've been helping young Michael all along. Ever since… since…." The priest tried to back away from me. "I…I can't be in service to the Devil!"

I tightened my grip.

"You'll be in service to *me*. Cross me, old man, and you might make it to those pearly gates someday, but only after I'm done with you, and I really doubt they'll recognize you when you get there. Understand? Now, where is he?"

The priest swallowed hard. "At the church's camp upstate. He's been helping to get the place ready. He's working under Father Ryan's tutelage. Your brother has taken a great interest in developing his faith. He's a good young man now."

I let go of the priest and backed away. Something about the church camp didn't sit right with me. In life, I had a gut instinct when something was about to go sideways. That's how I felt now.

The priest ran.

I didn't care. Didn't care about the Devil. Didn't care about my plan. My brother was all that mattered.

❖

A second after vanishing from the bar, I reappeared at that summer camp, outside Father Ryan's office.

Whether you gamble in the streets, play Three Card Monte, or bet it all on black in Vegas, there's only one rule: The house always wins. I should have seen it coming.

My career had always been a threat to Michael's life. I had spent most of my time between assignments watching out for him, waiting to see who was stupid enough to test me. So when Michael started taking an interest in the church, I allowed it.

My brother was slow. Not a retard or anything like that, but slow. I figured the church would keep him safe. I hoped they'd help save his soul. I never figured they'd be waiting in line to test me, too.

Everything in life is a test.

I always had a bad temper when it came to Michael's safety. One of the sisters had once told me that I was like a bad furnace. After the boiler overheats, watch out. She had said some other shit, too. About how I could control it and whatnot, but I never listened to her. I never listened to anybody.

There was always a quiet second before that furnace blew, like the calm before a storm.

When I opened the door to Father Ryan's office, that quiet stole the air.

Michael kneeled into the priest's lap, head between the priest's legs. Father Ryan opened his eyes and screamed. He pushed my brother away, then looked at me with his expression frozen onto his face.

My brother smiled. I guess he was happy to see me, but he shouldn't have been. The look on my face should've sent him cowering into a corner.

It's hard to pin down exactly what happened next. I screamed words that sounded like rolling thunder in my skull. I felt like the old me, deadly but without demonic powers.

I crushed Father Ryan's windpipe sometime between ripping him out of the chair and smashing his back against the bookshelves. That was too bad. I really wanted to hear him scream, and by the time I gouged out one of his eyes and showed it to the other, he had already drowned in his own blood. That was too bad, too. I wanted him to see what it had cost him, doing that stuff to my brother. In the end, it hadn't been all that much; it wasn't the priest's body in my hands…it was Michael's.

My brother's head slumped over my hand. His neck felt like a small bag of crushed glass. For the first time in my life, fear coursed through me; for the first time in my life, I hated what I'd done.

Father Ryan sat in the chair with his head tilted back, eyes frozen open, pupils blown.

I laid my brother on the floor, then covered his body with an old blanket I found lying by the fireplace. I took the time to tuck the edges under him. I hated that he was already getting cold.

I grabbed one of my knives and pushed the blade tight to my throat. The sharp edge broke my skin as I pulled it across, slowly. Hot liquid crawled down my chest. My arm wanted to stop, but as the serrated tips caught, I closed my eyes and pulled it the rest of the way, feeling the tug on my windpipe as I choked on my own blood.

❖

"I know," the Devil said, shaking his head in sympathetic disbelief. "I know, Mr. Stark." He leaned back into the red, sparkling vinyl backrest, stretching his arms along the length of it. "Priests, right?"

"You set me up," I said. "You knew I killed my brother all along and that I killed myself. You just made me relive it." My body fell numb. The fight had gone out of me. I was just like everyone else in this place now.

The Devil leaned forward. "That was the test! Had you listened to that little voice in your head and simply walked away without guilt, without remorse, and most importantly, without killing yourself, you would be a demon this very moment! But no. You had to punish your-self, Stark. Demons do not punish themselves."

He shifted in his seat, his features darkening again.

"So now you're just like the rest," he explained, gesturing at the staff and patrons of the diner. "Instead of an omelet, you're merely a broken egg. A real shame, too. I could have used someone like you! Monsters walk the Earth every day, but demons are hard to find."

I touched my face, realizing that I had been crying. Rivers of tears were pouring like a waterfall from my swollen eyes, and snot slipped from my nose in thick ropes.

I straightened up. "How do I know that this wasn't all a trick? At the summer camp…how do I know that wasn't just one of your illusions?"

The Devil reached for the tabletop jukebox, pushed a button, and turned the volume all the way up. The sound of me crying blared across the diner until the whole place went stone-silent.

After having his fun, he silenced the jukebox.

"Illusions?" the Devil asked, acting both surprised and insulted. "You see the world as you choose to see it! That includes this place. You see this place as a diner. As for Father Ryan, well he is, shall we say, more of a…traditionalist." The Devil leaned over the table. "But don't worry about him, Stark. You did the world a favor with that one."

"I don't worry about him. I worry about my brother."

"Ah, yes! He really is at the heart of this whole drama." The Devil sat back and folded his wings. "Well he certainly wasn't safe from you, now, was he?" he asked, exhaling heavily.

"He's safe, then?"

"I forgive him. What happened was not his fault."

"Forgive him? The Devil doesn't forgive."

"Your brother I can forgive," the Devil said. "You know something? I forgive you, too. But you'll remain here, I'm afraid. A deal's a deal, after all!"

"I never asked you for forgiveness. That wasn't part of the deal. I knew I was going to Hell for what I'd done."

"You most certainly did ask me for forgiveness." He smiled. "Think, Stark. *Think hard.*"

I closed my eyes.

"Remember now?"

The only time I'd ever asked for forgiveness was during my last moments on Earth with the knife under my chin. *God, forgive me.*

I opened my eyes to see not the Devil but blinding white light. It was beautiful. Warm.

"God?"

I saw Michael in the light, smiling and waving.

"My dear boy," a voice boomed, but there was a kindness in its tone. The Light began to fade away, leaving me behind in my eternal sorrow.

"Who ever said I was the Devil?" ◆

Dale Elster is a horror and dark fiction author living in upstate New York with his wife and two children. A chef for over 20 years, Dale was forced to retire due to medical reasons, thus moving his lifelong passion for writing to the front burner. Since then his work has appeared in anthologies published by NorGus Press and Collaboration of the Dead. Look for him in Deadsville *an all-new anthology he is co-writing with fellow horror scribe T.D. Trask, due October 2015. His house may or may not be haunted. But it probably is.*

BURKE.14

Artwork: Chris L. Burke

THE EXCHANGE

JASON PARENT

Ramsey covered his mouth, but the vomit had to go somewhere. It rose in his throat and forced its way through pursed lips, spraying out the cracks between his fingers. Recognizing the futility of his efforts, he gave up trying to stem the flow.

He sat Indian style on the floor–some floor, somewhere. Darkness surrounded him. Ramsey leaned forward and planted his goopy palms on the soft carpet. After he emptied his stomach's contents, he struggled to find his bearings. Though, even in the dark, he sensed some familiarity with his surroundings.

Where am I? How did I get here? He concentrated hard. His brain pounded from the effort. He tried to scan his surroundings for clues, but the darkness proved to be all-consuming.

Wherever he was, it was quiet and warm. He dragged his fingers along the carpet–soggy, not just where he'd thrown up but also underneath his buttocks. His skin radiated feverish heat. Ramsey went to wipe his vomit-coated hands on his jeans, but discovered that he was naked from the waist down.

He grabbed his t-shirt, letting out a breath of relief, as if this minute symbol of familiarity was enough to dispel his incomprehension. It made sitting bare ass on the carpet in the dark, covered in his own puke, somehow seem a bit more normal.

Rammmmsssseeeee....

"Huh?" Ramsey sprang to his knees, his arms slashing at the air in front of him.

*Rammmmsssseeeee...*the voice, like a whisper on the wind, flowed into his ear.

"Who's there?"

Ramsey waited for a response but none came. His head felt like a bomb had gone off inside it. Panic, and the sudden urge to flee, thrust his heart into overdrive. He leapt to his feet. His head connected with the ceiling, and he came crashing down. Dizziness and pain clouded his mind.

He rubbed his head where a bump had already surfaced. He reached up and touched a sloped ceiling.

My room?

Ramsey stood, this time slowly, and stumbled through the dark to where he hoped the light switch would be. Reaching out for the wall opposite the slope, taking baby steps toward it, Ramsey moved unimpeded. He followed the wall to the door and the light switch beside it. His bedroom illuminated. The light sent flashing pain behind his eyes so harsh he had to close them. After the agony subsided, he opened them a sliver, giving them time to adjust.

Gross, he thought, glancing at the remains of last night's dinner now deposited on his usually pristine carpet. The bulk of the mess pooled in front of the cutout entranceway to the attic behind the southern wall of his bedroom.

He tried to piece together the previous night, but nothing came to him. Puke clotted his short beard and stained his t-shirt. He followed its trail down to a used condom hanging off the tip of his penis.

"Where have you been?" he asked his flaccid friend. A stream of drool escaped from the corner of his mouth. He wiped the back of his hand across his lips, then ripped the condom off and threw it into the pool of vomit.

I'll clean it up later, Ramsey thought, shrugging. He needed sleep, some time to give his mind a chance to reboot. He tore off his shirt, staggered toward his bed, and noticed a perfectly chiseled specimen lying atop his sheets, exposed buttocks turned his way.

"And just who might you be?" he asked softly.

Ramsey's penis stiffened despite his drunkenness, despite the pain pulsating through his body and head. His eyebrows rose as well, and he turned around. He looked at the condom he'd tossed on the floor, which after a moment's debate, decided was beyond reuse.

He dashed out of the room, immediately regretting the sudden movement. A dry heave followed by an acidic burp forced their way up his throat. He entered his bathroom and stared at himself in the mirror. Bloodshot eyes complemented his greasy, unwashed face.

"At least you don't have bedhead," he told his reflection as he rubbed his clean-shaven scalp.

Old pipes protested with grunts as he turned on the hot water for a quick shower. The heat soothed his already warm flesh, sweat purifying his body, excreting alcohol from his pores. He closed his eyes, and by the time he opened them again the water had gone frigid.

He turned off the water and dried himself. He picked up the mouthwash and took a swig straight from the bottle. Instantly, the memory of drinking Jägermeister flashed through his mind. It felt good to remember something. He swished it around and spat into the sink. With his towel wrapped around his waist, he half-staggered back to his bedroom. He threw the towel over the filth on his carpet, turned off the light, and climbed into bed beside the enticing stranger.

Why clean up today what I can get this sucker to clean up tomorrow?

Ramsey pulled up a sheet and curled against the man. He grabbed his company's hip, excited by the feel of hard muscle beneath smooth skin, and kissed his lover's shoulder. An almost metallic scent, like iron mixed with musk and sweat, enveloped him.

"Burr," Ramsey said, stroking the man's arm. "Your skin is like ice. Poor thing. You must be freezing. Here, let me warm you up."

Ramsey's penis rested like a hot dog between the stranger's buns. He moved his lips playfully along the man's shoulder in a continuous path that led to the curve of his neck. Once there, he bit, a nibble at first, then hard enough to leave imprints. The man didn't budge.

This one likes it rough.

His excitement grew. He threw his arm around his lover and squeezed him.

"Eww," Ramsey said, withdrawing his arm from a sticky wetness. "You got sick, too? I mean," he stammered, then raised his voice. "You got sick in bed, too? What did we do last night…must have been one hell of a good time."

Ramsey's penis fell flaccid.

Puke on the floor is one thing, but in bed? This brings grossness of a whole new level.

"Come on, love. Let's get you into the shower." Ramsey shook the man again. "Damn, man, wake up!" Nothing stirred him. His unknown lover was out cold. Very cold.

Ramsey sighed. He stood next to his bed and flipped on the lamp atop an end table.

"Wake up," he commanded, his patience thinning.

He shook the stranger violently. The man rolled onto his back, his eyes wide open. Red stained his chest, and his neck looked as if had been torn apart by some wild animal; strands of shredded skin hung beneath his chin, his spine visible inside the gaping hole.

Ramsey bit down on his knuckle to stifle a scream. His eyes darted from the bed to the floor and to each corner of the room, not really sure what he searched for.

"W-W-What happened?" His lips quivered as he spoke.

What do I do? What do I do?

The question repeated in Ramsey's mind like a broken record skipping at a million rotations per minute.

Oh my God, did I kill him?

Ramsey slouched, his enfeebled legs buckling beneath his weight. His heart pulsated erratically. He could never imagine himself hurting anyone. Not like that.

The fact remained: A dead man lay in his bed.

Ramsey tried to settle his nerves, to consider the evidence. He didn't recall any blood on him before he showered.

Think, Ramsey! God, it looks like a bear mauled him.

Ramsey had heard of people doing all sorts of crazy shit while they were drunk, some kind of psychotic episode during a blackout. As disturbing a truth as it was, he knew he had to have killed the stranger. No one else was in his apartment.

Unless–

Ramsey gasped. His mouth hung open. His nerves tingled on high alert. Whatever haziness had clouded his mind earlier vanished.

He crept to his bureau, pulled out a pair of boxers, and threw them on. He dashed to the kitchen and snagged a steak knife from a drawer. There he stood breathless, listening for any sound, waiting for someone, anyone, to appear out of the darkness.

Ramsey reached for the phone, but his arm recoiled from its smooth plastic as though it were on fire.

Not yet. The police will think I did it.

Room by room, Ramsey systematically ruled out each potential hiding spot: a bathroom, a living room, a kitchen, a dining room, and a bedroom. He flicked on every light, opened every door. No one squatted within the kitchen cupboards. No one veiled himself behind the shower curtain. No one leapt from any of the closets. He made his way back to his bedroom. His closet stood open, but no feet filled the shoes inside.

Only the attic remained unchecked.

The attic door was really just a square panel with a handle to pull it open. Ramsey didn't like going into the attic. It always smelled worse than a nursing home. The air hung heavy. Pink insulation sprouted in patches from the walls and ceiling like puffs of cotton candy. Silverfish, alive and dead, filled every crack and crevice. Its sole light bulb, no matter the wattage he used, never illuminated the furthest reaches.

When he reached for the handle, he saw that the panel was cracked open. He stepped back, the knife in his hand jutting out before him.

"Who's there?" Ramsey asked. "If someone's in there, I swear to God I'll–"

The door exploded from its resting place, hitting Ramsey in the shin. He buckled from the pain. Quick to recover, he jumped back and fixed his eyes upon the exposed entrance.

"Leave now," Ramsey said, the knife shaking in his hand. "I'll tell the police I never saw your face."

A low rumble emitted from the opening, almost like the purr of a finely tuned motorcycle, but much softer, less mechanical. Ramsey back-peddled in slow motion, barely aware of his movement. His gaze never left the attic entrance.

The rumble grew louder, becoming a swishing sound, like an arrow piercing the air. A searing pain shot through his chest. He looked down. Three barbed prongs penetrated his body, their points disappearing deep beneath his skin. Cables were connected to the shafts that stretched back into the darkness of the attic.

The cords pulled taut, tugging at Ramsey's flesh. His skin tented as if he were suspended from fishhooks. He screamed and grabbed the cords. Fleshy and slime-covered, they pulsated. He couldn't grip them; the more he tried, the more his hands burned.

Unable to resist the agony any longer, he let go. Deep grooves striped across his hands. He dropped onto his ass, planting his feet and pushing backward. His attacker would have to drag him every inch of the way.

Whatever tugged him didn't stop, but Ramsey matched its action with an equal and opposite reaction. His flesh split. He believed that if he didn't remove those damn prongs, his skin would soon rip from his frame.

Despite how bad it looked, the pain faded. His fear and his fight went with it. The room seemed to slant, then sway. None of it–not the dead man in his bed, the prongs beneath his flesh, or the villain to whom they belonged–concerned him any longer. His lack of concern concerned him, but only briefly.

Black as space.

It was as if the attic repelled the light in his room. The intruder moved against the brightness like oil on water. The air inside the attic seemed alive. Ramsey stared at the black mass with curiosity, almost fascination. It began to swirl. He knew he should fear it.

The pain had all but disappeared. Somewhere in the back of his mind, Ramsey understood that he'd been drugged. The soft voice of his conscience still begged him to run, but his intoxication muted it and he moved closer to the attic's entrance, falling into the euphoria.

Like a baby learning to crawl, Ramsey shuffled on hands and knees toward the door. A broad grin curled up his face. Drool ran freely from his mouth.

He entered the attic.

The darkness engulfed him with all the comfort and warmth of a fur blanket. The attic became a safe and nurturing place, a womb. His mind surged with excitement. His heart beat strong and steady. There in the darkness, he believed he had transcended to his purest self, leaving his imperfect human form on the other side of the threshold. He never wanted to leave.

❖

Ramsey awoke in his bed. He scanned his room but saw no body, no blood, no disorder, no sign that a murder had occurred.

A dream?

The idea that it had all been a dream filled him with disappointment. If only a dream, how could he return to it, to feel once again those amazing sensations that had claimed his body and mind? They were gone now. Normalcy had returned, and with it, a sense of loss. He craved the euphoria. He *needed* to feel that way again.

He stared longingly at the attic, the door slightly ajar. Ramsey dismissed the false memories of the dead stranger and the murderous creature that lived behind his wall. They didn't matter. They were inconsequential figments, distractions from the euphoria that had swept him away.

Trying to recapture the feeling in the dream, he scratched at his chest. His fingers came away wet and sticky. Three welts mounded over his heart, each the size of a quarter, oozing a yellowish liquid. Red striations spread like an infection from the wounds.

He stared at his attic door, hopeful and terrified.

Noooo…dreeeeam…Rammmmsssseeee, a voice called from within the darkness.

Ramsey sat up, drawing the covers to his chest. For a moment he didn't move, not knowing what to do, then he sprang up and raced for the exit. His hand froze upon the knob.

If I leave, I may never feel it again.

He shivered and plodded back to his bedroom. Building up courage, he drew in a breath and approached the attic, his whole body shaking uncontrollably. His teeth rattled. Letting out the breath, he removed the panel from the wall.

A crunching sound came from ceiling, like someone walking on broken glass. Ramsey's eyes adjusted to the darkness. An arm hung from the insulation…a human arm dripping blood.

Ramsey froze. He dared not move or make a sound. His muscles ached from the strain of stillness.

The arm fell to the floor, shredded at the shoulder, muscle and tissue stripped from the bone. Jagged bone fragments protruded inches above the elbow.

Two spiny black appendages, sleek and slender, slid from the insulation. Sharp talons extended from webbed hands.

Ramsey screeched.

Run. Oh please dear God, run!

All the logic in the world couldn't will his feet to move. His eyes widened, locked on this thing emerging from the ceiling.

A face breached the insulation.

Ramsey's heart nearly stopped when two small, yellow eyes, cropped like a bird's on a bulbous black head, peered directly at him. Below poked a large upturned snout with nostrils the size of fists. Its skin stretched thin, silvery veins coursing through it. And its smell, a foul odor, far worse than a rotting corpse.

Still, Ramsey couldn't run. No matter how much he wanted to, his body would not obey.

The creature's lipless mouth wrapped halfway around its head. Its jaw lined with six-inch pointed teeth that interlocked like a bear trap. Red blotches stained each tooth and stringy chunks hung from the gaps.

The crunching sound came from the creature's mouth, those monstrous teeth gnashing and grinding, smiling wide.

Bone. This thing can chew through bone.

Hunnnngreeeee...Rammmmmsssseeeee.

Ramsey wasn't sure if it spoke the words at all or if he heard them in his head. He didn't know if it was offering to share its meal or if Ramsey was the main course.

One of the barbed cords coiled around his ankle. Its prong quivered like the backend of a rattlesnake.

"What the fuck!" Ramsey screamed. He tried to back away, tried to escape, but the cord twisted around his legs and he fell. He smashed his chin against the floor, immediately tasting blood. The wiry tentacle squeezed like a tourniquet around his shin. His bones cracked, and a sharp, violent pain shot up his leg. His vision blurred.

The thing tugged at him, the tentacle cutting like piano wire into his calf. Ramsey clawed his fingers at the carpet. The nail on his index finger caught in the rug and ripped clean off as he slid into the attic.

He reached for the wall and managed to brace himself for a moment. His fingers latched on each side of the doorframe. But the thing pulled harder, raising his body off the floor. The thin wooden wall splintered beneath his grasp. His fingers slipped and then let go.

"No!" he yelled. "Help!" He wriggled like a fish on the end of a line.

The creature reeled him deeper into the attic.

Ramsey came to a stop and rested his cheek against the dusty floor. A silverfish scurried away from him. The creature still gripped his leg, but the coils had loosened. Ramsey felt its presence above him, still heard it gnashing bone. The attic smelled of decay, of death.

Ramsey propped himself up on his forearms. He imagined the thing's mouth opening wide, his foot disappearing behind those rows of teeth. The gnawing would follow, the unimaginable pain of being eaten alive. Feet, then ankles, then shins, and so on until his body went into shock or he bled out. He closed his eyes and prayed.

Please just make it quick.

But nothing happened.

What is it waiting for?

Ramsey rolled onto his back, ready to meet his tormentor face to face. The creature stared down at him. Blood dripped from its teeth into Ramsey's mouth and onto his cheeks. Its appendages shot forward, pinning Ramsey to the floor. Then, it lifted him as though he were weightless and drew him within inches of its gaping maw.

Head first?

Sweat beaded on his forehead. Liquid warmth spread across his groin.

Something writhed like a worm along his stomach, passing over his navel and up his chest. A barbed prong appeared before his eyes and rattled. The tentacle and its arrowhead-like point thrashed lightning-quick, slapping Ramsey's neck, the prong delving into his jugular.

The walls and ceiling faded into darkness. Only the creature's face remained, surrounded by swirling black pools of that dreamlike substance that seemed to be more than a liquid but less than a solid.

Plasma?

His terror became a fleeting memory. That vile weaponry the thing called teeth came close enough to kiss, and Ramsey began to feel the euphoric high. The creature had once again elevated him to Heaven.

He smiled, staring dead into the creature's mouth. "Are you going to eat me?"

Noooo…Rammmmssssseeee.

Ramsey struggled for a clear thought. It took some time, but his next question slowly spawned from the muck. "What are you going to do to me?"

Moooorrrre.

The creature released Ramsey but he remained suspended in the air, the plasma substance billowing around him. It picked up the remainder of the arm and dropped it against Ramsey's chest. *Goooodieeeeessss… forrrr…goooodieeeessss.*

Ramsey scrunched his forehead. His mind fell into a haze, but he thought he understood.

"If I bring you more goodies, you'll give me this feeling in exchange?"

Yesssss…Rammmmssssseeee.

Ramsey felt superhuman, omnipotent, as he experienced euphoria greater than mortal comprehension. Human life seemed so infinitesimal, valueless.

How could I ever go back to my insignificant existence?

As the blissful tingling surged through his body, raising his senses to a higher plane, invigorating his very soul, Ramsey justified what was asked of him.

But what will I think when the drug stops working?

Nevvvverrrr…hassss…toooo.

Never?

The creature nodded, and Ramsey smiled.

Ramsey knew what that meant but didn't care. He would exchange as many lives as it would take for continuous access to the creature's utopia.

Guess I'll be going out tonight.

Another prong shot from the creature and burrowed into Ramsey's chest. His eyes fluttered, then came to a close, shutting out what remained of his humanity. ◆

Jason's fiction is born from darkness, finding its home everywhere from the supernatural and surreal, to the all-too-real iniquity of the human condition. His debut novel, What Hides Within, *a mystery/horror/dark humor blend, was published by Double Dragon Publishing in July 2012. It was an* EPIC *finalist in "horror," was named runner-up in the "Best Horror" category in eFestival's Independent eBook competition and has been named to several "Best of" lists for horror. Jason has published several short stories and has several more due for release in the near future. He is also finalizing four unrelated novels and hopes to have them completed soon.*

Artwork: Carrie Will

SKEIN

RHOADS BRAZOS

It was Rollo's idea to go to the abandoned house, wander around a bit, and shoot out some windows with their pellet guns. Rollo held a good one that looked like a .44 Magnum.

"It'll blow your head clean off," he bragged. *Ping!*

Most of the glass had already been shattered by other enterprising youths. Windows lined all three floors, yawning and toothy, as if the whole house grinned. Though only paltry targets remained, the two boys took careful aim and sent more than a little debris shimmering to the weed-strewn lot.

"Love the sound of plate glass in the morning," Rollo said.

Eddie took a bead on a shard no bigger than a postage stamp. It popped into a rhinestone spray.

"Nice!" Rollo drew the word out with a hiss.

"Like a sniper," Eddie said. "Might join the Marines after high school." He'd never considered it until that moment.

"Badass. I'm joinin' Blackwater."

"How you get in there?"

"Dunno." Rollo reloaded and aimed at his foot. "Hey, I'm a conscientious objector." A sharp snap. The shot went through the toe of his sneaker.

"Charlie wins again," Eddie said sadly.

Rollo's mother always bought him oversized shoes. By the time they fit properly, they were held together only by a sense of thrift. Eddie was certain that Rollo's mother intended this pair to see the next election.

"Hey, inside," Rollo said.

The door had been kicked in years ago. The doorknob had even been torn loose.

The boys milled about aimlessly, firing shots into the walls. Bottles littered the second floor–boozing sophomores, no doubt. Those oafs had given the two of them a bad time, reciprocating the grief they must have endured the year before. Thus, the cycle never ended.

"Coexist," Eddie said.

"What?" Rollo fired another round. The top of a bottle snapped into the air. Its body skittered and spun.

Eddie reloaded while Rollo set the target again.

"Nothin'," Eddie said. "Just thinking 'bout those hippie wannabes."

Rollo scratched his head. "Beatniks. Just copying commercials. Not like us."

True. Eddie and Rollo had an inarguably unique panache: Dixie with a dash of Motorhead. Eddie hadn't brought it up yet. Had to let enough time pass. "They mess you up Monday?"

Rollo shrugged.

"Man, I woulda helped," Eddie said. "You know that."

"Yeah. I got your back, too."

"Right."

"Always." Rollo gritted his teeth and emptied his gun at the remaining portion of the bottle. A few shots connected. "Hey, know what we should do?"

Eddie frowned. This felt sordid. Two freshmen rejects doing target practice and plotting violent revenge.

"You fucking idiot. Not like that." Rollo shook his head. "I mean... we should let the air outta their tires or something."

"Never work."

Rollo shrugged. "Just the back two. Leave them stranded."

"Someone'll see us, then—"

"Yeah, maybe so." Rollo let his gun dangle to the floor and scratched at his head. "Wish *I* had wheels."

"Hav'ta pay for gas," Eddie said.

Rollo grunted.

"And insurance," Eddie added.

"Whatever. Hey, upstairs."

They creaked out of the master bedroom and stalked to the center of the house. A chain hung from the ceiling, the remains of a chandelier probably scavenged by some shabby chic decorator. Regrettable. It would have been the mother of all targets.

Eddie's feet crunched over the floor. The surface of the ceiling had loosened, denuding a wooden lattice and powdering the floor below with a slick talcum. Heaped upon the mess stretched the rotted remains of an old staircase, the only route to the third story.

Rollo kicked at the boards. "Bet there's stuff up there." He sniffed and looked up toward the landing.

"What do you call that junk they insulate with?" Eddie asked.

"Fiberglass."

Eddie shook his head. "Naw, the old stuff. Gets you sick."

"Uh, asbestos?"

"Yeah."

"My uncle got it real bad from that," Roland kicked at a piece of debris.

"Well, should we—"

"Pff. I feel fine, don't you?" Rollo hunkered down and rummaged through the collapsed pile. "Look," he said, pulling a long pipe loose and propping it alongside the landing so that its top rested between the banister railings. "Keep it steady." He tapped the bottom on the floor.

Eddie held the pipe firm while Rollo hoisted himself up, like a fireman who'd forgotten his boots.

As he struggled upward, Rollo called down, "Quit checkin' me out!"

"Shut up." Eddie stared at the ceiling, attempting to avoid any follow-up witticisms. A piece of plaster fell, tumbling end over end and smashing into crumbs. Eddie squinted. There was something up there, caged behind the lattice—a shape, a shadow.

"Okay," Rollo said. "Got it from here. C'mon."

Eddie clambered up, giving only cursory thoughts to rust stains on his jeans.

"Hey, look." Rollo pointed to a painting in the upper hallway. Someone had created a landscape of the house. The place used to be white with red shutters. It had beds of flowers, shrubs, climbing vines with inky-purple flowers, and a grove of trees sentineling the lawn. There weren't even stumps out there now. Eddie traced a finger along the gilded frame, furrowing through dust.

"Think that's worth something?" Rollo asked, rubbing his nose mightily.

"Maybe. It's got a tear, though." Eddie pointed. A scratch cut through one of the top windows.

"Lessee what else there is," Rollo said.

As they poked about the upper rooms, they found a dresser and rifled through it—empty, naturally. Next, they rooted through closets.

"No–wire–hangers!" Rollo whipped a fistful at Eddie. Eddie yelled as they hit across his arms. He hurled them back and Rollo jumped aside, laughing.

They found a couple of old books on dusty shelves, the kind you got for a quarter at yard sales.

"Aw." Rollo's eyes grew wide. He rattled on the doorknob to the last room. "Not locked, but–"

"Push it open."

"Tryin'."

Eddie rolled his eyes. "Quit menstruating and kick it in."

Rollo chuckled, as if pleased by the insult. "Vice squad!" His over-sized shoe pounded into the door with a booming thud. The door pushed open an inch but slammed back shut.

"Something's behind it," Eddie said.

"Yeah." Rollo's eyes shone. "Bet nobody's been in there."

"Let me try," Eddie said.

He took his turn, kicking the door several times. After his feet numbed, he let Rollo try again. When it still didn't open, Rollo opened fire on the lock until splinters coated the floor.

"Not gonna do any good anyhow," Eddie said. "Handle turns easy."

Rollo ruminated. His beady eyes roamed up and down the door-frame. "Okay. Got an idea."

They set their guns aside and returned with a heavy dresser. Hoping to break it down, they lunged the dresser at the door, leaning into the momentum. A terrific collision thundered through the house. The door flew open with such force that its handle punctured the wall.

Rollo grabbed his gun.

"Don't shoot it up," Eddie said.

"Naw."

Eddie picked his up, and they stormed in.

A single bed sat in the corner next to a toy box. Picture books scat-tered the windowsill, and the room stank–musty, like Eddie's grand-mother's attic.

"Why was the door so hard to open?" Eddie asked.

Rollo sniffed and shrugged.

Eddie pulled the door free from the wall. "Nothing was behind it."

"Wood's swollen, twisted hinges." Rollo pushed a book cover closed with his toe. "Dick the Detective." He snickered. "This one's for you."

"Shut up. Think those are worth anything, like collectibles?"

"Maybe some."

"We should box 'em up."

"Yeah." Rollo's eyes roamed the room. "Hey, you see a bank?"

"Just pocket change."

"Naw. You're not thinkin'. Silver dimes, quarters."

"Hey, that's right!"

They thoroughly searched: marbles, a fork, more books, string, and a busted pocket watch.

"Not very old, was he?" Eddie asked, holding up a pair of thin, little pants.

Rollo scratched at his ear.

Drawings stuck against the walls, not taped or tacked, but slipped over splinters in the woodwork. The kid appeared to like drawing. No friends or family, like most kids...just himself. Kid on the lawn. Kid in the room. Kid on the porch. Kid on the roof. Eddie found a picture of a mouse, and in the next drawing, the mouse lay on its side, an X in place of each eye, and its pink tongue nipped between two long teeth.

"Loner," Rollo said. "Like something you'd come up with."

Eddie turned away.

Rollo cleared his throat. "Sorry."

"Yeah, this kid never drew his parents."

"Must not have gotten along."

Eddie looked over the pictures. He stared at the kid's rendition of the house–grey with jagged windows. "I guess."

"Huh." Rollo grabbed the end of the bedspread and yanked it aside. "What the hell's that?"

A soiled outline of a very small person smeared up the center of the bed.

"I donno," Eddie said, leaning closer.

"Sick. Looks like chow mein with beef. Kid was gross."

Eddie chewed at his lip.

The shape covered from toes to fingertips and up to the hairline, like one of those silhouettes they used to do in school.

Rollo coughed. "Don't even want to check under the mattress now." He pointed his gun at the blotch's head.

"Rollo." Eddie put his hand on Rollo's shoulder. Knowing that a young child had slept there, that he'd been there so long the bed sagged around his outline. "Don't."

One pop, then another. Rollo drilled two eyes through the stain's head. One high, one low. "Ho! Look at that. Like a chameleon or somethin'. Ever seen how they look around?" Rollo brought the gun back, muzzle pointing to the ceiling, trigger at his ear.

"You shouldn't ha–"

"Shh." Rollo sneered and turned his head.

"What?"

"Did you hear that?"

Eddie took in slow breaths, straining to hear something other than Rollo's breathing. "Someone downstairs?"

"No. I thought I heard–"

The sheets blasted up in a flapping blur. A dark, wet-looking mass smacked into Rollo and wrapped around his head and torso. Rollo screamed. It flowed up his chin and reached for his mouth. He spit and sputtered and tumbled to the floor, thrashing.

"N–No! G-G-get–"

Eddie fell back against the wall. A picture of a little boy crying slipped to the floor, big blue tears slinging off his face.

Rollo shouted and raked at the monster as it tried to enter his mouth. It oozed up his cheeks, curled through his hair, wrapped around his throat, and tore at his clothes.

Tufts of hair and scalp spackled outward. They stuck to the walls, some spattering Eddie. Eddie gagged. The monster gripped Rollo's lips and tongue between its tiny mottled teeth. For the first time, Eddie realized that the creature attacking Rollo resembled a kid. Tendrils reached up to Rollo's eyes, each strand tipped with yellowed barbs.

Eddie ran.

"N–No! Ed. He-hel–" Rollo's pleas melted into a gargle.

They had been through a lot together. Just two weeks ago, the sophomores had jumped Rollo. Three on one. When Eddie arrived, he didn't hesitate; he charged right in. The two of them had focused a full assault on the flimsiest of the thugs, mercilessly incapacitating him before driving the next sophomore to the pavement. The third fled.

Eddie ran for the door, his own screams drowning out Rollo's.

The monster released Rollo and slung itself behind the door, pushing it closed. The dresser sat jammed in the doorway, the only thing saving Eddie. Knowing what it had taken to get in, he somehow knew he would never open it again if it slammed shut.

He clawed his way over the dresser and tumbled out into the hallway. The door repeatedly slammed into the dresser, splintering.

A pounding struck at the floorboards behind him. Eddie turned to find Rollo crawling toward him, his face a mess of shredded skin. His lower lip flapped below his chin like a meaty apron.

"No!" Rollo screamed as the creature spindled itself back around him, twining up his body. "Ed. 'lease!" The monster wound around Rollo's torso, his body jerking forward. It twisted around Rollo's neck and arms before shrinking into a thick, soupy gruel. "Eddie! Help me!" Rollo said, still trying to reach for Eddie.

Eddie's eyes flickered from Rollo to that soupy mass. He grabbed Rollo's hand and yanked hard. The monster slipped toward Eddie's white knuckles. He tried to let go, ready to run, to give up, but Rollo held his hand in a viselike grip.

"'uck!" Rollo cried. "Ed! You–"

"Roland, I can't!"

Eddie pulled as hard has he could, and with another sudden jerk, he broke free and Rollo lurched backward. Eddie bolted. The cries began again in earnest. Eddie hurdled over the banister and came down hard ten feet below. His shoe pinched tight. Two steps across the floor and anguish screamed up his leg. He tripped and fell, then noticed the rotted board nailed through his foot.

Rollo's cries reached a rabid delirium. Eddie rose to a knee and, gritting his teeth, stepped on the board and yanked his foot free. He sprang up and limp-sprinted from the house.

He tried to ignore Rollo's shrill screams and cries of pain as he struggled down the front steps to the gate where the fence's bleached bones skewed from the ground. He turned and glared at the house and that upper room, its window shattered and its frame missing. In its outline, a lone figure slowly waved its arms.

Eddie sobbed. *I left him.*

He whispered, "Rollo." Then shouted, "Over here!"

He knew Rollo as well as Rollo knew himself. There was only one thing the guy would do.

Rollo turned, seemed to be staring directly at Eddie. Eddie waved his arms frantically and screamed, "Here!"

Rollo stood still.

"Here!" Eddie shouted again. "To me!"

Rollo charged the third-story window and threw himself into empty space.

❖

The next morning Eddie lay in his bed, weeping.

Gone. Just like that. Just like Dad. One morning you wake up and everyone's gone. Well, Mom remained, in her own way. Eddie listened to her bumping about the kitchen. He waited until she left for the motel, the screen door slamming like a shot.

Rollo lay out there, baking in the sun. Eddie's gun had been left on the premises, his footprints in the dust, blood too, from that nail. Even yesterday's clothes were damning, spattered with grisly evidence. An open-and-shut case. Another delinquent off the streets.

Eddie stumbled to his feet and grasped through the hazy murk. He fumbled through the kitchen, catching the faint scent of coffee and bacon. He reached the second bedroom and went inside.

The worst part was the blame. He wasn't a bad person, not really. But the papers would say otherwise. The kids at school. Rollo's parents. The whole world would hate him. He shouldn't have cowered. He should have told someone right away. They might have listened, but now it was too late.

Eddie cried. Tears pooled in his eyes but went no farther. He sat at the desk and scribbled a note as best he could. The letters he wrote blurred as if he were looking through a film of gravy. *We didn't mean to. I love-* And he was off the paper. He dropped the pen, too dejected to care.

How had it found him? It had sliced him pretty good, perhaps it followed that tag like a scent. His throbbing foot could have left a trail. Or maybe it just peeked through windows until it found where Eddie slept.

Eddie reached to his face and the monster snapped and hissed. Right.

His mother's gun felt heavier than his, more gravity of purpose. The safety sat in the same place. He could do it blindfolded.

Eddie wedged the muzzle under his chin and.... ◆

Rhoads lacks his wife's classiness, his son's genius, and his house cat's fearsome nature. His life is a simple one, Rockwellian with a touch of morbid fancy. Rhoads transcribes his dreams into prose and shares them with the unsuspecting. Somehow, his work has seeped into this anthology and other unknowing venues, including: Apex Magazine, Stupefying Stories, Gaia: Shadow & Breath Anthology, *and* Death's Realm Anthology.

Artwork: Carrie Will

ENVOY

HUNTER LOWE

Joseph Murich rocked back on his heels, pushing a thick cotton sleeve over his nose. Dead birds littered the ground around his muddy boots.

Hera, Joseph's dog, whined restlessly behind him, keeping her distance from the bird carcasses. That alarmed Joseph more than the event; normally, a field full of easily accessible birds would have looked much akin to a free buffet to the German Shepherd. Joseph sank to a knee, casting his eyes across the fallen animals.

❖

Four days ago, Beth had sprinted toward the house at full speed. Her blue sundress billowed behind her. Long, curly strands of grey hair bounced as she kicked off her sandals mid-sprint. She shrieked Joseph's name the whole way, jumping over twigs and tree roots. As she neared the screen door, she almost knocked Joseph down.

"The docks," she managed to say between wheezes.

Joseph put his hand on Beth's back, trying to calm her, but her chest heaved and the hair framing her pale face sat matted with sweat. Joseph knitted his brow and stepped outside to look at their small boathouse.

"What the hell is going on?" Joseph asked, not seeing anything from the doorway.

Beth faced him. "They're everywhere, filthy damn things!"

Joseph laughed. "Is it beetles or mosquitos this time?"

Placing a hand on her chest, she said, "You need to go look for yourself."

"Alright. Just get some water and calm down, okay?"

Beth nodded and went inside.

Joseph stepped off the porch and walked toward the water. The path that he had dug out in his younger years showed signs of disrepair. He walked down the bumpy, root-snarled road, taking in a deep breath of moist air. *Rain tonight probably.* He kept his pace slow and steady. At his doctor's behest, he was to take it easy, very easy–after his second heart attack, his chest held a ticking time bomb. As he approached, he noticed the quiet. No more than ten steps ago, the low thrum of crickets and cicadas had been chattering.

The lumpy silhouette of the partially-repaired boathouse had stood on the wrong side of a rotten tree last fall, and the insurance company was taking their sweet time to correct the situation. Besides the eerie quiet, everything seemed normal.

As he took a step forward, a crunch issued from underneath his boot and traveled up his body. He yanked his foot back, staggering.

"Oh, Christ."

Insects covered the ground, almost to the point of choking the path—thousands of them, all dead. At the sight of the insect holocaust, Joseph walked back to the house, his pulse rising to alarming levels.

He opened the screen door and pushed past Hera. Beth sat at the kitchen table, sipping from a glass. She looked up as he entered. Lines covered her pale face, resembling a page from a coloring book, begging for someone to color in what fear had stolen. Joseph thought she'd aged ten years in the short time he was gone. Her hands shook and her eyes seemed puffy. Her hair appeared glued to her loose skin, but her brown eyes looked very much alive.

Her left leg twitched up and down nervously. "Did you see them?"

"I saw 'em." Joseph crossed the yellowed linoleum kitchen floor, tugging off his cap. Most of his hair had abandoned ship before the remaining turned grey. "Maybe some kind of chemical got loose from a farm. I'm not positive. The sheer number of them was…." He stuffed the cap into the pocket of a coat hanging near the door.

"Fucked up?"

Joseph nodded. "That sounds about right. I'm going to give animal control a call in the morning. Let's keep Hera in for the night."

Joseph locked the front door for the first time in years.

❖

Shaken from his daydream by the pungent aroma of dead birds, Joseph marveled once more at the sheer amount of death, ranging widely in size and species. Joseph was no ornithologist, or even a birdwatcher for that matter, but he knew that entire clouds of birds didn't just drop from the sky.

Hera whined at him again. He reached down and stroked the big dog behind her ears.

"You're telling me." Joseph felt the hairs on his neck stand up. "Let's get out of here, girl."

Joseph retreated from what felt like a crime scene, his heart racing uncomfortably in his chest. Hera nosed her way in front of him.

Beth called from the living room window. "What is it now?"

Joseph sighed. "Honestly?"

"Honestly."

"Birds." Joseph entered the house and made his way through the small kitchen, into the living room, and approached the phone. "Whole hel-luva lot of dead birds." He picked up the receiver and dug a scrap of paper from his pocket. Sheriff Coughlin had offered his personal contact information during their last meeting, just in case anything else strange happened.

Beth turned back to the television and clicked rhythmically with her knitting needles.

Joseph punched the number into the phone, and after two beats, a voice answered. "Sheriff Coughlin."

"It's Joseph." No response. "Murich. Joseph Murich. The guy with all the dead bugs?" Joseph closed his eyes and massaged his forehead.

"Mr. Murich! I'm sorry, always been bad with names. Won't forget tramping around ankle-deep in bugs any time soon, though. Is every-thing alright?"

"It's worse," Joseph said. "Went for a look today, and the entire area has a fresh layer of dead birds."

"Birds?" Coughlin's voice took on a tinge of worry. "How many are we talking?"

"I don't know." Joseph lowered his voice, glancing at Beth, "Hundreds?"

"Oh," Coughlin said. "I'm on my way. I'll bring some of the animal boys to help clean up."

"Thanks."

Joseph hung up the receiver. He needed a drink.

❖

A couple hours later, Joseph stood next to three other men. Sheriff Coughlin wore his standard uniform and stood a head shorter than Joseph. Dark sunglasses covered his eyes and sweat ran down his face from the hairline of his black buzz cut.

The other two men looked like a series of mug shots come to life: big, tough, and ugly. They wore grungy jeans, and the larger of the two sported a black, sleeveless shirt picturing a grinning skull.

The three men carried shovels and several strange, elongated pieces of aluminum, each one topped with a metal hook. Joseph was less than keen to discover how they would be using the long, silver rods.

"You weren't kidding." Coughlin pinched his nose. "Jeeeesus, the smell." The two larger fellows didn't seem to mind the stench. "Get to work, boys; Joseph and I need to talk." He motioned for Joseph to step away.

"Anything this time?" Coughlin said.

Joseph scrunched his nose, his eyes watered. "No, nothing that either of us noticed. It was the same way with the bugs and the—"

"Fish." Coughlin finished for him. "That was something special, too. I'm sorry, I don't know what else we can do other than keep updating the report I sent to the state health department." He moved around Joseph, removing a camera from a pocket. "I'm gonna take some photos again, then I guess we'll get to work de-birding your property."

The small camera beeped, before extending its lens. Coughlin moved around the scene while snapping a few photographs.

Joseph removed his hat and rubbed a rough hand over his scalp. "It's moving up, isn't it?" He felt a chill.

Coughlin stopped and lowered the camera. "Moving up what?"

"The food chain." Joseph's heart jumped. "First bugs, then fish, and now birds? All of them around my boathouse? What the hell is going on here, Sheriff?"

"For now, let's just get this cleaned up. The faster we get that done, the easier you'll sleep tonight." Coughlin walked to his truck. "It's strange, that's for sure. Someone did take an interest after I reported in today." He reached into the truck's bed, retrieved a long pole, and handed it to Joseph. "A crew from the city is coming to have a look at the surrounding area tomorrow afternoon 'round one. They aren't the state boys, but maybe their findings will help convince someone at the higher levels to deal with whatever this is."

Joseph breathed a sigh of relief. *Finally*. He squeezed the metal rod and grimaced. "Let's go bag some birds."

Tools in hand, Joseph and Coughlin walked slowly across the yard, spearing bird after bird. In no time at all, gore covered the tip of Joseph's aluminum pole. "I knew I wasn't going to like what these did." He hefted another dead bird over to a growing pile near Coughlin's truck and shook it loose. It landed with a damp smack and tumbled down the mound of carcasses.

"Gonna take you all day if ya keep bringin' one at a time," the larger of the animal control boys muttered. He rested the tip of his pole on the top of the mound and slid six dead birds off with a bloody work boot.

Joseph shook his head. "I don't think I caught your name."

"It's Graham. Why?"

Joseph smiled. "I just can't get enough of that winning personality."

Graham spat on the ground, and walked back through a path cut through the dead birds. As he went, Graham wagged a middle finger through the air.

Coughlin passed the goon. "Hey Graham! How about a little respect for a taxpayer that makes sure you see a paycheck?"

Graham spat again, dropped his middle finger, and stomped deeper into the woods.

Coughlin shrugged and turned toward Joseph. "He's not a bad kid. Little bit of a temper and complains more than my grandmother, but not a bad kid. Now the other one, his brother Dwayne, he's a piece of work."

"I'm sure," Joseph said. He'd already dismissed the exchange, his mind mulling over the situation at hand.

❖

Graham had forgotten to put sunscreen on his head. He poked the top of his sweat-slicked scalp and cringed. "Hotter than shit," Graham said. "Damn dead birds everywhere."

He grimaced at a parade of ants crawling out of a crow's eye socket. Taking a step back, he hefted his aluminum pole and jabbed the sharpened point into the bird. Ants rained down as he swung the crow away from him, then a flash of movement in the trees caught his eye. An owl.

It occurred to Graham that he had never seen an owl before. The bird perched on a branch, its pale face turned toward him with large, yellow, unblinking eyes. The owl ruffled its wings and tilted its head. The bird moved down the branch, almost like it was trying to see around Graham.

"Can I *help* you, man?" he asked the bird. Its lidless eyes seemed to consider him once more. The white and brown plumage covering its body became still. "Hey!" He waved his hands, but the owl did not flinch.

Graham dropped the aluminum pole and scanned the ground. A large pinecone lay nearby, one side coated in dried mud. He hefted it in his right hand and looked around for the old man and that damned Sheriff.

The owl continued to stare. "Cut it out, man!" Graham aimed at the bird. He cocked his arm back, then sent the pinecone through the air. It hit the owl, tearing a chunk of feathers from its chest. Small dots of blood peeked through the skin. And it continued to stare.

Graham stepped back. "What the…."

The owl wobbled on the branch.

"The hell are you staring a–" The owl fell to the ground. Graham froze. The way the owl had fallen dead seemed…wrong. A chill climbed up his body. He felt as if something watched him, and he shivered.

The strange sensation turned to a sharp pain as if burning hooks dug into his mind. When Graham screamed, the pain increased in his head, embers smoldering behind his eyes. When he stopped, the agony faded to a dull thrum. The old man's dog barked in the distance and the pain increased once more. Images of dead birds and then the dog flashed through his mind. Paired with the barking, he couldn't help but think of Lassie.

"Dog. It's a dog. Let me go please, God, please don't kill me." Graham shrieked until the pain receded once more. Graham's mouth flopped open, and he managed to yell, "Dog!"

❖

Sheriff Coughlin crunched through the foliage. Light ran low as the sun descended. Dwayne had already stowed the gear and claimed "shotgun" for the ride back. They decided to call it quits for the day, but no one had seen Graham for half an hour or so.

Hera barked, followed by Graham's loud yell repeating "Dog, dog, dog!" Sheriff Coughlin sprinted in the direction of Graham's voice. He crashed through the undergrowth and came to a skidding stop before Graham. The boy twitched madly on the ground. White foam frothed between his clenched teeth. His eyes rolled around their sockets like marbles.

Coughlin unfastened his belt, pulling it from around his waist with a snap. He pried open Graham's mouth and forced the belt in between Graham's teeth. After the seizing stopped, Graham's skin became clammy and sheet-white.

"What happened?" Coughlin pulled the belt away slowly, letting it drop to the ground.

Graham opened his mouth. At first, only a wet choking sound came out. "The dog. It…." Graham took a deep breath. "It wants the dog." Graham trembled violently in Coughlin's arms then became still, blood running freely from his nostrils and down his cheeks.

Coughlin shook the boy. "Graham? Jesus, wake up!"

In front of Coughlin, something shifted, sending his heart into his throat. "Who's there?" Leaves drifted to the ground where the disturbance had occurred. Coughlin searched for any movement. *The dog.* "Oh no." He bolted to his feet. "Joseph, get away from the dog!"

❖

Joseph massaged his left shoulder; it always ached in the evening. The area looked considerably better. The small crew had cleared away most of the birds. He did not envy whoever had to tie up the giant plastic sacks of dead animals, especially not that boy, Graham.

Hera began barking from the side of the truck.

"Mind keeping a lid on the mutt?" Dwayne growled from inside the truck, sitting with his dirty boots on the dash. Joseph decided against responding; his recent chats with Dwayne had been unpleasant at best.

A sudden growl ripped through the air, then Hera whined and backed away from the truck, tail tucked between her legs. Her tongue flapped loosely out the side of her mouth; her breath came in loud, jagged gasps.

"Hera?" Joseph stepped toward his snarling dog. He heard a yell and glanced toward the woods. Hera growled low in her throat, strings of saliva dripping from her jaws. She moved closer to Joseph. Joseph stepped back. Her face tightened up into a snarl, and her eyes turned glassy.

Dwayne opened the truck door a crack. "The hell is up with your dog, man?"

A wheezing Coughlin crashed out of the woods. "Joseph." Coughlin inched his right hand toward the small leather strap holding his service pistol. "Get back to the house. Now."

Joseph lifted his hands. "What are you aiming to do, Coughlin?"

Dwayne pulled the door of the truck closed again. The locks clicked from within. "Shoot the fuckin' thing, Sheriff. It's rabid!"

"Graham is dead," Coughlin said. The leather strap snapped loose. "Last thing he said was, 'It wants the dog.'" He removed the pistol, leveling it at Hera.

Joseph waved his arms and stepped toward Hera. "Whoa, whoa, whoa! You can't shoot her!"

"I don't know what's going on here." Coughlin's voice broke when he spoke. "All I know is that a dying boy very clearly told me something wanted your dog, so yes, I'm sure as shit about to shoot her."

A shot rang out; Hera collapsed to the ground.

"Hera!" Joseph ran to his dog, dropping to his knees. He examined his dog. Aside from a small amount of blood seeping from her nose and ears, she appeared unharmed. The sound of truck doors unlocking caused him to jerk his head up at Dwayne.

The truck door creaked open. "Dead?" Dwayne unwound his six-foot frame as he stepped from the vehicle. "Did you say that my brother is *dead?*" His brown eyes bulged. "No way am I dying here, too!" Dwayne sprinted up the road.

Hera grunted, then something that sounded like, "*Stooooop!*" came from the dog's throat. The voice belonged to Graham.

"Holy shit." Coughlin raised his pistol again. Joseph kicked his feet, scooting away from Hera's talking corpse.

Graham's voice shouted through Hera's mouth: "Dwayne! Stop!"

Dwayne skidded to a halt and turned around. "Graham?" he said and took a few uneasy steps toward the truck.

Coughlin shouted, "Don't listen, Dwayne!"

Hera's jaws stretched into a wide grin.

"Dwayne, get back!" Coughlin fired three rounds into the dog. Blood and fur arched through the air.

Dwayne's jaw sagged open.

"Get back to your house, Joseph." Coughlin walked toward the driver's seat of the truck. "Go inside. I'm calling in help."

Joseph scrambled to his feet, carefully breathing in three-second intervals.

One…two…three.

He let his breath escape.

One…two…three.

He wheezed up the small incline to the house, pausing to take a few more breaths.

He turned back to find that Coughlin and Dwayne had vanished. The police truck remained unperturbed: the driver's side door had never opened, backup never called for.

The rhythm of Joseph's breathing fell to pieces. He sucked in air with sharp, jagged hitches, feeling a cold tingle spread from the center of his chest and radiating outward. He ran for the screen door and scrambled into the house. Joseph locked the door and flipped the porch lights on.

Joseph turned to see his wife snoring in the chair, the television blaring. "Beth!" he yelled. She didn't move. "Beth, wake up!"

Beth whipped her head around and rubbed at her eyes.

"Beth," Joseph said. *One…two…three.* "Lock all the windows."

She stood from the chair, yawning. "What's going on?"

"Just go lock up." He approached her and squeezed her shoulders gently. "I'll tell you after I call the station."

"Wait, we need to let Hera in."

"Elizabeth, don't."

Beth half smiled and shook her head. She pushed past him. "What are you going on about?"

"Hera's dead," Joseph said.

Beth stopped and turn back to him. "That isn't funny." She turned back to the door, but Joseph grabbed her shoulder and forced her to face him once more.

"It isn't a joke. Now go lock up. I'll explain after I call the station."

Beth nodded. She blinked rapidly as tears brimmed her eyes, and began locking all the windows.

Joseph approached the phone, willing himself to calm down. He snatched the receiver and punched in 911. Nothing. He hung up the phone, then lifted it to his ear again. Nothing. He slammed it into its cradle, then pressed the heels of his palms into his eyes. Brilliant colors ran across his vision.

Beth entered the living room at a rapid pace.

"Joseph?" Beth whispered. She walked slowly, sticking to the most interior wall of the house as if expecting monstrous hands to burst through the windows or doors and yank her through. "What's happening?"

Joseph approached the back door and slid the curtain open to find the police truck missing. He closed his eyes. *Dammit.* No truck. Not so much as tire depressions in the long grass of his back yard. Nothing at all. *Impossible.* "Remember the argument we got into about whether or not we should own a gun?"

"Joseph?" Beth squeaked.

"Go get the gun. You're about to be glad I bought it."

❖

Beth huffed up to the second story. The shadowy hallway filled her with a nameless sense of dread. She flicked on the lights and proceeded toward the master bedroom.

After noticing an open window in Joseph's office, she darted in and slammed it shut. The lock had a layer of paint over it, so she used the paperweight to pound it into position. Once done, she moved down the hall toward her bedroom, pushed open the door, and groped for the light switches. She flipped them all on, but the room remained shrouded in gloomy darkness.

She saw far enough to locate the closet.

She took a cautious step inside the room and made her way around their king-sized bed, careful not to crash into a bedpost.

Once at the far wall, she reached for the closet door. Cold metal brushed against her hand. She seized the knob, and paused. She didn't want to open it. In fact, she had never wanted to avoid something so badly.

Beth bit the inside of her cheek and turned the knob. Her heart raced. With a rush of confidence, she ripped the door open, ready for what hid inside, but nothing bounded out of the darkness to rip her limb from limb. She flipped the light switch. The bulb bloomed to life and shattered, sending a rain of glass and filament down onto the closet floor.

"Oh, Jesus!"

She blindly groped for the shotgun, finding it propped against the back right corner.

Beth seized the weapon and sprinted out of the dark bedroom.

❖

Joseph heard his wife scurrying back toward the stairs. He left his post by the back door and moved toward her. Eventually, she arrived at the top of the stairwell, clutching the dusty old shotgun. Joseph took two long strides and extended a hand.

Beth tossed him the gun.

"Thanks," Joseph said.

"What's happening?"

Joseph moved toward the kitchen. Crossing to the pantry, he checked to see if the gun was empty, then rummaged for the unopened box of shotgun shells. He pushed aside a few boxes of oatmeal.

"Something is out there," he said while snatching the heavy box out of one of the darker corners of the pantry. He plopped the box on the table, and set about clumsily loading the firearm.

Beth's eyes widened. "Something? Like an animal?"

"No, not an animal," he said. A shell slipped out of his grip and skittered across the floor. He paid it no mind. "Well, it could be I suppose. I haven't seen it, so I don't really know what to tell you." As the final shell clicked into place, he felt a surge of courage. "All I know is that we are staying inside until it's light. Nothing gets opened until morning."

"Why don't we just call someone?" Beth made for the phone.

Joseph shook his head.

She stopped. "No phone?" Her entire frame trembled ever so slightly.

He leaned the shotgun against a nearby cabinet and massaged the left side of his chest in slow circles. Beth was on the move before he could stop her. She returned with a small, orange plastic bottle containing his medication. Joseph smiled, accepting the small bottle, letting his fingers linger over hers.

He stepped away and went to the refrigerator, pulling it open with a soothing swoosh. The cold air against his face felt nice. He grabbed a bottle of water, snapped it open, and popped a few of the miniscule pills into his mouth. The medicine always helped.

Beth sat down at their kitchen table, the loaded shotgun on display instead of a home-cooked meal. Joseph joined her, and together they waited.

❖

Joseph stared at the oven's display.

Only three in the morning?

Everything remained pitch black and completely silent.

Beth lay sprawled across the table. Her hair covered her face.

Joseph yawned, his eyes felt itchy. He cracked his neck and stretched.

Beth mumbled something but remained asleep.

He stood as quietly as he could and grabbed the shotgun. He crept, footstep by footstep, until he stood inches from the small window in the back door. His hand shook as he began to draw back the blinds. The porch lights bathed the porch in a yellowish glow. Still, no sign of the Sheriff or his crew.

Maybe it's over. Maybe whatever came through has lost interest. Just maybe.

"I'm still here."

Joseph stifled a scream. The voice came from just outside of the back door. It sounded…wrong. He could barely understand the words, as if spoken by someone who had just learned a new language.

"You're not without kindness, Joseph."

Hair stood on the back of Joseph's neck. His hands quaked.

"You will have your night, what is left of it. I am no…murderer."

The strange accent began to fade, the voice becoming clearer, becoming more human.

"Yes, that is the word. Murderer. I have learned, I have deconstructed what your microscopic kind call feelings, emotions. It took time to understand, many suffered as I jumped forms, but now I know."

Coughlin appeared on the other side of the thin wooden door. His eyes rolled back, bloodshot. His lips shifted. *"I have analyzed your needless fear, your struggle."* The voice lowered. *"But do not be afraid."*

Graham stepped onto the porch and cried out, *"Soon you will join us!"*

Joseph staggered back, the shotgun bouncing wildly as he attempted to steady his aim. He heard footsteps retreating, followed by silence.

Beth lifted her head, pushing her hair out of her face. "Joseph...?" She rubbed her eyes, "What time is it?"

"Little after three." He lowered the gun and glanced at the back door. "Still a ways to go." He walked to the kitchen table. "Things have been quiet. Why don't we go get more comfortable?" He smiled, and she smiled back.

"If you really think it's safe." Beth stood up and followed him upstairs. "Oh good, the lights are working now."

"Maybe it was just the old house after all." Joseph shrugged. He crossed to his side of the bed and sat down.

"What about that *thing*?" Beth sat down next to him, resting her head on his shoulder. "That animal or whatever."

"How about we just relax for a while? Relax and talk?" Joseph threw his right arm over Beth's shoulder and pulled her closer.

They talked about their upcoming trip across the country. They talked about their children, long ago grown and moved off to start their own lives–all three of them more than proving their ability to handle the world. Beth kept falling asleep for a few short seconds, before waking back up with a start. Joseph smiled and pulled back the sheets on the bed. Beth quietly slid into them, fluffing her pillows.

He slid next to her, his right hand still entwined with hers, then glanced at the clock: *Five a.m.*

Thirty-five years of marriage had armed him with the ability to disengage from any of Beth's embraces undetected. He slid out of the bed and before leaving, leaned over and planted a kiss on her forehead. She stirred as if unconsciously acknowledging his love. Joseph took one final look at her, then walked across the room to the door.

He took a deep breath and hefted the shotgun onto his shoulder as he walked toward his study.

Nothing will touch her. Not as long as I'm here.

Inside the study, he kicked off his shoes, letting his sore feet enjoy the plush carpet. The air smelled like old cigar smoke. Joseph had taken up the habit a while back, much to Beth's displeasure. He recalled hours of smoky viewings of SportsCenter and drinking with good friends–many of whom had moved far away enough to drift into obscurity.

He avoided his desk and made his way to the leather armchair. After sitting, he flipped open a lacquered brown box, removing a cigar and lighter from within. He bit into the cigar and clicked open the lighter. His thumb flicked the ignition once, but no flame emerged. He huffed and flicked the lighter again. Nothing.

Joseph growled. "Muvrfuckr."

When he flicked the lighter again, the small TV in his office lit up. Static roared through the room, white light blinding him momentarily. The cigar fell from his mouth. He scrambled out of his chair, slapping at the buttons lining the side of the TV. The noise finally ceased, and his ears rang.

"Yeah, tough guy?" Joseph looked around, waiting for his assailant. He returned to his chair, then snatched the cigar and lighter from the floor.

He clicked the lighter open. This time, a bright red flame danced merrily. He moved the flame closer, puffing the cigar to life. Thick, oily fumes filled the room. He closed his eyes and allowed himself a moment of rest.

"Joseph."

Joseph's eyes shot open and he grabbed the shotgun. Nothing in the room moved. Cold fear pressed up his spine. He stood, breathing as calmly as possible, and worked toward the door. He pushed it open with the barrel of his gun and peered down the hall to see the silhouette of Beth still in their bed.

"Joseph!"

The voice seemed to come from behind him. He cried out and jumped, spinning and firing the shotgun. The spray tore through the computer on his desk. The blast shook him from head to toe.

"Son of a bitch."

He clutched his chest, then turned back to the hallway. He could no longer see Beth's sleeping body as their bedroom door was now closed.

"No! No! No!" Joseph ran down the hall and found the knob locked. He pounded his fists, yelling, "Beth, wake up!" When she didn't reply, he spun to face the empty hallway. "Don't you dare touch her!"

Only the faint sound of glass breaking from the kitchen answered. Gooseflesh danced up his arms. He raised the gun, ejecting the spent shell from the chamber. More glass broke from downstairs, followed by a strange grunt.

Joseph made his way slowly down the stairs, keeping his back against the wall. He held the gun at shoulder height.

When he reached the bottom, he looked into the kitchen. The screen door lay on the ground, ripped from its hinges. Blood streaked the white eyelet drapes dangling from the windows. Glass littered the floor.

Joseph screamed as something barreled into him from behind. Before sliding against the refrigerator, he caught a glimpse of his attacker: Coughlin.

The two men fought, and the shotgun came loose from Joseph's grip, clattering across the floor.

Coughlin shoved Joseph off of him and stood. *"Interesting."* The once sheriff's lips moved but the voice echoed inside Joseph's mind. *"Such specimens you are."*

Joseph crawled toward the shotgun, only to feel hands close around his right foot. His fingers squeaked across the floor as Coughlin dragged him into the kitchen, moving like a man who had spent far more time on a boat than dry land.

Joseph kicked out, striking Coughlin in the knee. Coughlin staggered and fell.

"Clumsy, however."

Joseph shrieked and backed toward the door, small fragments of glass shredding his palms, bloody handprints marking his way across the floor.

Coughlin regained his balance and stomped toward Joseph, his eyes rolling into whites. Bulging blood vessels appeared across the milky white surface of the sheriff's eyes while his jaw twisted in a muted scream.

"This one did not like you." Coughlin took a wobbly step. The voice changed into Coughlin's own. The paralyzed mouth said, "Crazy old bastard." Then Coughlin took another step.

Joseph shook himself free from his terror and searched for the shotgun.

Coughlin darted forward and pulled Joseph up by his collar. Joseph cried out and struck Coughlin in the temple.

"So much hate in all of you. This is what you all want, below all of your niceties and manners." Coughlin released his grip and dealt Joseph a thundering blow to the side of his head. Color exploded behind Joseph's eyes and he sagged, unable to re-orient himself.

"I've learned everything about you that I could possibly ever need to make my choice."

Coughlin backhanded Joseph.

Blood seeped from between Joseph's lips, and he rocked his head back and pitched forward, slamming his forehead into Coughlin's terrifying eyes. A satisfying crunch answered each blow. He dropped to the ground and snatched the shotgun. "What the fuck are you?"

Coughlin gargled what may have been a laugh. *"I am the first of many. The envoy."*

"What do you want?"

The cold voice said, *"I'm with your wife now."*

Joseph fired, and Coughlin crumpled backward, his torso shredded by the close proximity of the blast.

Coughlin's mouth still moved. *"All the same. All so violent."*

Joseph paid no heed and stormed up the stairs. His heart spasmed, sending arching pains through his left shoulder and arm.

So be it. If I'm going to die, at least my own body will do the job.

The door to the master bedroom stood wide open. The large window, no longer covered by curtains, revealed the sun peeking over the horizon.

"Beth? Oh God." His hand covered his mouth. Beth sat upright, her eyes staring out the window, tears streaming down her cheeks. The smell of urine permeated the air.

Joseph crawled onto the bed, letting the shotgun drop from his grip. He took her into his arms.

"Beth?"

Her green eyes met with his. "Joseph." Then a horrifyingly wide smile ripped across her face, twisting her features into something like the Cheshire Cat.

Her hands shot up, grabbing the sides of his head in a viselike grip. Fingernails dug into his scalp.

"Beth! You're hurting me!" Joseph attempted to struggle, but to no avail.

She wrenched her husband's head toward the window. "Joseph, look! It can all be over!"

He struggled, fighting her until the pain in his chest became too much to bear, resisting more than he thought was possible, until finally... he let go.

Outside, a massive form shifted in the brightening dawn.

Beth pressed her lips to Joseph's ear and whispered, "It wants to learn." ◆

Hunter Lowe is a 27 year old writing enthusiast currently residing in Los Angeles, California. After chasing the tails of a variety of passions including classic hand-drawn art to digital illustration and three-dimensional construction geared toward use in video games he realized he could never shake the constant drive from within to continue his writing. His time spent experimenting with such a variety of art forms lead to a stronger visual library for him to integrate into his writing. While working on his novel he loves to step into the short-story environment and intends to put out as many quality reading experiences that he can. While horror is where he is most at home, he has a number of stories in the works ranging from science fiction, fantasy, to amalgamations of all of the above. He will soon be relocating to the lovely state of Colorado to continue his writing in a nice secluded forest.

Artwork: Chris L. Burke

FOR FAME, FOR FORTUNE, FOR A COMMEMORATIVE STATUE

JAMES PARK

The feat was of a rare and unusual nature, the kind of accomplishment that doesn't hold a benchmark with the Guinness Book of World Records. It was a feat that more so secures a presence at Ripley's Believe It or Not! or like one of Madame Tussauds' sculptures. If Michael Milenko had it his way, a commemorative statue would follow his accomplishment.

It didn't matter that Lloyd Luchtenberg thought he was an idiot. Michael was going to be rich. Filthy rich. So what if his old fishing buddy and lifelong rival took a vodka-fueled piss all over the parade? Over a dozen witnesses could attest to his accomplishment. They'd watched the spectacle with ambivalence, straining to catch passive glances through squinted eyes, and Michael Milenko intended to compensate each of them in due time. But first he needed to engrave his name in the annals of strange and bizarre culture in order to join the ranks of Harry Houdini and Mabel Stark.

The compulsive stroking of his own ego started the moment he walked away from the certainty of death, and Michael wasn't about to stop now that he'd reached Las Vegas. It was time to sell his story; more precisely, it was time to sell pre-calculated portions of the story. Specific chapters would be withheld. That was crucial.

"The purpose of the tabloids is really quite simple," he gloated into his cell phone from a pink taxicab that carried him to the Flamingo.

"And what purpose might that be?" Lloyd Luchtenberg inquired, his stoic and uninterested voice muffled by raspy reception.

"They're bait," Michael continued. "I just need the tabloids to get some rumors stirring, you know, get my name out there, earn some quick cash. I'll start with *The Tattler*, then move on to *The Midnight* and *The Confidential*. I'll even let *The Enquirer* in on the scoop. Then the bigwigs will come knocking: *Life, Time, People…Rolling Stone*. I'll give them the full story or most of it, at least. Gotta save some details for the talk shows, my friend. I'm gonna milk this thing dry, and then live like a pig for the rest of my life."

"I wish you luck," Lloyd said. "But Michael, you need to be a realist here. How much time can you possibly have left? It's a miracle you've made it thi–"

"A *miracle*!" The pink taxicab lulled into the glitzy bulb-embroidered foyer of the Flamingo. "I survived, Lloyd. I survived! Do you even hear me?"

"Yes, Michael. I hear you. But I thi–"

"I survived and I'm in Las Vegas. The only ailment I have is a sore throat, you know, a desert cough. But Lloyd, I can't blame you for turning green with envy."

"Oh please, Michael. I'm not envious of you. If anything, I pity you."

"Hold on, hold on. What's that?" Michael asked, lowering the cell phone as the balding middle-aged driver opened Michael's door and muttered some sort of incoherent jibber-jabber.

"What?"

"Fifteen dollars," the driver shouted.

"Fifteen bucks? Sure." Michael handed over a twenty. He didn't instruct the driver to keep any change, but didn't much care that it wasn't returned. Grabbing the handle of his bag, he headed for the hotel's entrance, sand spilling from his sneakers with every step. He lifted the cell phone to his ear and said, "You know what, Lloyd? You can sleep with my wife."

"Michael, that's ridiculous."

"No, really. Sleep with Carol. I've seen the way you dote on her, and don't you for a second think that my filing for divorce *before* making my millions is a coincidence. I ain't givin' her a penny, not a single gawd damn penny. She can commit all the infidelity she wants. See if I care."

"You can't be serious, Micha–"

"Just make sure you take Buster for a walk afterward, and don't let Carol keep him locked in the basement, all right? Oh, and Lloyd, I'm hanging up on you. It's time for me to check in."

The line was painstakingly long; the conversation could have continued, but Michael Milenko had little patience for his fishing buddy and suspected lover to his wife. They'd spent their entire lives trying to one-up the other, from leisure sports, to women, to cars. Even petty accomplishments, like catching a slightly larger trout, carried bragging rights that lasted years.

Carol had always served as an unusual victory for Michael, being that she was skinnier and prettier than the prototypical floozy that Lloyd Luchtenberg was known to attract. Now she'd be a victory to Lloyd. But in the shadow of Michael's newfound fame, stealing Carol was a meager accomplishment, and Michael knew that Lloyd knew that he knew that it was just that: an insignificant little accomplishment. That's why Lloyd had urged him not to do it. And now that he'd done it, Lloyd kept telling him that he'd regret it.

But none of that held any significance. The only thing that mattered was checking into the Flamingo and cleaning himself up. The desert had taken a toll. His lips were dry and chapped, his skin sunburned, and his face was overdue for a shave. The odor lingering in his every pore yearned to be scrubbed clean with a pad of steel wool, and everyone seemed to notice.

"Sir, you're next."

A blonde directly behind him was gorgeous until she made a hideous face, as was a tan brunette with a tiny waist and endowed chest. She'd paced back and forth, cigarette in one hand, glass of wine in the other, but wrinkled up her peeling nose at the notion of standing in the same line as Michael Milenko.

"Sir, may I help?"

A pair of young Asian women–twins, presumably, as the lethargic eyes of Michael Milenko wished them to be–scooted to the back of the line. They grimaced at the unfavorable odor now surfacing from the front.

"*Sir, really, can we please help you?*"

The line of jetlagged arrivals shook their heads as Michael turned toward the desk clerk, and then nonchalantly shuffled his sand-crusted shoes to the counter. Plopping down a folded newspaper, he said, "Michael Milenko. I've reserved the Hunter S. Thompson Suite for the next two months."

The clerk's face underwent immediate transformation, her smile signifying acknowledgement that he was not an ordinary guest; it was almost genuine.

"Mr. Milenko, we've been expecting you. I do wish you'd have used the gold members' check-in. No need to wait in line with all of *these people.*" Her nose scrunched in disgust as the words plopped out of her mouth.

Michael yawned as he picked an indecipherable speck of crud from the corner of his eye. He could smell himself, and he knew it wasn't pleasant. But the woman standing before him was young, articulate, and attractive; picturing her naked was all Michael needed to forget the unpleasantness of his own condition. She smiled artificially while she swiped his credit card and collected his signature. The Hunter S. Thompson Suite awaited, with promises of a bathtub, soaps fragranced with honey, oils smelling of coconut, and various exotic gels.

❖

In Michael Milenko's opinion, a Las Vegas evening void of women and bourbon was a terrible misfortune. Unlike the dirt and grime that he'd washed away at first opportunity, however, the virtues of good judgment and sound discretion had to be preserved. It was crucial. His interviews depended on it.

Confined to the solitude of his suite, lights didn't flash, buzzers didn't buzz, and women didn't twirl around brass poles. But he welcomed the morning, for his brain was still sober and his body had embraced its first full slumber since the completion of his magnificent accomplishment.

He'd told Cynthia Janese of *The Tattler* over and over again, "I'll give you a twenty-four hour lead on the interview, but you'll be payin' for it, in cash. And I mean boatloads of cash."

She delivered, and she was dazzling. As Michael stood in the open doorway, wearing nothing but a white full-length bathrobe, his first impression was that Cynthia Janese deserved better than *The Tattler*.

She was pretty, CNN pretty, perhaps even *E! News* pretty. But when she opened her mouth, a set of grimy nicotine-stained teeth greeted him, providing a slight indication as to why this attractive young woman remained faceless behind the smutty pages of a checkout line magazine.

"This is Javier," Cynthia announced, motioning to the boulder of a man standing behind her. "He tags along whenever cash is involved."

Javier was enormous. His skin looked beaten and worn, like an old leather pouch. His unspoken dominance held the aura of a cage fighter or a professional wrestler, maybe even a hit man.

The only certainty was that he felt relieved when Javier unloaded the bags and waited quietly in the hallway. There was no reason for the goon to impose on Michael's first interview, especially if said interview provided the opportunity to become better acquainted with Miss Cynthia Janese.

She was so delightful, in spite of her chain-smoking, and her questions didn't stray from the previously negotiated topics. Michael's health rested at the top of the list, and he gave her the same scoop that he'd given Lloyd Luchtenberg: "The only ailment I have is a sore throat, a desert cough."

Michael thought about his statement. He felt an odd stiffness in his feet like nothing he'd previously encountered. It hadn't been noticeable until he'd sought refuge at the Flamingo. He'd traveled so many miles into the desert, with nothing more than the conversation of strange witnesses to occupy his time. So of course he felt stiff, and of course the colossal ball of mucus that he'd coughed up first thing that morning was unusually hard and slightly coarse. He was in the desert, and he planned on staying in the desert for some time.

Michael told Cynthia Janese: "I'll be in Vegas for awhile, you know, long enough to get some long overdue rest and relaxation."

She smiled wide, a gesture that showcased her grimy teeth, and undid her top button. Poignancy rested on her face as she asked, "What was it like out there? What was it like staring into the face of death?"

Having rehearsed in front of the mirror, Michael's response was cool and calculated, albeit slightly artificial. He'd traveled into the depths of Hell and was alive to tell the story. It didn't matter how scared he'd been or that he'd nearly shit his pants. This was *The Tattler*, and as far as Michael was concerned, the first publishing of his tale should hold the same degree of honor and masculinity as a Conan the Barbarian story. It made little difference that he was a short, balding man in his early forties. The chain-smoking hussy seated before him, dressed in a cheap blouse and short skirt, legs parted wider than they should be, was going to print whatever he told her.

"It was a moment of intestinal fortitude," Michael said with arched eyebrows. "I had to prove once and for all what kind of man I really am. Sure, I had my hesitations, but when a man has confidence on his side, there's really nothing that can't be accomplished."

Cynthia Janese blushed, then took a drag from her cigarette.

Michael clamped both hands over his mouth and sneezed, catching a handful of snot that felt oddly tough. Discreetly, he wiped it on the side of his robe, hoping the gesture would go unnoticed. And then he sneezed again. There was nothing he could do. The smoke attacked his sinuses without mercy. It had been years since his last cigarette and considerably longer since Lloyd Luchtenberg had first introduced him to what he now considered a disgusting habit. But Cynthia Janese made it look sexy, even natural, just like the girls had back in high school.

Wiping a second smear of snot against his robe, Michael pushed the temptation to ask for a cigarette out of his mind and said, "The whole feat was just a question of mind over matter. I held my ground and I created my own destiny."

"Tell me about this destiny," Cynthia requested as smoke seeped from her mouth.

Michael didn't hesitate to mention that his Saturdays spent fishing were a thing of the past. He was becoming a wealthy man and felt he should partake in the pastimes of wealthy men.

Cynthia raised both eyebrows and parted her legs further. "You mean scholarly pursuits?"

Michael chuckled, then pondered his response. He dared not mention his plans for womanizing, especially to a reporter. His fame would last longer if such gossip unraveled in due course. And he couldn't possibly mention his intentions of wasting away at strip clubs or flying to exotic lands in order to nibble at the delectable treats squatting in their brothels. Instead, he rubbed his chin and said, "Traveling. I see myself doing a lot of traveling."

"Any journeys like the one you just completed?"

"No, no." Michael laughed. "I've stared death in the face once already. I have nothing to gain by pressing my luck any further."

"You might change your mind about that. Evel Knievel didn't stop after his first stunt. Men of your occupation often have trouble bowing out gracefully."

Michael shook his head. "Evel Knievel broke every bone in his body. I don't see much point in going down that road. Besides, in this day and age, a man needs to learn from other men's mistakes. I'm willing to gamble that Roy Horn wishes he'd stopped performing at the Mirage long before Montecore ripped his neck open."

"But it didn't stop Siegfried & Roy from performing one last show with that same tiger," Cynthia said as she ground her cigarette into the ashtray. She undid another button.

Michael shrugged. He had no interest in being compared to seasoned professionals. He was the working man's daredevil, and it didn't matter if they made him out to be a one-trick pony. Tabloids turned nobodies into multi-millionaires. They could publish whatever garbage they want alongside their photos of Kim Kardashian's enormous butt. It didn't matter. Michael hoped the photographers would pester him until his dying day. He welcomed the nuisance, and the bad-press-is-really-good-press paychecks destined to follow.

In Cynthia's line of work, she probably saw this kind of greed every day. The only thing different about Michael Milenko was that he'd accrued the type of accomplishment capable of supporting his desires.

With a smirk situated atop her soft face, she asked, "What about your sex life?"

"That's not on the list of topics I agreed to discuss."

"It's an off-the-record question." She undid another button and spread her legs as far as they would go.

Michael sneezed, wiped a glob of snot on his robe, and admired Cynthia's thighs. He gave the thin stretch of fabric covering her privates a hungry leer. He couldn't have been happier that Javier had waited outside the room.

❖

The reporter from *The Midnight* wasn't the pleasant surprise that Cynthia Janese had been, nor were the reporters from *The Confidential* or *The Enquirer*; instead, they carried the poise that a generation of infomercial watchers inevitably carries. They had bad skin hiding beneath layers of cheap cosmetics. A lingering foulness of heavy perfume followed their every step. And their pudgy hands were crusted with remnants of chocolate truffles.

Presumably, they could at least jot down Michael's words and turn them into a published story. If not, plagiarism was a viable option, and that was bound to happen sooner rather than later. The headlines were destined to be nothing more than carbon copies from *The Tattler*. The articles would all be the same, with emphasis directed toward Michael's good health, how he felt on that death-defying day, and his obvious plans for a gluttonous future.

Michael never mentioned the unexpected twinges gnawing around his stomach. And why would he? They were reporters, not doctors, and it made little difference that they'd purchased the rights to report on his health. The pains were negligible, the distraction was moderate, and Michael Milenko wasn't going to let some minor discomfort spoil an otherwise fabulous blossoming new life.

The interviews were over, and the stacks of money he'd collected were tucked away in the spacious closet of the Hunter S. Thompson Suite. Outside, sunshine bestowed a layer of warmth atop the synthetic glow of flashing lights. Hobos begged for change and leftover food. Street entertainers hustled for tips: they sang Elvis Presley songs, imitated Liberace, and posed in superhero costumes for pictures.

Michael paid little attention, for his own agenda was of greater concern. He needed new clothes, loads of them, and he needed the expensive kind. Other people went to the Forum Shops at Caesar's to stare in awe at the cloudy blue-sky ceiling, take their photographs with the statue of David, maybe dine at Spago. Michael Milenko was there to spend money with the assumption that an endless stream of interviews and guest appearances rested securely in his future. And he extracted a perverse notion of sexuality from the saleswomen that helped him in and out of his new attire. They blushed and giggled when he removed his pants, and stood closer than necessary as he stepped into their recommended selections. They knew who he was. *The Tattler* had hit the newsstands, and competing publications would start popping up any day now.

Michael relished in the attention he received behind the privacy of dressing room doors. Even for high end stores, Michael's kind was a rare breed. The women were used to old money and they were used to stolen money. But new money went to the craps tables and the strip clubs, rarely to overpriced boutiques.

The phone call made to Lloyd Luchtenberg was nothing more than a formality. The walk from the Forum Shops to the Flamingo was relatively short, yet Michael happily paid an inflated delivery fee to avoid carrying his own bags. It wasn't a choice, but a necessity. People were noticing him. Even street performers turned and stared, watching the tourists snap photos of a real personality standing right there in the flesh.

Dressed in designer denim purchased at Calvin Klein, a Ted Baker button-down opened to mid chest, and a pair of leather shoes, Michael held the cell phone firmly against his ear and said, "Lloyd, I think you know why I'm calling."

"Michael, if it's more of this nonsense about Carol, then I'm going to be frank with you. I haven't the slightest intention of ever slee–"

"Lloyd, my friend," Michael interrupted. "You underestimate me. I called to gloat, not to accuse."

"I see." Lloyd's voice was low, unnaturally monotone, seeping with simulated disinterest.

"Have you been to the grocery store this week?"

"I've seen *The Tattler*," Lloyd confirmed. "Very impressive, Michael. You've joined the ranks of circus geeks. Bitten the heads off any chickens lately?"

"Don't be jealous, Lloyd. You know I've raked in more cash this week than any circus performer earns in a lifetime. And you should see the clothes I'm wearing or the women I slept with last night. Better yet, Lloyd, you should see the women I'm going to sleep with tonight. Shall I send you a picture?"

"Sounds like you're spending the money just as fast you make it," Lloyd said, his voice still low and uninterested. "What are you going to do when it's gone?"

"It won't ever be gone." Michael ran his stumpy fingers over his balding head of greyish hair and adjusted the Saddleback leather belt that cinched his designer denim. "The real magazines are next, after that the talk shows. And you know what I think I might do in a few years? Just guess, Lloyd, just guess."

"Oh, please share. I'm dying to hear what the magnificent Michael Milenko has in store for round two. Wait, let me guess. They're going to fill your pockets with raw meat and drop you in a cage full of tigers. Or maybe they'll cover you in honey and hurl bee's nests at your head. Which is it, Michael? What's your next stunt going to be?"

"You can make fun all you want, but I'm going to write a book. Not just about my accomplishment, but about the life of excess I'm living thanks to that glorious accomplishment."

"A *book?*"

"That's right, a book. Just like the rock stars write, so the whole world can read about my fabulous lifestyle. That's what Americans care about, you know."

"Yes, yes," Lloyd said, a hint of liveliness seeping into his voice. "In this current age of economic uncertainty, America wants to read about how rich you're becoming. Sure, that's what we want. That's why *Lifestyles of the Rich and Famous* was discontinued all the way back in the mid-nineties."

"Don't be a smartass," Michael said.

"Me? A smartass?" Lloyd chuckled. "You underestimate me. I wish you nothing but champagne wishes and caviar dreams."

"Lloyd, it might be time to hang up on you. But before I do, just one question: have you been walking Buster like I asked?"

"Why on earth would I go over to your house to walk Buster?"

"I just thought that after you slept with my wife you'd have the decency to take Buster for a wal–"

"Michael, I'll be the one hanging up this time. Give me a call when your head's out of the clouds, alright? Maybe we can go fishing."

The cold silence of a disconnected line followed. Michael didn't care. It wouldn't be his last opportunity to get the final word. His old buddy was probably at his house right now, sharing intimacies with Carol, lounging around in one of those gaudy robes he always wore on Saturdays when he wasn't fishing. The stench of cigarette smoke was probably irritating Buster, and Lloyd was undoubtedly acting like a douche, puffing through his long cigarette holder with a dirty martini resting on the nightstand.

Michael was no stranger to watching Lloyd Luchtenberg hold himself to high standards, even on his bookkeeper's salary. The man didn't have a family; up until now he didn't have a woman like Carol to suck the change from his pockets. He probably hadn't even bothered to take Buster for a walk, but Michael didn't care so long as someone fed him. Carol would see to it. She wasn't that cruel, at least.

Michael exhaled a deep sigh that made his lungs ache with stiffness.

As he shoved the cell phone back into his pocket, a riveting pain rose from his hand and crept up his arm, causing an unexpected soreness to linger around the shoulder. The grossly abnormal sensations reminded him of the newfound stiffness in his feet, a tenderness that had accompanied his every step since returning from the middle of nowhere.

Michael was tired and needed rest. An afternoon void of interviews and worries was long overdue. There'd be women by the pool, hordes of them, in groups and by themselves, lounging on plastic recliners in tiny swimsuits that scarcely concealed their unmentionables. Michael wiped the sweat from his forehead, his worries dissolving as perspiration dripped from his fingertips onto the cemented walkway of Las Vegas Boulevard. By sundown he'd be sipping cocktails more expensive than any drink that had ever soiled the lips of Lloyd Luchtenberg, with his free hand pinioned between the thighs of an escort.

❖

It occurred to Michael Milenko that the women standing on either side of him had probably seen the fountains outside the Bellagio shoot spears of water in synchronized rhythm to Viva Las Vegas more times than they cared to remember. He knew the flesh of their cheeks had spent so many hours scrunched into simulated displays of enthusiasm that remnants of artificial joy would be forever molded below their mascara-embroidered eyes.

Michael had yet to tire of watching the show. With an arm wrapped firmly around either woman's waist, he watched with the passion of a tourist while his escorts seemingly resisted the urge to yawn.

Neither woman wore underwear. Michael's hands had solved that mystery shortly after making their acquaintance, and for the amount of money that they'd extracted from those same hands, they'd soon be wearing nothing more than plastic smiles.

They walked casually toward the Flamingo. The evening was just beginning its progression into night as the fountains fired their final shots and the accompanying lights slowly faded into nothingness. Hints of darkness crept between the glows of sparkling casinos. Michael tried not to acknowledge the pain in his legs or the odd sensations moving toward his knees. The women on either side of him were of greater importance, and the discomfort of walking too quickly proved to be a minor distraction.

His hands were on their backsides before they reached the hotel, and their hands were all over his shoulders and chest as they entered the casino and weaved through the gauntlet of slot machines. In the elevator, they kissed his cheeks and his neck. Upon reaching Michael's floor, they stumbled down the hall with their heels in hand, giggling like school-girls. They nearly ripped the shirt from Michael's back before making it inside the suite. When the door closed, their dresses were on the floor before Michael could kick off his shoes and pour a drink.

Scratches lined his back from the night before. Additional marks littered across his chest and shoulders. They were inconsequential, nothing more than temporary battle wounds that Michael wanted to grow worse before healing.

The women rubbed his shoulders while he fondled their backsides and kissed their ears. The shorter of the two gave his penis a long stroke before falling back onto the bed. Spreading her legs, the look on her face made suggestions that no words could adequately articulate. Michael gave each of her feet a kiss, then ran his mouth up her body until his lips were pressed tightly against her neck. Long locks of blond hair brushed his face. As Michael slid inside, her long red nails tore into his back. He planted kiss after kiss on the woman's neck, hearing a noise like nails scraping along a blackboard.

The unoccupied escort sat on the corner of the bed, scrunching her eyebrows. The escort Michael was screwing ran her hands through her hair, and Michael noticed that her nails had disintegrated and only bare fingertips now roamed up and down his body.

Michael ignored the fingernail chippings and panted like an out-of-shape old geezer, gasping for air between the deliverance of impersonal kisses that landed atop her cheeks and shoulders but nowhere near her lips.

The unoccupied escort brushed her palm back and forth across Michael's calf and then his thigh, eventually traveling across his ass and over the hardened flesh of his back. She pulled her hand away, and without uttering a word, scooped her dress from the floor, stretched the expandable fabric over her young body, and then stepped back into her heels. Taking her Prada handbag from the table, she ruffled around inside, and then discarded a wad of cash. The door shut quietly behind her as Michael released a final, pleasurable scream.

He rolled off his temporary companion, then stretched his arms as sweat trickled from his greyish hair, dampening the pillow.

"What the fuck?" the woman said. "What the fuck happened to my nails?"

Extending her hands, she peered at her fingertips, and then scoured the bed with uncertain eyes. Chipped nails coated in red polish were strewn about. As the flustered blond woman cast vehement eyes on Michael, he felt his blood begin to boil. It warmed his head, his cheeks, and his chest, leaving a sour taste in his mouth. But the heat didn't circulate all the way down his legs or to his hands. The twinges that gnawed at his stomach returned. The pain perpetuated in the uncomfortable silence, as they both peered around the empty room. Neither mentioned that the other escort had gone or that she'd left her money on the window-side table. The unspoken silence created a breed of discomfort that words could not have cured.

The escort slipped back into her dress, found her shoes, and grabbed her purse. The door slammed behind her, and the sound of her brisk footsteps soon faded into an undisturbed stillness.

The afterglow that Michael had paid for was overshadowed by aches and pains. He'd felt so young the night before. Making women scream while he slapped their asses and called them names had rejuvenated him. And now it did just the opposite. He wasn't a young man. Even in his prime he'd never pleasured women by the pair. The over-indulged acts of youthfulness were bound to extract a toll from his sedentary self. Michael hurt. The pain moved all about his body. At his age, gallstones were a reality, as were kidney stones, even ulcers. It was nothing more than an impediment of passage. He didn't know what caused his stomach to throb, and he didn't care to speculate beyond common problems that could be relieved with common medical procedures. The broken nails weren't his defect. There wasn't anything weak about his keratin. His outsides had never felt stronger or more unbreakable.

It was time for a drink. Michael knew nothing better suited to wash away worry than a stiff bourbon on ice. He dressed significantly slower than the women who'd fled from the intimacies of his tough exterior and then took a moment to admire himself in the mirror.

Michael liked what stared back. The features were well proportioned, even attractive, and were accentuated by the refined dignity of receding hair that contained a modestly greyish quality. The new clothes concealed the imperfections of his unexercised body, and his entire look seeped with the residue of wealth. Even people who didn't yet recognize his face could tell that he was somebody.

His muscles ached on the stroll to the elevator, throbbing with an unfamiliar stiffness. He pressed a big round button, and then watched the overarching numbers count down to lobby level.

Diving headfirst into a new lifestyle had been foolish. Michael longed for rest; he wanted more than just a day by the pool. Maybe he'd get a massage in the morning and spend the afternoon lounging at Cheetah's, bourbon in hand while an endless parade of twenty-somethings waved their asses in his face. He needed to build up the anticipation, crave the forbidden fruit for a while instead of bloating his body with as many bites as he could muster.

More than that, he needed exercise, but not tonight. Tonight he needed cigarettes and bourbon, the ingredients for distraction. He'd gone long enough without smoking that an isolated binge shouldn't hurt anything. Besides, Lloyd Luchtenberg wasn't around to say, "I told you you'd start again someday."

The flapper girl selling smokes was delightful, in a Cynthia Janese sort of way, and the smile on her face suggested that she recognized Michael.

All sorts of people were beginning to recognize the Magnificent Michael Milenko. They pointed him out to their friends over spilled drinks and hastily placed bets. Bells and whistles around the slots grew quieter as he walked by, heads turning in his direction.

Michael helped himself to a seat in front of Blazing 7s, slid a Benjamin Franklin into the machine, and then ordered his drink from a doll of a waitress. With a cigarette perched between his lips, Michael played the highest bet, repeatedly, as the night progressed with an ashtray and a collection of empty rocks glasses.

The weight of watching eyes rested on the back of Michael's head, and he could hear their whisperings. When a member of the paparazzi popped up, he gave the camera a polite smile and a brief wave and then ignored the man altogether, leaving him free to snap all the pictures he wanted. With a crumpled matchbook in hand, Michael drove one tobacco-filled nail after another into his coffin, the pack growing smaller as the hours slid by. His mind entered a strange vortex where nothing tangible seemed to matter save for the pouring of fresh drinks. Money slowly disappeared from his pockets, but it made little difference. He didn't even reach for his phone when it vibrated. There was nothing he cared to discuss with Lloyd Luchtenberg, and he didn't much feel like gloating. It would be better to leave Lloyd in the dark, let him think he was tied up with the press, or negotiating his first talk show appearance.

Besides, it couldn't be real. None of it felt real. It was just nervous anxiety. The pain would only be temporary. He wasn't used to the desert, the enduring episodes of sex, and his body had a strange way of adjusting. That was all.

❖

Kimberly came highly recommended. The desk clerk had nothing but kind words to say about the short redhead. She was cute, in an alluring way that often necessitates lewd comments, inappropriate suggestions, and the occasional misplaced hand on her backside.

After everything he'd been through, Michael just wanted the massage and nothing more. Sprawled helplessly atop the massage table, his face was tucked snugly into a padded opening at the head, a towel tossed carelessly over his midsection. Michael hardly noticed the warm sensation of oils dribbled over his skin, and he barely acknowledged the hands kneading his flesh like unbaked bread.

If Kimberly hadn't cursed before stepping away from the table, extending her parted fingers as Michael lifted his head, he'd have never known that she'd broken her nails.

Kimberly gave her hands a final stare before shifting her attention toward Michael, her intruding eyes inspecting his body as though he were a lifeless dummy that had suddenly mutated into an amorphous blob of flesh and bone.

Rising from the table, Michael paid no mind as the towel fell to the floor. His limbs felt heavy and strangely lethargic, almost unwilling to move as he proceeded to the window-side table. He didn't count the wad of cash that he scooped up, but he had a rough idea of the amount. It was enough to make women shed their clothing and taint their purity, and likely amounted to five or six times the cost of a massage.

Kimberly avoided eye contact as she snatched the wad from Michael's hand, but allowed a quiet "Thank you" to pass between her lips.

Michael shooed her away like a river rat. She folded up her table. He stepped into his boxers, followed by a tattered pair of shorts that he'd owned prior to his wardrobe update at the Forum Shops. Opening his pack of smokes, he could hear Kimberly quietly closing the door behind her, and he sighed at the sight of one remaining cigarette.

He hadn't planned on smoking after the pack was gone, but the virtues of self control no longer held any importance. Room service could send up another pack, and the minibar was stocked with an adequate selection of bourbon.

Michael stood before a wall mirror and examined his back. The collection of sores and scratch marks was gone. There wasn't even a trace of redness where Kimberly's nails had brushed against his shoulders, rather chalky indentations that were small, almost unnoticeable. He shrugged and stepped onto the balcony. Every muscle in his body stiffened as he parted the blinds and gazed down upon a city where hope flourished amongst encrusted scraps of despair. The degenerates were all ignored, sitting on street curbs like garbage that should have been ushered away, and the hopeful cared not to learn from the mistakes of the wretched.

Placing the cigarette between his uncharacteristically tough lips, Michael knew he could do the same. Nothing was happening that couldn't be ignored. Besides, it wasn't real. His surroundings weren't even real. It was just an elaborate mirage in the middle of the desert, a man-made illusion constructed for no other purpose than to make his wallet lighter.

Michael saw little reason to stay any longer. The heat was affecting his judgment, and the women weren't what they should have been.

It was time to wake his brain up with a drink and enjoy another pack of cigarettes while he pondered the possibilities of a limitless future.

❖

"*Motherfucker!*" Michael shouted.

The taste of booze lingered subtly about his mouth submerged beneath the stronger residue of cigarette smoke. His tongue tasted like an ashtray. It had been years since he'd quit, but even back then the balls of mucus he coughed up didn't resemble the alien artifact that he'd just spat into the sink.

He'd been smoking for two weeks now, but the younger version of Michael Milenko was no stranger to coughed-up blood in the morning. Lloyd had given him his first cigarette when he was only fifteen, and he wasn't even halfway through high school when the two of them started associating the pastime of pilfering trout from the river with the enjoy-ment of smoking one cigarette after another. But he'd never coughed up blood in such quantity, with sanguine liquid coating his mucus, even dribbling from his lips. He didn't want to touch what had come out, not with his bare hands. And it couldn't be washed down the drain.

Michael knew exactly what he'd spit up, but he still felt the need to poke at it, just to be sure. It wasn't just one pebble, but several, each of them black as tar and tough as marble. They made coarse contact with the tip of his finger, though he hardly felt the friction.

Michael digested the scene splattered before him. A hoarse cough erupted from the pit of his upset stomach, causing a second spattering of pebbles to let loose, a rich coating of mucous preventing them from making a clank as they hit the side of the sink and were immediately suctioned into place. Larger spurts of blood gushed from his mouth, coating his fingers as he touched his trembling lips. With shivers tickling the length of his spine, he couldn't even feel the wetness of the blood.

"Motherfucker," Michael repeated, slamming his fist down with such might that the countertop cracked beneath the blow. Jagged shards of granite bounced into the air. An indentation of his curled pinky was left behind, though he didn't feel a thing. There wasn't even a hint of numbness.

Stepping back, violent pains shot from his knees, as though bone was rubbing against bone. He'd never before suffered the malady of arthritis, but this felt real, too real. Pain climbed all the way up his thighs and cascaded down his shins. He didn't feel it below his ankles. He couldn't even move his toes. They were null and void to sensation, just like his fingers. But at least he could wiggle his fingers. He could hold his hands in front of his face without a shred of feeling.

Michael gazed into the mirror, reluctantly making eye contact with his reflection. He quietly pleaded for nothing to be out of the ordi-nary. He'd been in the desert for three weeks, so of course his throat was hoarse; it burned from a dryness that was gradually easing down his esophagus, tainting his digestive track with an inflammation that seemed to harden his interior.

"Snap the fuck out of it," Michael yelled.

He fumbled with the knobs on the sink, eventually managing to release some warm water. Cupping both hands beneath the faucet, he couldn't feel the accumulated wetness. Splashing it over his face to wash the blood from his lips, there was no sensation at all. He needed to quit smoking, stop ordering room service that was piled high with bacon and eggs, lay off the booze, and most importantly, get out of the desert. If he did all that, he'd feel better. He had to. Whatever was attacking him from the inside would go away. He could live the rest of his life any place he wanted, and he'd be stinking, filthy rich.

Michael's body ached when he turned the faucet off. His knees screamed in pain as he hobbled out of the washroom. He lacked the wherewithal to gather up his cash and leave. He was sick, and he didn't expect to get better until someone helped him escape from this horrid desert air.

Picking up the cell phone was a reluctant gesture, for he knew only one man who could help.

Lloyd answered on the first ring, as though he'd been expecting the call. Michael could just picture him, staying over at *his* house, reading *his* newspaper, and drinking *his* booze while seeking comfort in the arms of *his* wife. *Had he even bothered to walk Buster?* Michael doubted it. The man had nothing to one-up him with by walking a dog.

Lloyd Luchtenberg was a man of superficial actions, and Michael was reminded of this by his tone of voice: "Oh, Michael, calling again already, are we? I'll save you a little time. The answers to your questions are, no, I'm not sleeping with your wife, and because of that there's really no reason why I'd take Buster for a walk."

"Lloyd, let's cut the bullshit." Michael paused to clear his throat. The mucus lining of his throat felt like concrete. "I'm sick. I'm really sick."

"You sound it, good friend."

"It's the gawd-awful climate out here. It's so hot, so dry. And I haven't taken care of myself, not just now but for years, and it feels like it's catching up with me. I need your help."

Lloyd didn't respond immediately, as if he was searching for the right words to fill the uncomfortable silence. Michael knew what he wanted to say, but he also knew that his own voice was weak, raspy, and even Lloyd Luchtenberg knew better than to kick a man while he's down. The long silence finally broke: "How can I help?"

"I'm at the Flamingo, still in the Hunter S. Thompson Suite. Room nineteen seventy-two. One. Nine. Seven. Two. Everything I've earned these past three weeks is in cash, stuffed in the closet. I ain't got the strength to pick it up and get it myself out outta here. Lloyd, I need to leave this filthy city. I've gotta get out of the desert and get myself some-place where I can rest and recuperate."

"Michael, I'm on my way," Lloyd said. "Just hold tight an—"

Michael Milenko let the cell phone slide from his hand and onto the floor without bothering to disconnect.

❖

Lloyd Luchtenberg arrived at the Las Vegas airport at three o'clock in the morning. The flesh on his back was still raw from Carol's fingernails, just as the flesh beneath his ear still carried teeth marks from kisses planted too hastily.

He caught a pink taxicab to the Flamingo, the driver weaving in and out of traffic while the glitter of fluorescent lights sparkled on either side. A full moon shimmered overhead. The air was cool, particularly for late summer.

Passing through a gauntlet of gold and pink lights, Lloyd entered the hotel and made his way to the elevator, mentally disregarding the on-slaught of bells and buzzers, the proverbial yawns and lazy sighs emerg-ing from craps tables as hard-earned income diligently became property of the casino.

The door to room one-nine-seven-two was ajar, and Lloyd shut it quickly behind him, ensuring that it was locked and he wouldn't be disturbed. The sight made his stomach churn, though it didn't surprise him. None of it surprised him save for the piles of cash stuffed inside the closet. He had a rough idea of how much was there. Michael had gloated endlessly about his earnings, and Lloyd only had one question: How much had yet to be spent?

The answer appeared favorable. The stacks were piled high, all in large bills. Lloyd shook his head and laughed. America really wanted to read about Michael Milenko's little stunt, and the fruits of this strange and bizarre fascination stood before him.

Biting his lip, Lloyd scooped the cell phone from his pocket and placed a call.

"Carol," Lloyd said, his tired eyes glued to a stone statue once consti-tuting the mortal being of his good friend and lifelong rival.

"Yes. Lloyd, is that you?"

Lloyd Luchtenberg scratched his temple and shook his head. The money behind the statue never strayed from his eyesight.

"We're through, Carol. Do you hear me? We're through."

"What? Lloyd? Why would you say such a thi—"

Lloyd dropped the cell phone back into his pocket.

He inspected the statue of Michael Milenko. His old friend had hardened with a macabre expression chiseled into his face, pure terror captured in his unbelieving eyes. The arms were straight, resting at the side, as though he'd given up and just stood there, no longer trying to fight it.

Ashtrays littered the room, stuffed tight with cigarette butts. The walls expelled an odor of mildewed smoke. Unfinished room service was strewn about, just beginning to acquire mold around the edges.

Lloyd suspected that he'd find an empty bottle of booze for every pack of cigarettes, a near-empty bottle of wine for every entrée. It was a miracle that Michael hadn't burnt the place down, given his newfound stiffness and the collection of half-burnt cigarettes on the floor. The stacks of money were clean, but everything else carried layers of filth. Even Michael's new wardrobe had been flung around the room.

Only one piece of luggage rested within the spacious walls of the Hunter S. Thompson Suite.

Just like Michael, Lloyd thought. *He came here to collect millions, and only brought one suitcase.*

Lloyd didn't trust armored car services, not in a mob-infested town like Las Vegas. More suitcases would be necessary in order to get all of that cash to a bank. He didn't yet know where he'd move, what he'd do, or how he'd live. But two absolutes had certainly become manifest: Carol wasn't going to be a part of it, and Lloyd would never do anything half as stupid as Michael had. There weren't enough riches in the world to tempt him into a stunt like that, and he could do without the fame, not to mention the undesired side effects that would transform him into his own commemorative statue, just like his old fishing buddy.

Looking Medusa in the eye was clearly not worth the risk, even if Lloyd Luchtenberg thought he could pull the stunt off with greater success than had the Magnificent Michael Milenko. ◆

Artwork: Chrissy Spallone

THE RESURRECTIONIST'S BOX

JACK MADDOX

1875

Edmund Carnaby sat in the front of the empty lecture hall, silent as a church mouse, while Professor Darius drew on the blackboard–a diagram of the skull, each of the separate plates labeled in his unmistakable scrawl. Edmund glanced at the examination table. A body waited under a sheet.

"So I hear you'll be leaving us at end of term, Master Carnaby," the skeletal teacher said.

"Yes, sir," Edmund replied, staring at his hands. Last night, he had bitten his nails to the quick. The nightmare had been bad; an army of half-dissected cadavers chased him down Piccadilly Circus.

"I must admit my disappointment," Professor Darius said, still chalking. "You are one of the hardest-working students I've seen in years. Maybe not the most academic, but your drive is remarkable. It would have carried you far in medicine."

"Thank you, sir."

"I took the liberty of looking through your records. Your father is a coal miner, your mother died in childbirth. You were raised in Whitechapel, where–unlike other youths who became exemplary criminals before their teens–you were an outstanding student with perfect attendance. At seventeen, you are the youngest man ever be admitted to Guy's Hospital. Tell me, what could be so important that you are willing to toss all that away?"

"Not my choice, sir. My father's wiped out his savings.... He gambles, and he doesn't have another lifetime to save money for my schooling."

"Ah." Darius finally put his chalk down. He looked at Edmund, his eyes softer than usual. "I apologize. I didn't understand your situation. Come, look at something with me."

Edmund joined the professor by the covered corpse. The air smelled of formaldehyde.

Darius grasped the sheet and whipped it away.

An ape stared up at Edmund. Half of its face had been removed, revealing yellowed teeth and a blackened tongue. The fur was orange and ragged. The chest had been marked with X's and dotted lines, awaiting the next lecture. *The circulatory system*, Edmund remembered.

"It cost our hospital a thousand pounds to ship this specimen from New Guinea," Darius said. "Multiply that by the dozens of apes we go through during a semester. That amount would pay your tuition ten times over."

"It would only cost two pounds for a Lancashire pig," Edmund muttered.

"What was that?"

Edmund hesitated. "In biology, I've noted that the pig is our closest physiological relative, despite what the Darwinists say. Perhaps we should be dissecting pigs instead."

Darius' eyes twinkled as he replaced the sheet. "We *should* be dissecting human corpses," he said. "But our government, in all their wisdom, has sanctified rotting bags of meat as unimportant to the advances of science. Tell me, have you heard of body snatching?"

"I haven't, sir."

"A phenomenon in the more lurid newspapers of late. It seems a squadron of enterprising young men have been digging up the recently deceased and selling them to the highest bidder. Collectors have been lining up, despite the illegality of the process. Such a hobby might prove profitable...to a young man down on his luck."

Edmund said nothing.

"Also," Darius continued, "if such a man were to bring bodies here, thereby helping to advance the medical field...perhaps he would find himself picking up some education free of charge." He looked Edmund over. "Hmm. You have a strong build. Good muscle in the arms and chest. Have you considered physical labor after you leave our school, Master Carnaby?"

"Actually, I was thinking of grave digging, sir," Edmund said.

1880

Edmund Carnaby sat in a rocking chair outside a tavern called the Butchered Pig when Collins, Professor Darius' newest assistant, approached him. Five years in the streets had hardened Edmund to a statue in a long black coat and tall hat. His eyes burned with fierce intelligence above a ragged pale face.

"Hello, sir," Collins said, then sniffed at the air.

Edmund held a bottle of ale in one gloved hand and gestured at the street with the other. "I imagine this is what some of my *clients* wake up to–a world of blood and shit. What's the old man got for me, sweetheart?"

Collins cleared his throat and drew himself up to his full five-foot height. "Professor Darius has requested…the…personage of an older male, between seventy and eighty years of age. He specified that the teeth should be as intact as possible, and of course, the fresher the specimen–"

"The higher my payment," Edmund said, swigging from his bottle.

Collins blushed.

"I'll make the appropriate inquiries." All traces of the Cockney accent had vanished, and Edmund now sounded like the fearfully intelligent young man who'd left Guy's Hospital five years prior. "I shall procure a specimen within seventy-two hours. And do tell Darius that I thoroughly enjoyed our conversation on the transfusion of bone marrow. It comes to me every time I dig up a new set of bones."

Collins face screwed up, his eyebrows knitting together. "Professor Darius insists that I refer to you as The Resurrectionist…. Would that–"

Edmund burst into laughter, almost spilling his drink. "That's rich. Yeah, sure…call me that. The Resurrectionist it is."

Collins backed away slowly. He nodded, then turned and ran.

❖

Edmund had sources in the Metropolitan Police, and a young sprat named Wheeler had told him about one Mr. Harrison Blake, found dead in his apartment in Shoreditch the night before, seventy-one years old, killed by a heart attack.

Edmund often hired independent muscle to do the digging, but he didn't anticipate acquiring Blake's corpse would be a problem. As midnight rolled around, Edmund was hard at work in Bunhill Fields, his lantern resting on his pick as he moved soft earth. Fog laced over the ground. The gravestones loomed as he dug deeper, an army of unblinking stone judges catching him in the act.

After an hour of non-stop digging, the satisfying clunk of shovel striking wood echoed from below his feet.

Edmund brushed the remaining soil away, his breath steaming the air, body lathered in sweat. The coffin had a brass nameplate with the letters H C B imprinted on an intricate font. Beneath the initials: SOME BOXES REMAIN UNOPENED.

The message may have once startled Edmund, but he had grown immune to such penny-dreadful philosophies. He traded the shovel for the pick, and minutes later he'd hacked open the coffin lid.

Harrison Blake's face resembled a shrunken head Edmund had once seen, with a lipless mouth and leathery skin. The old man had been buried in a ratty dressing gown, and the mortician hadn't been particular about preservation; pancaked makeup had been smeared around the old man's countenance, calling attention to liver spots, sunken cheeks, and grey complexion.

His hands clasped an object.

Edmund reached down and tugged a box from his grip, letting Blake's rigid hands thump to his hollow chest.

It was heavier than it looked. A different character had been embossed on each side of the hinged lid, resembling the *kanji* handwriting used by the Chinamen Edmund bought opium from. The lettering was bright red, like arterial blood.

Edmund tried the lid, but it wouldn't budge. He turned the box over. A piece of parchment had been pasted to the bottom. I BELONG TO YOU.

❖

"And what exactly is this?" asked Professor Darius.

Edmund grunted and hoisted a suitcase onto the operating table. He raised the lid. Harrison Blake had been bent to fit inside, his heels touching the back of his head.

Darius pried open Blake's mouth. "Hmm. A nonsmoker. His teeth are in good enough order. I'll throw in ten pounds atop your usual fee."

Normally they traded bits of academic rumor and obscure medical facts while Darius retrieved his checkbook. This time, Edmund had raised a different subject. "Collins told me that I'm The Resurrectionist now."

"Seemed fitting, what with all you do." Darius fumbled with the papers on his desk.

A pang of frustration ran through Edmund. "Tell me, sir, what do you make of this?" Edmund presented the box.

Darius examined it, moving it back and forth under the light. "The construction is fairly new," he said. "Not much damage to the exterior. It has been handled with extreme care. The figures on the sides have several characteristics common with the Chinese language but also contain something of the Cyrillic. Linguistics was never my strong suit. Where did you get it?"

"Buried with the specimen. He held it in his hands."

"Well, the elderly do have their eccentricities, which, unfortunately, I now know from experience. Would you like to hold on to this?" Darius offered the box back.

"The madman image is a smokescreen," Edmund said. "I don't keep trophies, but if you manage to get the lid unstuck, I'll take half of whatever you find inside."

"Hell," Darius replied. "After my dental presentation tomorrow, you can have half of Blake's teeth. They'd make a wonderful necklace."

They both laughed.

❖

Professor Darius removed Blake's lips, slicing through them with a scalpel before dropping them into a jar of formaldehyde. He was so engrossed in the process that he had forgotten the box on the table beside him.

It clicked open, the lid rising on silent hinges.

Darius squinted and leaned toward the box.

❖

In his room in Whitechapel, Edmund dreamed.

The box is huge, so big it fills the world, but somehow he is even bigger. It opens like a music box.

God's holy body is stretched out on a slab of black stone. His innards have been removed, labeled, jarred. His left eye is missing, and in the empty socket, Edmund can see God's brain.

God whispers, "It belongs to you now."

❖

After reading the headlines in the morning newspaper, Edmund rushed to Guy's Hospital. Collins sat in Darius' office, cleaning out the desk, packing books and papers into a wooden crate. His eyes were bleary and red.

"What happened?" Edmund asked, storming into the room.

Collins jumped, one hand going to his heart. "What are you doing here? If the Dean sees you—"

"I think our arrangement won't affect the professor's career anymore. What happened to Darius?"

Collins collapsed in a chair and started sobbing. "He worked late last night. No one came in or out. The watchman has already been questioned by the police, so...what happened...the professor must have done to himself."

Edmund resisted the urge to seize Collins by the throat and throttle the life out of him. Instead, he kneeled, took the little fellow's face in his hands, and murmured, "Show me."

Collins explained that the lecture hall had not yet been photographed, nor had the medical examiner come down to look over the body. Two beefy patrolmen stood on either side of the entryway.

Edmund carefully came out of the trapdoor behind the blackboard, sure to not disturb the guards, when the scent hit him—the unique, iron-shaving smell of a body freshly cut open.

Professor Darius lay on the autopsy table, spread-eagled. His face had been carefully peeled away in strips, revealing a manic smile, the raw red tissue striating his skull. His exposed eyeballs stared up at nothing, a fierce, uncompromising blue. A large incision had opened him from sternum to groin, and the spleen, a lung, and most of the small intestine had been piled at his side. Blood splattered the floor around the table in a crazed Rorschach pattern.

On the chalkboard behind the body, the words were written: 'IT BELONGS TO YOU NOW'.

Darius held a scalpel in one palsied hand. In the other, sat the box.

1881

Edmund Carnaby hadn't quite drunk himself to death, as far as the chambermaid could tell, but he was getting there.

He'd been renting the room a long time before she had started working at the Butchered Pig, and it showed. The place was a sty and stank of opium and puke. She kicked old bottles aside and gathered the sheets for laundry.

He might have been handsome once, she mused as she laid fresh sheets on the mattress, *but that time had ended*. Now Edmund had the haunted, harried look of a sleepwalker trapped in a nightmare. He'd inherited some money from an old professor, back from his schooling days, and promptly set about drinking all of it up.

The man himself was out, probably digging up a corpse, and the chambermaid found herself wondering if old Edmund had maybe squirreled some cash away. No sense to the idea; the man rarely bathed and downed gin like it was going to be outlawed. Still, she found herself looking through dresser drawers a scant minute later.

In the bottom, buried under a month's worth of tattered, filthy clothes, she found a box. The symbols carved into the wood reminded her of notes she'd sometimes carried back and forth between the Chinese sailors for a few extra shillings.

She had just decided to take the box to market when the lid clicked open.

❖

Edmund trudged up the stairs, disappointed that he hadn't found a drink that would kill him.

He'd hated every bloody damn second of life since the night he'd dug up the box. By all rights, he should've starved to death in a gutter. He could've shot himself months ago...or turned to the noose or a bottle marked with a skull and crossbones. But he hadn't, and hated himself.

All because of the box. He had never found a way to open it. The damn thing was just wood. It should've splintered the night he'd smashed it with a crowbar or when he fired a bullet at it one fine drunken evening. Nothing. Not even a chip.

If only Darius had told him how to open it, then perhaps Edmund might not have thought about the box morning, day, and night.

He climbed the last steps, turned the corner...and froze.

His room door was ajar.

He burst through. The chambermaid stood with her back to him, humming. A distant part of his brain recognized Tchaikovsky. *Where the hell would she have heard that?*

The maid held one hand up to her face. The other gripped the opened box.

Edmund forced himself to remain still and said, "I don't mind you being in my room, honestly, but I need you to hand me that box, right... now."

She continued humming as she turned. Edmund gasped. The chambermaid had stitched her eyelids shut. The needle still hung from her left eyelid on a length of black thread, swinging back and forth.

"I don't need to see anymore," she said, smiling. "The inside, I saw...I saw...."

"What?" Edmund growled, taking one step forward. "What did you see? What was inside?"

She suddenly leaped backward, crashing through the window. Edmund grabbed for her and tore a piece of her white apron, which fluttered from his hand like a flag of surrender.

The chambermaid lay still in the street, neck crooked, blood in her hair, and when Edmund reached the ground, a crowd had gathered. No one seemed to notice him bend over the body and grab the box before vanishing into the crowd.

1883

Edmund Carnaby had quickly become one of the most feared professors at Guy's Hospital.

His knowledge of anatomy was unparalleled. His sharp tongue was the subject of myth. His endless fascination with the limits of the human bodies was spoke of in awed whispers.

Still, other rumors followed him through the halls–stories of a past in debauchery and grave robbing; lurid experiments involving physics; dissections late at night in the vivisectorium.

No one bothered talking to the school's custodial staff, a crew of eighteen wizened matrons who scrubbed blood off the floor on their hands and knees. Edmund paid them to assist with his experiments, nothing too bizarre or even interesting. He had them play with a little wooden box and patiently waited for something to happen.

1888

Edmund Carnaby screamed from the shadows.

He's not paying enough. Not for this bollocks. Not by a long shot, the footman thought as he ran through Leicester Square. Somewhere nearby, a dog barked, and the footman almost yelped in response. His footsteps echoed off the cobblestones. *Filthy business. First the other two whores, and now two in one night....*

The footman found Edmund lying on the ground, sobbing, only recognizable by his hair: stark white, thinning far too early for a man of his years, and skeletal claws beating at the ground.

"I almost saw it," Edmund said, choking on his words.

"We got to get moving, guv'nor," the footman said, looking around. "They'll 'ave 'eard the noise, and Old Bill might be on 'is way already. We 'ave to go!"

The footman yanked Edmund to his feet, then noticed a prostitute, her legs clad in torn stockings, one shoe pulled partway off. Blood filled the gaps between the cobblestones.

"I gave it to her," Edmund gibbered.

The footman raised his hands to his mouth. "You don't pay me 'nough to get caught up in this, Carnaby," he told Edmund, directing him to his carriage.

Edmund continued raving. "She had the box…and then she tried to steal it. I heard it click open, do you understand? *The box opened!*"

1900

Edmund Carnaby had found the Shanghai summer to be hotter than Hell.

The room surrounding him was paneled with bamboo and cherry wood, the air sweetened with opium smoke. Businessmen lay on silk couches, smoking the pipe and chasing the dragon, each attended by lovely young Chinese girls, hair blacker than sin, some clothed in iridescent kimonos, some naked.

The sorceress sat atop a throne, mahogany skinned and tattooed with hundreds of *kanji* symbols. Her hair was tied back with a leather thong, and her nails were filed to killing points.

Long strips of flesh had been torn from Edmund's back, revealing the red muscle beneath. His fingernails were gone. His chest bore several brands, still smelling of cooked pork. Before him, marked with his own bloody fingerprints, lay the box.

Edmund licked his swollen lips and spoke in Mandarin, the language alien and uncomfortable on his tongue. "Please. I've heard tales about you, my lady. In the slums and docks they whisper of your abilities. To find lost things. To reveal the invisible…to open that which was not meant to open."

The sorceress seemed to consider him with her dark eyes, her lips twisting in cruel amusement. She whispered something, and Edmund thought the voice came from within his own head. *"You have come a long way, Westerner. So few survive my followers. Your resolve is strong, though your body is failing."*

"I've done…terrible things over the years. I've studied the human anatomy in all its glory, mastering the effects of pain and ecstasy. I have learned of quantum physics, and cryptozoology, and arts so black they tarnished my soul. I've climbed Nepali mountains and spoken words that can stop a man's heart. But…I don't know what's inside."

Edmund caressed the box lovingly.

"It's always been there," he continued, "hiding its secret from me. This box has caused the deaths of sixty-six men and women over the course of my life. I'm old. I'm tired. But still I must know."

The sorceress stood. A hush fell over the opium den as she circled the box, her tattooed legs flexing. She bent and touched it with one long finger. Her tongue flicked out, caressing the bloody wood. She took Edmund's face in her hands and kissed him slowly.

"I cannot tell you," she said. *"That is, I cannot tell you…what. However, I can tell you when."*

Edmund listened.

1933

Edmund Carnaby lay in a bed he hadn't left for thirty-three years.

The room was spacious, every shelf and table occupied by medicine bottles, suspensions, and pill jars. The air smelled of alcohol, human sickness, and spoiled meat.

He lay on his side, his back a mass of raw bedsores. It didn't matter how often the nurses turned him. His hair was gone, as well as his teeth. The rot he'd contracted in Shanghai had run its course, and the doctors had amputated both of his feet and his left arm to the elbow. Three decades earlier, they'd told him he wasn't expected to live.

Edmund smiled, his skin stretched taut and yellowed. He felt the arrhythmia in his chest—the icy pain of a heart finally giving up.

He stretched, reaching for it, always on the nightstand, never out of his sight. His love. His only reason for being.

The Resurrectionist's long nails touched the box…and the lid clicked open. ◆

Jack Maddox is the author of The Dog: Necrophagus, *and his stories have appeared in* Splatterlands, Dark Moon Digest, *and* The Last Diner. *He likes clockwork, insects, and sculpting evil heads from clay.*

Artwork: Chris L. Burke

THE STEEPLECHASE FLOURISH

PATRICK MEEGAN

"Can't I stay up a little longer to watch?"

Mark frowned at the boy. "Sorry, Andrew, time for sleep."

"Aww." Andrew turned from the bedroom window and climbed into bed, pushing aside the top sheet, which bore the emblems of all the Major League Baseball teams. "But it's summer, Dad."

Mark paused at the window as a streak of light flashed across the night sky, then went to his son's bedside. "That may mean sleeping late for you, but I still have to go to work tomorrow. If I have to go to bed, so do you." He tousled Andrew's hair.

"That's not fair."

Mark pulled the covers up over his son. "I agree. Hmm. Well, I guess as soon as you finish school, you can go to work and I'll stay home. Deal?"

Andrew crossed his arms. "Dad, I'm only starting second grade."

"Really? You seem much older."

Andrew laughed.

Mark finished tucking him in and began picking up the stuffed animals and toys scattering across the bed. "Which one?"

Andrew pointed to a floppy sheepdog.

"Ahh, Rufus. Our faithful watchdog." He handed the stuffed dog to Andrew.

Squeezing Rufus tight, Andrew asked, "Will we be able to see the shooting stars again tomorrow night?"

Mark picked up the rest of the toys and went to a chair by the window. "Not just tomorrow but for at least another week. Maybe this weekend, we can get up early to see them at their peak." He dumped the toys onto the chair. A wayward clown doll fell to the floor.

"Dennis Dunham says that shooting stars are angels."

"Well, I bet your friend heard that from his grandparents." Mark bent to retrieve the colorful clown. "Long ago, people would explain things they didn't understand as an act of God or angels." He held up the clown doll, its blue glass eyes staring out from a white face, its nose a bright red bulb. "Those stories became folklore...superstitions." He touched one of the green pom-poms that ran down the front of the ruffled green and white costume. "I remember my grandfather telling me that shooting stars were the souls of bad people sent back down to earth so they could redeem themselves. Sort of a second chance."

Andrew's eyes widened. "Is that true?"

❖

Roland–The Magnificent–stood alone on the moonlit beach, his high-gloss Oxford shoes sinking into the shore just above the surf line. Sand dusted his tuxedo's trousers. He idly rolled a half dollar coin across his knuckles. On every other pass his hand went palm up in a flourish, and the coin vanished, reappearing in his other hand. He had been doing this for hours: standing in the sand, looking up at the night sky, contemplating the shooting stars. Wondering what each one had done. Why, like him, they had been sent back down to earth, instead of going on into the light.

A gravelly voice came from behind him. "Hello, Dummy."

The others had begun to arrive, as they always did. Returning to the deserted stretch of beach before sunrise. Roland wasn't even sure if the place was real or somewhere in between worlds, a way station where they gathered again before returning to their punishment. He faced the new arrival. "Hello, Red."

❖

Mark dropped the clown onto the chair with the rest of the toys and went to sit on the edge of Andrew's bed. "Of course it's not true. Stories like that continue because people like fantastic stories more than the truth." Mark pushed the boy's fair hair from his eyes. "Shooting stars are just debris falling off the tail of a passing comet. Ice and rocks. Nothing but space dust."

"That's boring."

Mark chuckled. "Exactly."

❖

Red wore ragged clothes with exaggerated tears at the cuffs of his dark pants and large patches on his mismatched coat. Beneath his worn derby, his face was unshaven, circles of white greasepaint were smeared around his eyes and mouth, and the end of his nose shined a bright red: the Hobo Clown.

Roland held up his coin. "If, by dummy, you mean a ventriloquist's mannequin, I'm not." He waved his hands and the coin disappeared. "I found a child who still appreciates magic."

Red adjusted the frayed rope holding his pants up. "Probably turn out to be a dipshit, like you."

Roland sighed, wiping at the grains of sand that clung to his sleeves. The coin reappeared and tumbled across his knuckles.

It was how the group always appeared: clowns, magicians, children's playthings. Dolls. They were cast from the light as spirits; ghosts returning to the world where they didn't really exist, where they were only dreams. Or more accurately, nightmares.

❖

Mark pointed at the bedside lamp. "On or off?"

Andrew crinkled his nose. "Off."

"All right." Mark turned the light off and walked through the dark room. From the chair, the limp clown's blue eyes watched Mark pause at the bedroom door.

"Night, Dad."

"Goodnight, pal." Mark closed the door.

The green and white clown doll sat up straight and turned its head to the boy.

❖

Red dragged a dirty sleeve across his nose, leaving a streak of mucus and red paint. "I scared a shitload of 'em tonight. Twenty, maybe twenty-five. Scared the hell out of these twins, two flouncing little shits. They'll be afraid to go to sleep for years." He laughed, low, dark. "How many you do?"

Roland matched his stare. "I did enough." The coin kept rolling.

"How many?"

The coin disappeared. "Enough."

Red cocked his head. "Horse shit." He took a step toward the magician. "You didn't even do one, did you?"

Roland rolled his eyes.

"What the fuck! You didn't even work one kid?" Red jabbed at Roland as he spoke. "We get one night to make them sorry. One night to torment the innocent." He balled his fists and dropped them to his sides. "You came right here, didn't you?" His mouth hung open as he paused. "So, what did you do all night, Magic Man? Make things disappear up your ass?"

From behind Red came a burst of high-pitched, lunatic laughter. A blubbery clown appeared, wearing a costume of white satin. The outfit shimmered as his body quaked, a cackle erupting from a circular face that choked from the folds of a ruffled collar. White paint covered his face, fine black lines riding high above his eyes in gleeful arcs. A pointed white hat sat atop his head. Blood splattered the front of his costume. "Up his ass! Hehehehee!"

Red continued to stare at Roland. "Pucinello's back. I bet he did the right thing. He's probably covered in blood."

Roland gave a weak smile to acknowledge the gore-covered clown. "Of course he is."

Pucinello's smile forced folds of flesh up around his eyes. "I ate their pets!" Dark stains covered his teeth.

Roland nodded. "Of course you did." He turned back to Red. "Why don't you go compare notes with him?"

"I don't have to. He's with us. He knows his place. Pooch does the right thing." Red turned and walked to Pucinello. "I know you did good tonight, didn't you."

The white nightmare clasped his bloodied gloves together at his chest, hopping from foot to foot. "Ohhh yes, yes, yes! Hehehe! I scared them all so much, Red! I jumped up in their beds! I put snakes on their heads! They cried out in fear! But...no one could hear! Hehehehe! Then I caught them in nets and…." He stopped dancing. "Do you know what I did then, Red?"

"What did you do, Poochy?"

"I ate their pets! Heheheeee!" He clapped his hands and ran in small circles, sand flying from his oversized shoes. "Heeeheeee!"

Red applauded and barked out his own harsh laughter. "You see, Magic Man! It's easy. We may not get to stay here long but we sure can scar some kiddies for life!"

Roland turned his back on them and faced the ocean. He stared out beyond the rolling tide to the horizon, the place where the sea meets the sky.

The Ballerina appeared beside him, her feet planted in the sand in ballet third position. One hand slid around Roland's back to rest upon his shoulder, the other arched up above her. The layered netting of her tutu played against his leg. She brought the scent of lavender. Her lips moved close to his ear, "You'll never get to see the sunrise, you know."

Roland continued looking across the ocean. "Always the beautiful ballerina."

"Yes," she whispered, sibilant steam.

"But not a kind lover."

"No." She performed a slow pirouette, ending in first position. "Why have you drawn away from us, Roland? What has happened to make you feel apart?"

Roland faced her but did not meet her eyes. "Do you still believe as they do?" He nodded toward the cackling clowns. "That each time we are sent away, the only answer is to make others suffer?"

"Yes, Roland. We are the darkness to the light."

"And you? Tonight? Did you ruin the lives of the innocent?"

"Oh yes." She raised one leg straight into the air. "I went to them in their dreams as they lay beside their women, their true loves." Her hands reached up to her ankle. "I enchanted them and they came to me." She ran her fingertips down her leg in a slow caress, stopping at the top of her thigh. "And then they loved me." She closed her eyes and moved one hand beneath the folds of her tutu and sighed. After lowering her leg, her hands came up above her head. "The seed of infidelity grows inside them now. It will tear them from their vows." She returned again to the first position, facing Roland, her smile sultry. "Oh, the tears that will be shed for their wandering lust."

Roland saw that she held no compassion for those she cursed.

"They don't deserve that." He pulled back from her. "I don't belong here."

"Don't you?" She arched an eyebrow. "Each time we go up to the light, we are all cast back down here, judged unworthy. We get one night to enjoy being evil before we are returned to the darkness. You belong with us Roland. You've just lost your way."

"Why do we go up at all then? And all this?" He pointed in the direction of the clowns. "We'll never move on acting like this." He paused. "I'll forever be teased by the light, only to meet back here with them… and you."

Her smile broke, and her eyes darkened. "You're no better."

He was not moved by her anger. "Maybe we all are."

Red's voice rang harsh, "Hello, Daniella!"

Her eyes burned into Roland a moment longer before she turned from him and went to the others. "Hello, Red."

She put a hand on Pucinello's shimmering white sleeve, resting it just above the splatter leading from his bloodied gloves. "Pucinello, you look so handsome."

He brought his hand to his face and tittered.

Red grabbed Daniella's arm and pulled her toward him. "Why do you talk to *him*?"

"He's one of us, Red."

"He thinks he's *better* than us. He's gonna make us all look bad by not doing his part."

She looked back at Roland. "Give him time. Don't forget how wicked he once was."

Red snorted.

"Or, do you just want us all to turn on him so you can move closer to leading our little family?"

Red let go of her arm. "No one leads here."

The ballerina glanced around. "True," she said, turning back to Red. "Is Cesar not here yet?"

"Ho! Ho! Ho! Hate to be late, but I did bring a gift!"

Pucinello turned to the voice and his face ballooned into an excited smile, his hands flew to his chest, clapping.

Cesar.

His costume was green and white satin, large green pom-poms ran down the center like, giant green shoes slapping the sand. His white face gleamed like porcelain, the lower half painted red in an exaggerated smile, a halo of green hair shooting out wildly around his head.

Even from afar, Roland saw his blue eyes sparkling. He dragged a sack, leaving a smooth path in the sand. "I got tired of going back empty-handed." He swung the bulky load in front of him, watching it sink into the beach. A small cry came from inside. He held the edges, the colorful bag decorated with the emblems of Major League Baseball teams. "I think it's time we started playing in the big leagues!"

The others gathered around the squirming sack. Daniella crouched before the bundle and poked it. The contents whimpered and flinched at her touch. She pulled her hand away and turned to Cesar; her voice held a touch of awe. "You've taken one."

Pucinello leaned toward the sack. His hands formed a steeple, fingers tapping each other, as if praying. "Is it a dog? A cat?" He looked to Cesar. "May I eat it?"

"No, Pucinello. This is so much better. "

Pucinello's fingers stopped tapping.

Cesar smiled. "I've taken a *child.*"

Pucinello bolted upright, his fingers clasped each other. He spun to Daniella, then to Red, and back to Cesar.

Roland moved closer to them and looked down at the bundle. "No."

Red turned toward him, sneering.

Roland paid him no mind. Time after time he had been cast back down to earth. He and the others had one night which they used to stalk the earth as specters, to meddle in the minds of men and act as demons. A night to vent their anger on the best of them, torment them. But never had they dared to touch one, much less take one. He faced Cesar. "This isn't right! We can't do this!"

Red kicked sand at him. "Shut up, Roland!" He paused, then turned back to Cesar, scratching absently at the back of his hand. "We can do this…right?"

Cesar's eyes glinted. "What's going to happen? We get sent back to the darkness?"

The others joined him in laughing. Roland remained quiet, stepping away from them.

Cesar encouraged the excitement of the others as he hollered over their laughter. "I'm not gonna come down here anymore just to raise a little hell! I'm gonna start dragging some of these sheep back with me!"

The others roared. Pucinello clapped and ran in small circles.

Cesar crouched down over the bundled sheet, adjusting the loose ends. "Come and see." He held out the edges and placed a finger over his lips.

Pucinello and Red each gripped the sheet, standing close around the quivering sack. Daniella leaned in, too.

Cesar whispered, choking back his own laughter. "Let's introduce ourselves." Cesar looked up at them. "3…2…1…." They yanked the sheet open and screamed, their faces pressed together in a crazed mass of greasepaint and horror.

Inside curled a little boy. His eyes shot wide in terror, and he screamed.

They closed the sack and laughed riotously. The sheet rippled and snapped as the boy thrashed inside. Cesar twisted the edges, tightening the bundle again. The group took turns jabbing at the squirming boy, howling with glee.

Roland squeezed his coin, watching as they screamed in delight, encouraging each other, celebrating in depravity.

Cesar finished tying a knot and dropped the twisted ends atop the bundled child and approached Roland. "I can't believe you manage to find magicians anymore." Roland offered a weak smile. Cesar sighed. "Why aren't you with us on this?"

"This?" Roland raised a hand toward the others. "This is no good, Cesar. We're getting worse."

"Good? Worse? We're bad, Roland. That's why we're here. That's why we're made to suffer the dark place." He ran a hand across the bald part of his head. "I'm done coming here every time they cut us loose just to be a nightmare for a few people." He waved his hand toward the others. "Look at us. We're not even allowed to be real. Dolls! We're nothing but scary stories to them, Roland…ghosts."

"Pucinello eats their pets, Cesar."

"And what happens?" Cesar tapped his foot, waiting for an answer. "In the morning Mommy holds her whimpering simp." He pitched his voice to a feminine tone. "'It's okay, baby. Fluffy must have gone out the open window. He'll be back.'" He lifted his hands to his face, raising his voice higher. "'But the clown, Mommy. The clown….'" He lowered his hands. "'Just a bad dream, dear, that's all…just bad dreams.'"

Roland looked to the ground. "Maybe we're meant to be something else."

Cesar stepped closer to Roland. "That's right. That's why I'm done with bad dreams. If I'm not good enough for the light then I'll show them *real* bad."

Roland shook his head. "No. I don't believe it anymore. I'm not evil, not like this."

Cesar laughed. "Ho, ho! My friend, the things you did in life? They sounded pretty bad to me."

Roland spoke slowly, thinking. "I did bad things. But I'm not that person anymore. Not at heart. If I was, I wouldn't question myself, wouldn't have regrets." He looked to the others and back to Cesar. "All of us here, we do these terrible things out of anger. Don't you feel doubt though?"

Cesar's eyes narrowed. "Don't start preaching about right and wrong now. It's too late." He reached into his costume and retrieved a stone the color and size of a lemon: brimstone. "The night is over, and we all still have these. You know where they're going to take us? Back to the cold darkness where we'll suffer for a lifetime, and when we get a chance at going up to the light, what will happen? We'll get cast right back down again." He dropped the hand with the stone to his side. "No one cares about us, Roland. No one is ever going to give us a chance."

Roland glanced at the bundled sheet in the sand.

"This is what they get, Roland. They deserve it. That stone of yours? Is it getting warm?" Roland ignored him. "Yeah, it is. You're with us because you're no good. None of us are, so stop thinking you're somehow better. Let that go and be what you're supposed to. Be who you really are." Cesar's voice deepened. "The sun is coming. We need to be together now so we can bring our prize back with us." He gripped Roland's shoulder, "Do the right thing, Roland."

Roland slipped a hand inside his jacket, feeling the warmth of his own yellow stone.

Cesar walked past the others. "Follow me; we need to find a good spot."

The others exchanged glances and fell into step behind him. Roland followed, though he kept his distance.

"It needs to be just right." Cesar walked slowly down the beach, stopping occasionally to shift the sand with an oversized shoe. "It needs to be perfect." He stopped and glanced all around. "This is it." He turned to the others. "We'll place our stones in a circle and put the boy in the center. That should bring him with us when we're taken back."

The others spread out, each producing their own stone. They set them in the sand, forming four points.

Roland stepped between the two and hefted the bundled sheet into the center.

Cesar smiled. "Welcome back." He looked down to the sheet-covered mound then back to Roland. "Take out your stone, my friend. Close the circle."

Roland took out his yellow stone. He held it before him, and as the distant horizon line burned from the approaching sun, the stone began to smoke. He dropped it to the sand and stepped back. All five stones smoldered, their rough edges becoming smooth as they began to melt.

The sun boiled over the horizon, and the stones popped as blue flames burst from them. White-hot centers illuminated the five faces gathered around the bundle. The first light of day raced across the water and touched the group. Blue flames arced out from four of the stones, licking and then engulfing the costumed spirits. Roland remained outside of the fire, touched only by the light of dawn. His own stone sputtered blue arcs of flame that fell short of him.

Searing flames consumed the others, and they screamed as their skin puckered and burned.

Red raised a blazing arm and pointed at Roland. "What's this? What's going on?"

Cesar's face blackened and his lips burned away, his teeth and jaw glistening. "No! You're one of us!" His eyes fell to the bundled sheet, the blue flames arcing around it. "What have you done?" He reached for the mounded sheet, but his feet remained in the sand. The flames roared in a white blaze.

Roland looked down at his stone, the flames still sputtering weakly as it melted into the sand. He took a tentative step over it and entered the circle.

Red screamed, "You're coming with us!" He reached for Roland. His features became a blur of white fire.

Roland stepped through the blue flames that surrounded the bundle and grabbed it with both hands. He pulled the sheet away in a stageworthy reveal. All that lay in the sand was a bundle of driftwood and brush.

Pucinello clapped vigorously as he melted into the sand.

Daniella wrapped her arms around herself as if hugging the fire. "Roland, do you think we can be better?"

Roland watched the fire devour her. "Yes."

The Ballerina folded in half, consumed by flames, and dissolved into the beach.

Red and Cesar collapsed into heaps of fire. Roland watched them burn until all that was left was blackened sand.

❖

Roland–The Magnificent–stood alone on the brightening beach, the sun turning the sky orange. The warmth of the sun engulfed him and he smiled. The sheet with the baseball emblems hung from his hand. He spoke over his shoulder, "You can come out now." He turned toward the dunes and scrub brush.

A small face peeked out from behind a tangle of driftwood.

Roland nodded and waved at the boy. "It's okay. They're gone." He turned back to the blackened sand and the one remaining yellow stone. His stone. Low blue flames still danced across its bubbling surface. He watched as a final burst of weak blue fire reached out to him before seeping into the sand, leaving a final black mark.

The boy appeared by his side, his expression blank. Roland tried to wrap the sheet around him, but he flinched away, bringing his hands up and slamming his eyes closed.

Roland knelt in the sand. "I'm sorry." He touched the boy's shoulder. "Forgive me."

The boy opened his eyes. His voice came out high and frightened, "Where'd they go?"

"To another place. A dark place, far away."

"Is it where they come from?"

"No." Roland looked at the horizon. "It's not." His voice fell to a whisper as he squinted in the light, "They've forgotten where they come from. What's your name?"

"I want to go home."

"Yes, I can take you home." Roland held his hand and the coin appeared. "Please tell me your name. I want to remember you. You are the one who has shown me *my* way home."

The boy sniffled. "Andrew."

"Andrew.... Thank you." Roland held out his hand and rolled the coin back and forth across his knuckles. It glinted in the sunlight as it flipped in a smooth rhythm. "Watch the coin, Andrew."

The boy's eyes followed. His features softened and his shoulders slumped as the coin rolled back and forth, back and forth.

"It's time to remember what's real. Remember your home, remember your bed. Remember what was real before you fell asleep. All of the things that happened after that...the bad clowns, the beach, they were all just nightmares. Bad things that happened but none of it was true. That place where you live with your family. That place is made from love. That's what is real. Remember what that feels like. Remember how happy you are each day. That's what is real."

The boy's eyes fluttered.

"Now sleep, Andrew." Roland snapped his fingers and the boy fell into his arms. Roland wrapped him in the bedsheet and sat in the sand to face the rising sun, smiling as the warm light embraced him. ◆

Patrick Meegan lives in Orange County, New York. His work has appeared in the anthologies: 100 Doors to Madness *and* Twisted Boulevard. *He does not like the beach.*

Artwork: Luke Spooner

GILLIAN

KRISTOPHER MALLORY

Liquid death boiled as the candle flame scorched the bottom of a silver spoon. Using a hypodermic needle, the Alchemist loaded the poisonous brew into a syringe, leaving the impurities caught in a tiny ball of cotton. A black sweatshirt hung loosely off his body like a robe, the hood casting his sallow face in shadow. He twirled the needle in a bony hand, then poised the sharp tip over the track-marked arm of his most loyal customer.

Jackson bit down on the end of the tourniquet tied around his bicep and pulled it tight. Like magic, the outline of thick veins protruded at the crook of his arm, each bulge scarred from abuse and infection. He nodded to the Alchemist, and the needle penetrated his skin.

Taking in a sharp breath, his jaw released the band, and the familiar burn began its journey. A soft moan reminded him that Gillian sat beside him. She reached out and stroked his shaved head, a syringe still stuck in her flesh, dangling like jewelry. Jackson turned to embrace her, but the first wave of the drug hit hard and sudden. A tsunami of pleasure swept him into the waiting arms of oblivion.

❖

The drug-induced dream played like a movie. Scenes flashed by as Jackson floated above himself, a mere spectator to the glimmer of nightmarish events.

FLASH

Gillian was on top of him. She kissed his neck and tore at his clothing. Her body gyrated and thrusted, while the Alchemist and several other afflicted souls sat around the drug house. The dead-eyed fiends groped at the two lovers, drool stretching from scab-covered lips.

FLASH

They walked together through the warm summer night, peering into parked vehicles as they went. Gillian stopped. She placed her finger to his lips. The wind blew back her long, auburn hair, revealing a mischievous grin as she threw a stone through the side window of a caravan.

Jackson dove in, slicing his already scarred arms on the shattered glass. He rifled through the center console. Then Gillian tugged at his waist, cursing.

The car alarm had sent a man rushing like a minotaur from a nearby townhome. Jackson tried to brandish his weapon as a warning, though he had reacted too slowly—a fist landed a crushing blow against his face, knocking him aside.

Gillian turned to run but the man caught her by the dress, ripping it as he pulled her closer. His hands wrapped around her neck. Her complexion turned purple, tongue protruding from her gaping, soundless mouth. She clawed at the hands killing her.

Knife in hand, Jackson rushed the man from behind.

FLASH

The spotlight of a circling helicopter swept the streets and alleys as sirens drew nearer. Out of breath, Jackson and Gillian ran into the front yard of a small cottage—his grandmother's house. He hid behind the bushes below a bedroom window. Sweat poured down his face as he used a blood-covered blade to pry out a familiar pane of glass.

As a teenager he had done that very same thing a hundred times. Nana had forbidden him to see Gillian, so sneaking out was the only way they could spend time together.

Red and blue lights illuminated the block as a police cruiser turned the corner. Gillian ducked behind Nana's thick lilacs. Jackson took a chance and climbed up the stucco. He tumbled through the window into his childhood bedroom. Then he quickly reached down and took Gillian's hand, pulling her up the wall just as the spotlight from the cruiser scanned the house.

They held their breath. Jackson wondered what prison would be like. He imagined officers kicking down his grandmother's door, guns drawn. They would rip Gillian from his arms and carry him away in cuffs. The blood on his hands was proof enough. Jackson couldn't handle the thought of never seeing Gillian again. Maybe the cops would shoot them both dead? At least then they would still be together.

The purr of the engine faded as the police continued their search. Gillian let out a relieved sigh, and Jackson pulled her close, breathing in her scent. His heart rate slowed as the high tapered.

As long as she is mine, everything will be all right, he thought.

He found comfort in the sound of her steady breathing and slipped into the waiting darkness. Though he slept, part of him felt Gillian's warmth fade in the night.

Shortly thereafter, the screaming began.

❖

Jackson was startled from a bad dream by Gillian kicking him in the ribs. In the nightmare, Nana had been calling for him, and though he'd wanted to go to her, his body had refused to obey.

Gillian kicked him again. He swatted her away, wanting to slip back to sleep, but his arms were too weak to defend.

He mumbled, "Let me be."

"Jack, get up. We have to go. We're in real trouble, baby."

"I'm tired."

Voice trembling, Gillian said, "This is bad. This is really, really bad."

Lifting his head from the floor, a sliver of sunlight shining through the crack in the curtains triggered an unbearable pounding in Jackson's skull. The left side of his face stung from temple to chin. His entire body throbbed. Worse, the sickness churned the rotting contents of his stomach. He needed a bump more than he had ever needed anything in his life. Confused, he glanced around the room at various baseball trophies and first place blue ribbons, all of which had his name inscribed in gold leaf.

His eyes went wide. "How did we get to Nana's?"

Gillian sighed and fell backward on the bed like a rag doll. She shook her head.

Flashes from the previous night came crashing back. *No,* Jackson thought, noticing the dried red stains on his hands.

"Gill…Gill, you all right?" He rolled onto his knees and brushed her hair from her pale face.

Voice barely audible, she said, "Dead."

"It was self-defense. That guy was going to kill you."

Jackson thought about the beast that had attacked them. He strained to remember what happened, but a thick fog covered his memories. All he recalled was slashing and stabbing like a madman, doing everything in his power to protect Gillian.

"Besides," he added, "we don't know for sure that he's dead."

"Not him," Gillian said, her eyes dark and unsettling. "While you slept, I killed the thing pretending to be your grandmother."

Jackson swallowed hard. "What?"

Gillian stared at him.

The weight of her words felt too real, too dark to be a ruse. Nana couldn't hear very well. She wouldn't have known someone had broken into the house unless one of them had left the room during the night.

Gillian's hands trembled, and her blue sundress was damp with sweat and blood.

"Show me," he said, doing his best to hold back the sickness screaming to be free of his throat.

"We should leave, baby."

"We will. But first I need to see for myself. I hope you just had a nightmare, too."

Gillian nodded. She stood, and led him from the safety of his childhood treasures.

Splintered wood—what was left of the coffee table—was strewn about the living room. The sofa and recliners were overturned. The old television had been smashed, a phantom image still rolling underneath the static. The entire room, even the ceiling, was speckled red.

"I saw her for what she was…I used your knife…but she didn't die easily," Gillian said.

In a state of shocked disbelief, Jackson ignored her and followed a trail of gore to the basement door. The steps descended into pitch black. He tried the light switch, clicking it off and on, but the darkness simply laughed at him.

A ghostly cry echoed from the grim depths. *"Please, help Nana, Jackie! Help me, I'm diiieeennng."*

Jackson blinked at the reaching shadows. "What do you mean *she didn't die easily?* Gill, what did you do?"

Nana's voice wasn't real. Hallucinations were common with his mix of narcotics, but this all felt different, like a fading dream trying to come back. He pinched himself hard enough to prove he wasn't still dreaming.

Gillian crept up behind him with a flashlight and shined it down the stairwell. "Look," she said.

At the bottom, a chalky white foot with long, yellow nails rested in a pool of congealed blood. Jackson thought he saw the dead toes twitch. He tried to convince himself it was just a trick of the light.

"You've seen them, Jack," Gillian said. "When death courses through your veins, the truth becomes clear. But she was different. Something was wrong with her. It wasn't your grandmother."

The hair raised on his arms. Jackson couldn't deny that he knew what she meant. Sometimes people are more than they appear. A picture of the Alchemist formed in his mind. He shook the thought away, then slowly descended the creaking stairs.

Nothing in his life as a degenerate drug addict had prepared him for the carnage in the basement.

"Oh, Christ," he said.

The woman who raised him lay desecrated in a pool of black gel. The skin of her arms and legs had been sliced open, exposing the muscle and tendons beneath. She had been scalped. The white of the skull perfectly matched the white of her rolled back eyes. Her neck had been slashed open, and her tongue had been pulled through the wound in a grotesquely comical manner. "She didn't die easily, Gillian? You fucking *flayed* her!"

"A monster wore her skin. I swear. Baby, let's…let's take the rest of the jewelry and go. No one knows we were here."

Gillian dangled a necklace in front of the flashlight. Clasped to the thin, silver chain, was a heart-shaped pendant, adorned with a translucent black diamond. The light refracting through the gemstone created nightmarish shadow creatures that danced along the walls of the stairway.

"I'm keeping this one," she continued. "It's special. You can pawn the rest."

She turned away, leaving Jackson alone in the dark.

"I'm sorry, Nana. Gillian didn't mean to hurt you. It was the dope," he cried to the dissected corpse. "Please forgive us."

Eyes adjusting to the darkness, Jackson stared at the mangled body. Her wrinkled face reminded him that she had lived a long life. He wasn't sure how old Nana had been, certainly over ninety, maybe over a hundred.

He remembered the day they'd met. Jackson was seven, and Nana had stood next to him at his mother's freshly dug grave. Even then she had seemed ancient.

"You shall come live with me, Jackie," she had said. "I raised your mother and your mother's mother. I taught them to take proper care of their bodies but silly children always refuse to listen." Tears welled at the edge of her eyes but her voice grew furious. "Opium! A ridiculous way to die! Things will be different this time—yes, very different! Now, come along, child." Nana had grabbed his hand and pulled him away from the casket.

She had worn that heart-shaped diamond pendant. In fact, he had never seen her without it around her neck. Now her neck was practically gone.

Nana deserved better. But what could be done? She was dead, and he believed it was all his fault.

"I'm sorry." Jackson turned away and raced up the stairs after Gillian.

Room by room, they tore through bookshelves and drawers looking for anything of value.

Jackson found a revolver under Nana's mattress. He flicked open the cylinder. It was loaded. After slapping it closed again, he stuffed it into his jeans.

Gillian emptied the jewelry boxes into a duffle bag. It would be enough to keep them high for a very, very long time.

Will it be enough to make us forget what we've done? Jackson wondered.

"One more thing, then we can go," Gillian said, walking into the kitchen.

Jackson followed. After extinguishing the stove's pilot light, she turned on all the burners. The rancid smell of natural gas quickly drove them from the house.

❖

Gillian sought refuge at the only place they were welcome. The Alchemist allowed them to hide out in the condemned house and kept them supplied with as many drugs as they could handle, providing they forked over cash, of course.

Jackson pawned all the stolen goods, save for the necklace and gun. Money wasn't a problem, but the explosion in the suburbs was all over the news. To his relief, the newscasters made no mention of the mutilated old woman the police had surely found in the basement. He hoped the whole thing would be forgotten in a few days.

The Alchemist claimed the police had listed Jackson as a person of interest, that his face was plastered on fliers stapled to telephone poles around the city.

Worried one of their fiends would give him up, Jackson begged Gillian to skip town, perhaps find a place to hide in the forest.

Pressing another needle into her arm, she said, "Where would we go, baby? We don't know how to survive outside of the city. Besides, we've got to be close to our medicine. This is the best place for us. Unless the cops tack on a reward, we'll be safe here."

She nodded out before Jackson could protest. Safe wasn't a term he would use to describe the den of horrors in which they were trapped. Addicts came and went all hours of the night, most too strung out to know what was going on, yet still capable of spilling someone's guts if it meant them securing another fix.

The Alchemist couldn't be trusted either. Jackson had caught him greedily eyeing the necklace that Gillian refused to take off.

Gillian was the worst of them all. She was different somehow, completely despondent most of the time. After spiking a vein, she would sit on the floor, staring at the rats crawling around the discarded containers of rotten food while other beasts with beady, red eyes stared back from the holes in the walls. For hours, she mumbled to herself, slowly rocking back and forth.

Jackson wanted to escape the trauma of that night, but not through the needle. Dope was like quicksand though, and Gillian seemed as if she preferred to sink.

He tried to keep his head clear, and discovered how difficult it was to fight the sickness. He might have found the strength if not for Gillian tempting him back to the dark side.

When Jackson was coherent, Gillian acted as if he were invisible. He hated it, but he realized she was lost in the real world. They could only be together in that fantasy realm where consequences never matter and Nana wasn't dead. So once again, he rolled up his sleeve and accepted the Alchemist's terms of surrender.

Stoned out of their minds, they sat next to each other on a stained mattress in the graffiti-covered bedroom. The lock didn't work and junkies would stumble in from time to time. Jackson had to fight them off, threatening them with his knife or pistol.

During the night, the bravest pressed their luck. They crept in, hungry for a piece of Gillian, only to retreat when she attacked them like a rabid wolf. She was always ready, happy to rip flesh from bone.

After each attempted assault, she seemed more alive, more like her old self. Then the needle would come out again and she would regress back to mindless mumbling, the siren-like chant forcing Jackson to join her.

Drinking condensed soup directly from cans and sipping brown water from the bathroom sink barely kept their bodies alive. It seemed that every day Jackson poked a new hole into his belt.

As for the drugs, Jackson had reached his peak. He worried the next shot might be his last, and only took enough to keep the sickness at bay.

Gillian, however, refused to slow down. Spurred on by the violence of ripping another addict's face to shreds, she pulled the syringe from her purse then loaded the biggest fix that he had ever seen.

Jackson wanted to stop her, but the Alchemist had already injected a dose of death into his arm. "Don't," he uttered.

Gillian grinned. "Nana told me to do it."

Nana, Jackson thought.

He had loved her so much. She had been his family once. Consciousness dimming, he watched the massive hit flow into Gillian's ravaged vein, and then the darkness took him.

The next morning he found her lying in the tub, puke dripping from her chin, bugs crawling over her body. He swept the roaches off her cold flesh, picked her up by the arms, then dragged her back into the bedroom.

Jackson draped her arm over his shoulder and held most of her weight. He tried to get her to walk around the room. "Gillian! Wake up!" He slapped her face. "Come on, you have to move." She protested, but Jackson wouldn't relent until she was mostly taking steps on her own.

"You almost died!"

She laughed. "So?"

After that, the days and nights blurred together. Regardless of the ways Jackson struggled to curb her use, Gillian kept injecting herself with ever-increasing amounts. During the day, he watched her closely, making sure she stayed away from the Alchemist. Eventually he needed to get himself right, then while he was too high to stop her, she purposely overdosed once more.

Again and again, Jackson revived her. Gillian's temperature never was as warm as it should have been, and her complexion never changed back from the sickly grey color. He hadn't witnessed anything like it before. No matter what he tried, her usage increased, and so did her madness.

What had begun as drug-fueled mumblings had turned into full-blown rants. During her worst bouts, Gillian raved to the junkies about Jackson's dead grandmother. They listened to her preach, nodding along in agreement when she claimed that a wraith haunted her, that the old woman never left her side no matter how deep she stuck the needle.

Jackson had enough. Using a roll of duct tape, he tied her up, binding her hands behind her back. It was the only way he knew to protect her.

The intervention didn't work. After he had fallen asleep, she broke free and purchased more dope. The Alchemist was always happy to oblige a paying customer.

Distraught, Jackson finally gave up. *She needs to hit rock bottom. Then she'll let me save her*, he thought. Though he despised himself, he refused to interfere with Gillian's downfall any longer. He turned away from her pain like every junkie turns away from his or her own suffering.

Even when the infection set in, and the wounds on her arms festered, he remained silent. Even when bone and tendons were exposed, maggots biting at the dead skin, he kept himself on the outskirts of her insanity. Still, she refused to stop, shooting up whenever she could. All the while, she rubbed at the gem around her neck and swore Nana was a monster.

When the money dried up, the Alchemist's good will disappeared. Gillian refused to trade him the heart-shaped necklace, and they were forced back onto the streets.

"I need more, Jack. You don't understand!" She pounded her fists into his chest. "You promised you would always take care of me!"

Gillian's plea finally broke him. "How?" he screamed, ashamed. "You won't let me!"

"Find a way!"

Without any other options, Jackson suggested that they fall back on the oldest hustle in history until he could find a more permanent solution to their problems.

Gillian agreed. She promised him no matter what happened, this time would be the last time.

Jackson knew it was a promise that wouldn't be kept but lying to himself had always been so much easier than accepting the truth.

❖

Jackson sat at the bar staring at a reflection he resented. A machine pumped smoke that swept across the neon-lit floor. Crumpled dollar bills littered the small stage. The music pulsed through his body, reminding him of the first time the Alchemist had opened his vein.

"We got a treat for you tonight!" the DJ said into the microphone. "Please give it up for Anastasia."

Gillian walked around the stage to the beat of a kick drum. Holding on to the dance pole, she leaned back and looked out over the crowd. The strobe lights flashed on the heart-shaped diamond pendant.

"That girl's something, isn't she?" Jackson asked the man on the stool next to him, amazed at how Gillian's makeup hid the worst of the damage. Long, white satin gloves covered the places where the flesh had rotted away.

She was gorgeous.

Jackson remembered how she had looked in high school, back before drinking led to pills, pills to powder, and powder to needles.

The man sipped his drink, transfixed on Gillian's swaying hips. She slipped out of her dress. Her naked body twisted like a serpent around the pole.

Jackson leaned closer to the man, breathing in the smell of cigarettes mixed with cheap cologne. "Anastasia told me that she'd like to get to know you better. She said you could have her. She said you could do *whatever you want.*"

The man sat in silence, still mesmerized. Jackson waited. He knew better than to press.

When the song was over, Gillian collected the money on the stage, then walked back behind the red curtain.

The man downed the rest of his drink. Head bowed, and spinning a gold wedding band between his fingers, he seemed to contemplate the offer. After a moment of silence, he whispered, "How much?"

❖

Smoking a cigarette outside the hotel room door, Jackson listened as the headboard crashed into the wall, over and over again, a fake moan of pleasure following each thud.

Jackson stared contemptuously at the cars going down the block, the drivers scanning for a date. Everyone knew the place charged by the hour.

One day it will all be behind us, he thought.

He crushed out the cigarette and banged on the door. "Time's up, pal. Get dressed and get out!"

When the headboard continued to thud, but the moaning had stopped, Jackson cursed under his breath. He threw open the door, drawing the gun from his waistband. Leveling it at the back of the man's head, he said, "I told you to get out."

The man lay on top of Gillian, shaking. She clawed at his back with one hand, long trails of blood oozed through the sheets. Jackson swung, striking him in the head with the barrel, but the man did not stop.

Gillian cackled. Her other hand was wrapped around the man's windpipe, holding him on top of her. The man had been struggling to free himself, but was trapped between her legs.

"Let him go!"

She released his neck, thrust her fingers deep into his eye socket, and pulled his face down. The pillows muffled his scream.

Jackson grabbed him by the arm and threw him to the floor. Blood flowed down his chest from the puncture wounds in his throat. His dislodged eye rolled across his cheek, dangling by a thread of optic nerves.

Gillian lunged after the man.

Jackson grabbed her by the hair and threw her back on the bed. A tuft of flesh ripped free from her scalp.

Gillian kicked back the bloody sheets and smeared the red gore over her breasts. A low-pitched growl rumbled from her parted lips.

"Gillian! Stop!"

The man tried to pull himself up but slipped in the growing puddle of blood. The eye slid back and forth across his face. "She...tried to kill me."

Jackson kneeled. He pressed his hand to the wound in the man's neck, but when the blood continued to pulse between Jackson's fingers, he shook his head.

The man's terrified expression told Jackson that the he knew it was the end. He opened his mouth but no words came out. His limp hands fell from Jackson's wrists, and his head lolled forward. The eye in the socket seemed to be locked on Gillian, still rubbing his blood all over her body, while the other stared at the bloody carpet.

"Wrap him up in the shower curtain and leave him in the bathroom," she said.

"Why the fuck did you do that?" Jackson clenched his fists. He stood and turned toward her.

Gillian traced a bloody circle around her navel. "To feel alive."

"I can't help you on my own! We need *real* help!"

"Help? I'm okay, Jack. Nana is with me. She was lying in the bed next to me the whole time that monster had his way." She laughed. "Besides, you can't blame me. Nana told me to do it."

"We have to run far, far away…somewhere people won't know us. Rehab!"

Gillian laughed again.

"We can get through it if we stay together," Jackson said.

She shook her head. "It's too late for that."

"No, it's not. We'll get clean. We'll find work…rent an apartment… be a family. Please Gill. We can break free from this madness."

"I said it's too late, Jack. Look." Gillian held up her left hand, waving it like a magician. With her right, she dug her fingernails into her wrist, hooking a vein with her thumb. She slowly pulled out the long strand, then reached for another.

Jackson retched.

"There's no pain. I don't feel anything anymore. Do you wanna know the truth about your grandmother, baby?" Gillian caressed the gem around her neck. "Nana told me everything. She was already dead. Had been for a long time before we broke in that night. Now I'm dead, too. I'm a monster wearing Gillian's skin, and her rotting flesh itches so badly."

"Don't say that. You are just dope sick. We can get through this, I promise. Everything is going to be all right."

Jackson laid his head on her breasts, and she cradled him in her arms. Her body was so cold and her heart beat so slowly that he wasn't sure if he could really hear it at all. "Nana forgives you for what you did. I forgive you, too. And I love you, Gillian."

"She doesn't forgive me. She said I took away her link to life and now she's punishing me like *a silly child*. I don't care, though. The necklace is mine."

Gillian slid from Jackson's embrace. Blood glistened on her naked body as she limped across the room to her purse. The makeup had been smeared away in different places exposing the bruised flesh beneath. Jackson could only watch as she cooked up the last bit of her stash and injected it directly into her neck.

Pupils constricted to pins, she crawled across the bloody floor like a wounded animal. Jackson cringed as she pulled herself back into the bed and cuddled next to him.

"Wake me from the nightmare when you are ready to leave, Jack. We can sell his wedding ring to buy more death."

Jackson held her cold body for hours, staring across the room at the dead man, eyes unblinking. He wasn't sure if the stench came from the corpse or from Gillian.

All his life, he had never subscribed to the supernatural. He wanted to believe her affliction was a combination of mental and physical illness, some sort of disease that doctors could treat, though his mind couldn't rationalize the way she had changed. The things he had seen defied all logic. His last hope was to accept that something, some dark force, had power over her.

"Gillian," he whispered. When she didn't respond, he thought of his grandmother. "Nana? You were an addict just like the rest of us, weren't you?"

He traced the black heart pendant with his finger before gripping it tightly in his palm. Jackson yanked the necklace, breaking the silver chain.

Gillian lurched forward, eyes wide and bloodshot. She clawed at her chest, screaming in inhuman retching sounds.

Jackson clasped his hands to his ears in an effort to drown out the horror. The piercing howl went on forever. Déjà vu struck and he remembered hearing the same horrific scream from that night—Gillian must've ripped the pendant from Nana's neck.

Eventually her lungs gave way. She sank back to the bed, a slight smile lingering on her blue lips. Jackson pulled her closer. Her muscles clinched under his hands. Spasms contorted her into a twisted mess. Her body twitched and lurched, spine cracking as her back arched further and further backward. After what seemed like an eternity, Gillian finally went still.

Jackson cried. He wondered again about the diamond clamped in his hand. It held life somehow. Why would such a thing exist? For what evil purpose? A word passed through his mind though he didn't know the meaning, or where the thought had come from: *Revenant.*

Like all addicts, Jackson refused to confront the reality of a lost supply. Wiping away the blood and tears, he said, "I don't care what you are, Gill. I need you."

He told himself that he could learn to control her, to mask the rotting flesh, and to curb her dark urges. He put the pendant back around her neck and waited.

When Gillian did not stir, dread set in. He called her name but she did not answer. He shook her but she would not wake. He tried again, and again there was only cold death.

Jackson screamed.

He begged for her to come back. He pleaded for the life together that they had always planned. All the while, he knew it was too late. Hard and fast, they had lived the junkie lifestyle. Their relationship had always been destined to end in suffering.

There has to be a way, he thought.

His mind went though a dozen impossible scenarios, as if life were a fairytale and the sleeping princess could still be saved.

In the real world, he found only one option: suicide.

Jackson placed the gun barrel to his temple. While looking over Gillian's lifeless body, he took in a last breath, his eyes pausing on the sparkling black gem.

Suddenly, he knew the answer.

Jackson lowered the gun and kissed Gillian for the final time. "This isn't goodbye," he said, then fled the motel with the heart-shaped pendant firmly grasped in his palm.

❖

Jackson stumbled through the dark alleys of a city he no longer recognized. Shuffling through the dredges, he stared at the nickels and dimes in his palm. It wasn't enough, no matter how many times he counted. It wasn't enough. The rules had changed. Money could no longer pay for what he needed.

Looking for his next fix, he considered breaking into a car, maybe a house, if he could gather the nerve.

That might work, he thought. The alternative was doing what he had promised himself he would never do again, and the memory brought a horrible taste to his mouth.

He shuddered. Promises, after all, were meant to be broken.

Now that Jackson no longer used a needle, he simply went through the motions, living life on the streets because it was the only life left for someone like him.

He still sought a high, though he had finally come to terms with the fact that it was never the dope he craved. What he needed was something else altogether. His true addiction cost him more, and was harder to come by, than anything the other wandering addicts could possibly imagine.

Each day, he forced himself a little farther down the path to hell for a chance to get closer to the demons he desired—each deed slightly more horrific. But when the feeling came, Christ, it felt so good.

A silhouette appeared in the alley, surrounded by a dim, red glow cast down by the neon sign of the strip club. Jackson stepped back into the cover of darkness, terrified.

He listened closely.

The figure came toward him, footsteps growing louder and louder, then stopped suddenly in front of the shadow of the dumpster.

"Buyin' or sellin'?" the man asked.

Jackson knew the voice. His heart raced but he did not move from the darkness.

"You can't hide from me." The voice was gruff, as if the man had smoked two lifetimes' worth of cigarettes.

Jackson was cornered. It was impossible to escape with the way his limbs were shaking.

Besides, why run?

Nothing could hurt him anymore.

He took a hesitant step out of the darkness, feeling the strands of long, dingy hair stuck to his face, wet from perspiration, or worse. Though his clothing was ragged, the t-shirt and jeans stained so badly that the original colors could not be guessed, Jackson wore the dirty tatters of a brown corduroy jacket almost proudly.

"Buying," he said.

"You look a mess, boy."

Jackson shrugged. Yes, he was a mess. He should go home and clean up.

When had Nana thrown him out, anyway? Months, years, or decades ago? He couldn't remember how long he had been on the streets, but he still remembered Nana's expression when she found out Gillian had turned him into a junkie.

Gillian.

The Alchemist, much older than Jackson remembered, stared through him with unreadable eyes.

Jackson anxiously shifted his weight from foot to foot. The itch was growing stronger, the urge more intense. The scabs on his face driving him insane. He reached up and scratched until his fingers came away wet, exposing the part of skull above his right eye in the process.

The Alchemist took a step back. "It's been a real long time. Guess you've been shooting up without me?"

"No."

"Then what happened? Where's that girl of yours?"

"You wouldn't believe me if I told you."

The Alchemist laughed. "Well, I still got what you need," he said. "But you ain't got nothin' I want," he added, looking Jackson over from head to toe.

Jackson's skin crawled again, but it wasn't from withdrawals. He shoved his hands into his coat pockets.

Soon, Jackson thought. *The fix is coming soon.*

"Maybe you do," the Alchemist said, and pointed at Jackson's chest.

Jackson looked down at the black heart pendant hanging around his neck.

Footsteps approached from behind.

Ah, yes. Finally.

Nana stepped up to his left, her tongue still pulled through her neck, twitching. Gillian stepped to his right, her head twisted back from rigor mortis, skin several shades of black decay.

"What do you say then? Trade?" the Alchemist asked, holding up a bag of death.

"Do it, Jackie. Do it, do it, do it," Nana whispered.

Gillian's grip tightened on his arm and, in turn, his hand tightened around the pistol.

"We're family now, right?" Jackson pleaded, the gun sliding out of his pocket.

"Yeah Jack, of course we're family," the Alchemist said as he walked toward Jackson with a needle gripped in a pale, bony hand. ◆

Kristopher Mallory has no interest in mastering kung fu or underwater basket weaving, but he does enjoy throwing out the occasional random non sequitur. As for favorite animals, he's a big fan of sloths and hedgehogs. In fact, he once owned a hedgehog named Princess Pokey. He hasn't devised a plan to obtain a sloth…yet.

When it comes to writing, Kris enjoys horror and sci-fi. He's actively trying to be a gooder writer and hopes to one day join the SFWA*. Another focus is the* Daylight Dims *horror anthology, and Stealth Fiction publishing.*

Outside of writing, he traveled the world while serving as an aircrew member in the Air Force and currently works in I.T. around the D.C. area. He lives with his Wife, Son, Daughter, German Shepherd, Golden Retriever, Beta fish, an imaginary Easter Bunny, and with luck someone will give him a Sloth.

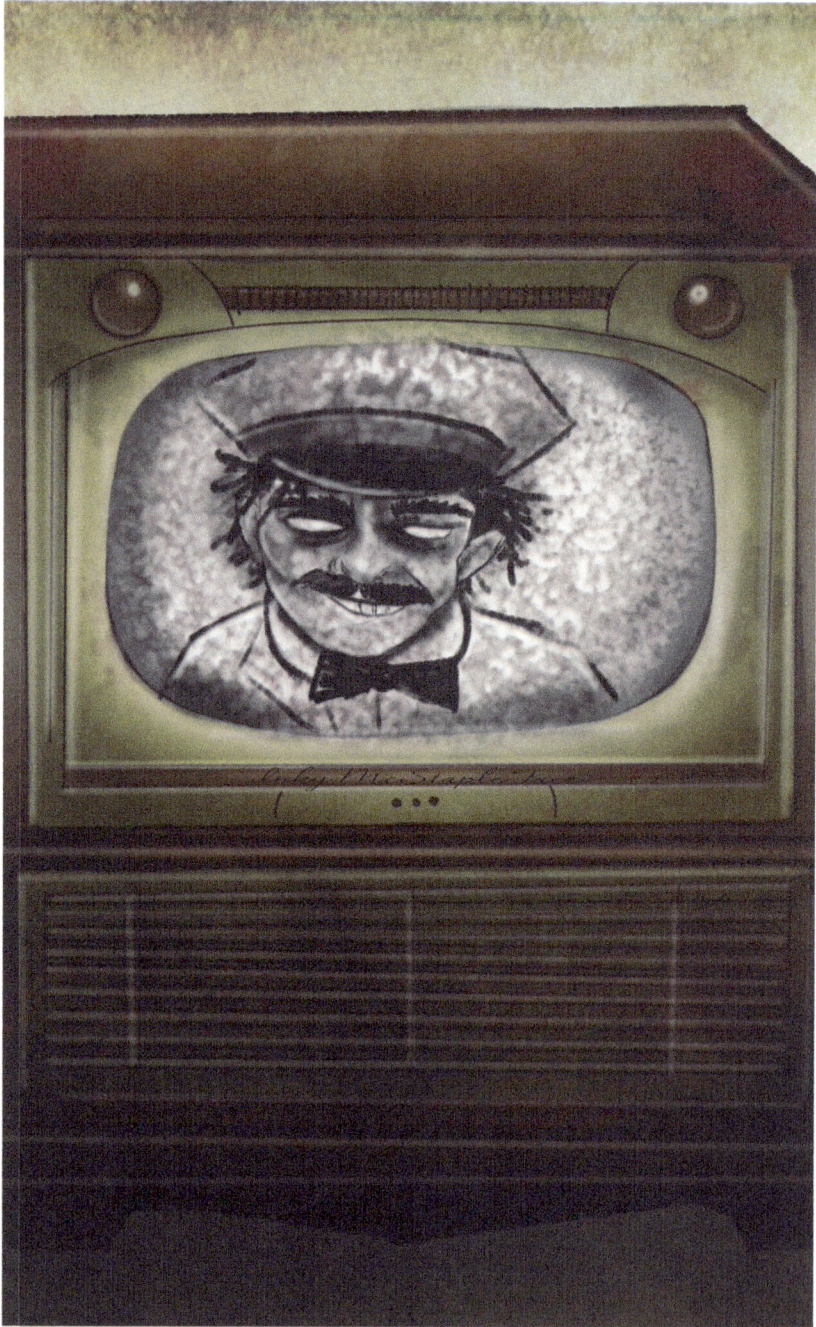

Artwork: Inky McStapleface

SPECIAL DELIVERY

J.W. ZULAUF

A thump struck against the door so loudly, it threatened the dusty picture frames lining the kitchen walls. Arthur Richardson, standing over the sink, didn't flinch along with it. He knew that the noises he heard weren't always there. While rinsing a bowl, a much longer series of knocks echoed through the air, catching his curiosity.

Arthur dried his hands as he left the kitchen. He opened the front door, leaving his hand on the knob for balance. He lifted his other hand to shield the sun's powerful glare and focused on the stranger standing so eagerly on his deck.

"Hell–" The words broke from the stranger's mouth. "Hello, s-s-sir."

The man in front of Arthur stood tall and sported a fireman's mustache. His clothes hung loosely, flapping like a flag caught around a skinny pole. The stranger's face held the subtle remains of an ancient acne problem, and his brunette hair hung over his ears, wiry as a frayed broom. Arthur gaze rested on the man's eyes but couldn't quite find a description to fit and decided that he didn't like the man.

The stranger shuffled his feet. "I'm h-here to d-deliver this."

"What's this about? Why you trippin' over your words?"

"M-m-my name is Corbin T-Turner. I'm here to drop off this t-television." He smiled and signaled to his right.

Arthur lingered on the broken-looking box, focusing on the dust and scratches covering its surfaces.

"Is your name Artttthhhur," Corbin caught his breath, "Rich-chardson?"

Arthur started to close the door with a scowl. The man reached out and stopped it. "Is that y-you, sir?"

Arthur pulled the door open and swatted toward the man. "Leave on out of here and take that piece of junk with you! My son tried for years to give me one of those Godforsaken things, and I'm going to tell you just as I told him: I don't want nothin' to do with it! That is the workings of the devil, making our world lazy and stupid."

Arthur tried to close the door again, but Corbin stopped it with his foot. "But th-that's just it, sir. I'm h-here delivering this from your son, K-Keith R-Richardson."

Arthur's heart leapt in his chest. "My son's been dead for seven years, you prick. Now get the hell out of here!" Arthur threw the door shut, but it bounced off of Corbin's leg.

"I have it r-r-right here, sir." Corbin removed a folded paper from his brown tweed jacket and fumbled it open. "There is a message, t-t-too. 'Get with the t-times, old man.'"

The phrase stung Arthur like a swarm of bees. It had to be a bad joke, but who would do such a thing? Instantly, his neighbor's face flashed in his mind. "Marty," Arthur cursed under his breath. "That son of a...."

Corbin lowered the paper and stared at Arthur.

"I know what you're up to!" Arthur's voice rose. "You tell Marty that this is out of control and uncalled-for."

Arthur nudged the man away from the door and slammed it shut. He marched to the living room and fell into his recliner. The situation exhausted him–that phrase. The same exact phrase his son used whenever he attempted to convert Arthur over to the new world: cell phone, television, new car. He flipped through his memories like the pages of a photo album.

Get with the times, old man.

He thought of Marty and their first real problem. Shortly after Marty had moved into the farm next door, he discarded a dead cow down the long ditch that met at Arthur's property line. The horrible scent of rotting flesh and the pallid, emaciated look of the animal had gripped Arthur's gut and held on for nearly thirty years. Sitting in that chair, Arthur's stomach churned and his face flushed. He could still smell the decay.

"Prick. Thinks he can play games with me. Well, I'm done with it." Arthur stood and made his way out the front door. As he stepped from the house, he saw that Corbin had left the television on the porch. Arthur snorted and pushed past the electronic contraption.

The walk proved to be arduous for Arthur. His frail lungs and weak knees stopped him every few steps.

Marty must have seen him approaching because he greeted Arthur from the steps of his house. When Marty spoke, his words came in heavy, wheezing breaths. "Arthur! How are you?"

"Don't *Arthur* me, you old crone!" Arthur poked his cane toward Marty. "I know exactly what you're up to, sending that challenged boy to my house. You're lucky I don't drive my mower right through your damned garage!"

"Arthur, I thought we put all of that stuff behind us." Marty's jowls jiggled as he spoke.

"Why did you do it?"

Marty wiped sweat from his brow. "I don't know what you're talking about, Art. Is this nonsense all you came over here for?"

"I can't believe the nerve," Arthur said, turned, and walked away.

Nearly twenty minutes later, Arthur slammed his front door shut and went into the kitchen. He sat at the table, fiddling with his cane, taking long, deep breaths. Once his heart slowed, he stood to make a cup of tea but stopped mid-stride. He heard voices from his living room.

"Art's going to be home soon. You better have this cleaned up before he does."

Arthur faced the living room to see a bluish hue flickering off the wall.

"It's clean. Plus he isn't going to care," Keith responded.

Arthur shook his head and wiped sweat from his face.

"Arthur! Arthur, come quick. You're going to miss it!" his wife's voice called from the living room.

Arthur jolted forward, nearly tripping over himself, and when he rounded the corner, he froze. Before him sat the archaic television, with the screen displaying Eleanor's beautiful face. The black and white picture instantly captivated him.

"Arthur," she called again, yelling off-screen.

"I'm here! I'm right here!" His voice cracked as he flew at the screen, throwing his hands on either side. His palms burned. His flesh sizzled and melted into the surface, and he couldn't pull away. The buzz of electricity filled the air, and seconds later, Arthur flew back, landing on the coffee table in the center of the room.

His head struck first, blood trickling down his nape, and the borders around his vision blackened. A pain shot up his chest to the base of his neck. Arthur attempted to lift his head, but his vision closed in until everything fell black.

Arthur woke to a silent and dark room. He remained still until he felt grounded, until his head stopped spinning. He pushed himself up but fell right back onto the remains of the cracked table. His hands burned as if they were on fire. He used his elbows to prop against the couch, unsure how long he'd been unconscious.

Fire shot through his palms. Raw tissue, muscles, and tendons were all that remained. His stomach churned. Once the nausea passed, he managed to stand, knowing he had to clean the wounds before they became infected. He climbed the stairs to the medicine cabinet.

While wrapping his left hand, he thought about a burn he had received while in the depths of an old Navy ship. The pain from accidentally brushing against a steam pipe so many years ago echoed through his open palms.

Voices called once more from the living room. Arthur had only half-wrapped his right hand, and when he pressed it against the wall for support, he left a sticky, red streak. His skin burned fresh all over again. The picture glowed so brightly in the dark room it appeared to be floating. Arthur skirted the television and sat on the couch.

Slowly, Arthur became consumed with the television, the show, his family. Everything he had ever wanted lay bundled before him. Time disappeared as he watched.

"You might as well not even ask. I understand he's your friend, Keith, but you know how your father gets. It's Christmas Eve. What else can I say? He will flip his lid when he—"

"My friend has nowhere to go! Why can't he just come over? I hate how Dad is! I hate it! It's not fair. Who cares if he has long days at work? Guess what, I had a long day at school. I hate it, and I hate him!"

Eleanor slapped Keith.

Arthur had never seen her strike their precious son.

"Don't you ever, and I mean *ever*, say that about him! He's a good man, and he loves you. He might be a little thick, but damn you for saying that. That man…." She tried to catch her breath. "Go. Go to your room, now."

The image switched to fuzzy snow, snapping Arthur from his trance. He tried to make sense of what he had seen, but another picture washed over the screen, stealing his attention.

Keith appeared older. He sat in the living room alone on the couch. Someone knocked at the door, but he continued to stare at his lap.

"I'll get it," Eleanor called from the kitchen. She walked across the living room, past Keith, drying her hands on a towel as she went. She stood on her tiptoes to see who knocked, turned to Keith, and said, "Go to your room for a bit. Marty's come to help me sort out how much we owe him for the vegetables."

Keith stood, scoffed, and said, "I'll bet." He disappeared off the screen and stormed upstairs, each footfall echoing through the speakers.

"Excuse me, *boy*, mind your mouth. I won't have that talk in here," Eleanor yelled at Keith, who stomped up the stairs.

She turned back to the door and before she could turn the knob, he replied, "You don't think I know what you do? I'm sixteen, Mom. I'm not a child! And you're a whore."

Eleanor's face fell, distorted with shock.

Arthur's fists clenched. His nails dug deep, producing blood spots in his bandages. He mumbled under his breath, "You don't talk to her like that."

Eleanor wiped her face. As she did, another knock rapped on the door, followed by Marty's voice. "Hello? Elly?"

She opened the door wide enough for Marty to walk into the living room. Before he could fully enter, she threw her arms around his shoulders, hugging him.

The television blinked, then focused on Marty and Eleanor in the kitchen. Eleanor leaned against the counter, crying into her hands. Marty extended his arms to console her, but she stopped the embrace with a hand on his chest and said, "This needs to stop."

Arthur leaned forward, confusion tearing at his mind as Marty made another attempt to scramble Eleanor's resolve. The screen blinked back to snow.

Stop what, Arthur wondered. He stared at the snow, different images like some sort of Rorschach inkblot test—his wife crying, his son storming off, and Marty entering the house.

Suddenly, Corbin's face floated toward him. Arthur closed his eyes, squeezing a tear down his cheek.

He had fallen asleep at some point, trying to avoid the images flying at his mind. It wasn't pain that woke him, but a soggy feeling in his pants. When he edged forward on the couch, the television flicked back on.

"Get the hell out of my house!" a much older Keith yelled from the screen. Even through the black and white, Arthur saw his cheeks were flushed. He shoved Marty toward the front door.

"Go destroy your own life. I'm done. I sat here for years while you guys did this to Dad, and I'm putting my foot down!" He cocked his arm back and launched it forward like a piston. A half-nude Marty tripped on the rug, fumbling to keep hold of the shirt in his hands.

Eleanor ran down the stairs wearing only a towel. Keith slammed the door behind Marty and turned to his mother, tears wetting his face. He opened his mouth to speak but before he could say anything, the television flicked again, changing the scene. Now Keith and his mother sat at the table in the kitchen.

"Keeeeiiiittttthhhh," Arthur heard his own voice call from another room. "Keith, buddy!"

The television focused in on the hatred displayed on Keith's face. "I'm in the kitchen with Mom."

Art entered the scene, years younger, wearing his old shipyard clothes. He glanced between them. "Everything okay?" the ghost of his former self asked. Keith's face cleared in an instant. He jumped up and wrapped his arms around Arthur.

Arthur glanced from the screen and down at his bandages, wondering how long it had been since he'd hugged his son. He remembered coming home that day and how happy he was to see Keith's bags by the door on the kitchen floor.

Someone knocked at his door, and the moment it happened, the television shut itself off.

Arthur reached out at the display with a silent cry. He wanted to be with his family, and the empty, dark screen made him want to cry. "Damn it," he mumbled under his breath, pushing himself from the couch.

"Art, open this door!" Marty wheezed from the other side.

Arthur glanced from the television, to the door, then to his palms. The blood had soaked through the poor bandage job. After another wave of knocking, he rose from the couch, and worked to open the door.

"About God calling time you old—" Marty cut his own words off. "Jesus Christ in a Chevy. What's happened to you?"

Marty's eyes passed from head to toe and after a moment of silent consideration, he asked, "Did you piss yourself, old man?"

"What do you want, you two-faced bastard? Come for your television? Well, it just so happens that the joke's on you because I like it. And I'm keeping it."

Marty's eyes fell to Arthur's hands. Arthur pulled them behind his back. "It's nothing."

"I'm taking you to the hospital," Marty said, forcing himself into the house. "Now before we get to cleaning you up, I just want to clear the air with you. I'm not sure what earlier was about."

Arthur slammed the door. Marty jumped at the noise and removed his hat, twisting it in his hands. He glanced from the television up to

Arthur. "I want you to know that I've not meant to upset you with any-thing. I honestly don't even know what it is that I've done. I just want to make sure we're on the same page. We are in way too shaky health to be keeping enemies."

Arthur responded quickly, "I'm sorry, too. Would you mind helping me out? I need to clean these." Arthur cast a smile at Marty and lifted his bloody hands.

Marty's shoulders relaxed, and he replaced his hat. "Well, alright. Let's get you taken care of then. Where's your medicine? Upstairs or kitchen?"

"Up."

Arthur watched Marty work his way upstairs. Once Marty cleared the top step, the screen flicked on, taunting Arthur. The scene of Keith hitting Marty, Marty stumbling, and his wife entering the picture sped up and played over and over until Arthur's chest raced with anger.

A loud creak sounded as Marty began his descent back down the stairs. The television switched off at the very same moment.

On the couch, Arthur swallowed hard as Marty removed the bandages. The soggy cloth had been floating on a mixture of pus, ointment, and blood. Once the new bandages sat secure, Marty said, "You need to change your clothes, Art. You smell like an outhouse."

"Alright, well, I'll go change."

Arthur worked his way to his bedroom, entering the closet. He wasn't looking for clothes. Instead of a new pair of pants, he grabbed the shotgun leaning in the corner and reached for a shoebox on the shelf above him. Batting dress shoes aside, the box tumbled to the ground, shells bouncing everywhere.

Moments later, Arthur returned wearing the same bloodstained clothes. Marty's eyes traveled to the gun gripped in his bandaged hands.

"You screwed my wife," Arthur accused, stepping toward Marty.

Marty's face screwed up. "I did no such thing!" He stood up from the couch and backed away a step.

"Don't lie to me, Marty. I saw everything." Arthur glanced at the television. The blood and charred handprints made it look as though the television smiled.

"Calm down, Arthur," Marty said, backing toward the kitchen. "I don't know what's got you all stirred up, but put the gun down, and we'll go to the hospital."

Arthur forced Marty into the kitchen. "I saw it. You would come in while I was out working at the shipyard!"

"I'm telling you that you got facts wrong, Art."

Marty slipped past Arthur to avoid being cornered, coming dangerously close to the gun.

"You don't tell me nothin'!" Arthur yelled.

His head pulsed so hard it felt like it might burst. Marty disappeared into the living room with Arthur pursuing. As Marty ran for the front door, the television flicked on, showing an image of Marty and Eleanor naked on Arthur's bed, arms wrapped around each other, smiles cracked on their faces.

Marty stopped and slowly faced Arthur. "I...I'm sorry."

Arthur lifted the gun, squeezed his eyes shut, and pulled the trigger. The recoil knocked him into the kitchen's doorframe. He slid to the ground, grabbing at his chest.

The scene on the television focused on Marty's face, blood running from the corner of his mouth. "You shot me, you son of a bitch," Marty gulped. The camera pulled back enough to show the spreading stain where the bullet entered Marty's chest. "I can't believe you shot me."

The camera zoomed out to show Marty standing next to Eleanor, his hand gripping her throat, his knuckles bleeding lines of white.

Eleanor tried to speak: "Arr...th...rr, Hhhlllp."

Arthur rose to his feet and lunged at the television. "No! Get off her!" He cocked his fists back and swung. Both of his hands went into the screen as though he had punched water, waves rippling to the borders. He tried to pull his fists out, but the television wouldn't let go.

"C-c-come on in, Arth-thurr," a strange, familiar voice stuttered from the speakers.

The television pulled him in to his elbows, then to his shoulders. Arthur tried with all his remaining strength to pull away. The television was too strong, like a million little hands pulling him inward. As Arthur slipped through the screen, the television went blank, catching the bottom of his old loafer and popping it off and back onto the living room floor.

❖

Rose prepared dinner for her children when she heard a knock at the front door.

"Jess, set the table. James, put your schoolbooks in your room," she said as she pulled the door open.

"H-hello ma'am. I-I…my name is C-Corbin. I'm here to d-d-drop this t-television off from your neighbor M-M-Marty." Corbin pointed behind him as if to signal up the street.

"I see," Rose said, passing her eye from the man to the television. "Well, we really don't need another one. Do you mind letting him know that for us? But we appreciate the kindness."

Corbin lifted his hat and bowed slightly. "Well ma'am, I was only d-d-doing him a favor. You'll have to reach out t-to him. I best b-be on my w-way now."

"Wait. What is it you do, Mr. Corbin? For a living. Maybe someone there could use it."

He smiled, his mustache lifting up like a wiggling caterpillar. "Oh, bless your soul, but I s-seriously doubt that, ma'am. I'm only a…a kind of a d-d-delivery man."

Rose frowned. "Well, I think it might be best if you go on and get that television out of here. Like I said, I kindly appreciate it, but we don't need it."

"Cool!" James yelled as he slipped between her and the doorframe. "Can I put it in my room? I can play my games there! Pleeeeease?"

"It s-seems like maybe you can use it a-a-fter all." Corbin turned and walked across the yard.

A shiver went up Rose's back and bumps ran down her arms. "Well, if you want it, help me bring it in."

James squeaked happily and grabbed one side of the television. ◆

J. W. Zulauf wears many hats while walking the streets of the writing world. He started with a focus on the short story, first winning the Marjorie Flack Award for Fiction. Then he became one of the editors for Daylight Dims, *which has grown into an annual anthology. He now works as an author with Evolved Publishing, creating the children's series,* The Balderdash Saga, *beginning with* The Underground Princess.

THANK YOU

The Daylight Dims Team

Thank you for reading *Daylight Dims Volume 2*. It was an honor to bring you another fine collection of stories and artwork. If you've enjoyed this anthology, we would love for you to rate and review it on your favorite site. We appreciate all feedback. You can also help with our exposure by telling your friends about *Daylight Dims* and sharing our information through the social media outlets.

Don't forget to check out our partner, Chilling Tales for Dark Nights. They provide fully produced, high-quality narration of the *Daylight Dims* collection, released throughout the year.

As a special bonus, we've created some Daylight Dims goodies: Bookmarks, Screensavers, Desktop backgrounds, Prints, and other merchandise. You can find everything and more on our sites listed below.

❖

DAYLIGHTDIMS.COM

FACEBOOK.COM/DAYLIGHTDIMSANTHOLOGY

TWITTER.COM/STEALTHFICTION

YOUTUBE.COM/DAYLIGHTDIMSBOOK

❖

Once again, thank you so much for joining us. We'll see you again soon!

J. W. Zulauf • Kristopher Mallory • Amber Whelpley
Paul Drager • Jason Adams • Katie Abernethy
Autumn Moreland • Chynna Laird

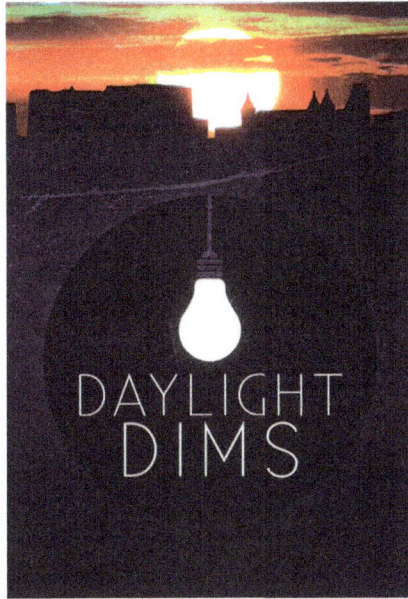

Daylight Dims: Vol 1

"These are original stories from authors of the macabre. From dark fantasy and pure suspense to classic horror tales, it shows the extraordinary scope of fantastical fright fiction. The stories in this anthology are a tour de force of fear, which will haunt you, terrify you, and stay with you."

S. MAHAFFEY

CPSIA information can be obtained at www.ICGtesting.com
Printed in the USA
BVOW11*0207201014

370987BV00008B/9/P

9 780989 757225